To: Karen

Tena Louise Atkins

Thank you

HOPE

TENA LOUISE ATKINS

HOPE

This is a work of fiction. All of the characters, names, incidents, organizations, and dialogue in this novel are either the products of the author's imagination or are used fictitiously.

iUniverse books may be ordered through booksellers or by contacting:

iUniverse
1663 Liberty Drive
Bloomington, IN 47403
www.iuniverse.com
1-800-Authors (1-800-288-4677)

ISBN: 978-1-5320-7823-1 (sc)
ISBN: 978-1-5320-7824-8 (e)

Library of Congress Control Number: 2019909845

Print information available on the last page.

iUniverse rev. date: 07/30/2019

Dedicated to my recently passed father-in-law
WHP retired Colonel W.O.Oyler and
my brother-in-law, WHP retired
Colonel Jess Oyler
both from Cheyenne, Wyoming.
For their 57 combined years of dedicated service
Also my own father,
late Ralph L. Atkins who was with WHP
as a dispatcher for 20 years until he retired.
THANK YOU ALL

PROLOGUE

Back to a simpler time when life was easy. When people took their safety for granted, and didn't notice weird strangers watching.

When kids especially were carefree and the only worry was who was going to be their friend, or whose turn it was to host a sleepover, and chasing butterflies or fireflies in the back yard. Playing red light, green light, or dodge ball and kick the can in the street. Even after-dark games, like hide and seek, or flashlight stop and go.

Nowadays it's all video games indoors. Hardly anyone knows their own neighbors for fear they are serial killers. That very well may be true, because we never really know people. It's always the normal looking ones that turn out to be the bad guys.

If you're not safe in your own home or neighborhood, how do you expect to feel safe on the open road; with all the rest stops, truck stops, and road rage violence happening?

Never take for granted; the value of any young life, the value of family, the value of marriage, the value of love, or the value of peace and quiet. There is always the possibility of someone out there who that can take all that away.

Hope is when you have the heart and perseverance to continue through adversity. There is hope for all our dear loved ones, young and old; keep them close, love them always.

CHAPTER 1

The weather was horrible, with the wind blowing snow across the highway so he could barely see the road. Too many idiots were out here in this blizzard of the year to be able to drive anywhere safely, so the stranger pulled into the nearest truck stop area, planning to wait it out.

This truck stop happened to be in the middle of nowhere, so maybe this would be the perfect time to find that special someone wandering around lost.

As it turns out, there are not very many law enforcement officers at these remote areas of Wyoming; therefore, he wasn't too worried about being stopped for doing something inappropriate. And he planned on doing a lot of not very good things to young girls; especially the cute one he was looking at near the restrooms, down a hallway near the back doors—perfect.

There had been several opportunities like this one over the years, and he had always been successful. However, this time was proving not to be that way, as he had noticed several people hanging around the hallway at the same time he was, and he didn't want to look too suspicious. Well, there was always next time. It was way too cold and windy out to be trying to drive away with someone tied up in the back of his truck anyway.

There were many, many miles of highway to travel along I-80 in Wyoming and Utah, with rest areas and truck stops to watch. There were also hundreds miles of I-90 in Montana and over into Idaho,

1

that had also proved to be lucrative. The stranger decided to take his time and wait it out.

Since he wasn't having any further luck with finding anyone, he stayed at the lunch counter and dreamed of what could be and what was to come.

He always liked the younger prepubescent girls who, preferably, were virgins (these days you never knew for sure)—because it was a symbol of a sacrifice to be a virgin, at least in his mind.

Once he found what he was looking for, there was a ritual he always performed: he tied them around the neck with a red ribbon to choke them and, as they were dying, he raped them repeatedly.

So they wouldn't be discovered right away, he would bury them deep in the desert, where he was sure they wouldn't be found for years. Sometimes, there were circumstances when he had to hurry, and during those times he was always afraid an animal would dig down and uncover the body. So far that had not happened, and he had been doing this for close to ten years now. Oh, the memories.

Good thing he always had the pictures to look at to remind him of his favorite ones, or of the ones who got away. He still took pictures of them all, no matter what because, who knew, maybe he would see them again, down the road somewhere, and think to himself, 'yeah, she's the one.'

He would keep hunting, maybe the next truck stop would provide another opportunity. There was always another one down the road. The vastness of Wyoming appealed to him the most, and that's why he stayed along I-80 while hunting.

CHAPTER 2

A my sat in the back seat alone, wondering what the heck she was doing somewhere in the middle of nowhere. Some strange place called Little America—where is that? Great, another truck stop, how boring could it get? She had no clue; they had stopped for gas and a bathroom break and now the car wouldn't start.

It had been a snowy day, with little traffic because who, in their right mind, would be out here, in the middle of nowhere, in the middle of winter? She was. Nothing to do, no radio, no one to talk to, as she was an only child. Forever lost and trying to find her place in the world of so called adults—-yeah, right. Boring. When you're 17, it's easy to become bored.

Her parents were older than the parents of her few friends were, by almost twenty years. They were Professors at some University in Boise, Idaho or something like that, she thought. She didn't much care anyway, and never paid attention to them because they pretty much didn't know she existed. She knew, fairly early, that she had been a mistake. She came along late in their lives and they didn't quite know what to do with a child.

Amy had always felt out of place anyway, not having anything in common with anyone, so she pretty much kept to herself. Her thoughts wandered and her dreams were scary sometimes. She didn't tell her parents about them, they would have locked her up long ago.

She was a cute kid, with medium length, brown, wavy hair, and beautiful hazel eyes that seemed to change with her mood.

Her personality was quiet and shy, but only because she didn't want anyone to think she was a weirdo.

As she sat in the car contemplating her life, or lack thereof, she didn't know someone was watching her from the inside of the little building where her Dad was trying to find out if there was a mechanic in this place. Her Mom came back and told her it was going to be awhile, so she may as well get out of the car, and go inside the restaurant to wait with her.

Amy thought it would be more interesting to walk around and explore a bit, so she said, "No thanks, I'll walk a bit. I'm tired of being cooped up in the car."

Her Mom said, "Okay, honey, be back here in an hour. It's still snowing out there, you know."

"Whatever," she grumbled, as she walked away.

She walked down a sidewalk toward what looked like hotel rooms and more pine trees. She felt someone was following and watching her from a distance, but when she looked over her shoulder, she didn't see anyone.

Amy thought what a place this is, with a gas station, restaurant, hotel rooms and a lot of semis parked around, and where there was nothing else, as far as she could see, in either direction. Driving here, they had seen no other towns for miles. Her Mom told her they were in Wyoming, but that didn't tell her anything. Where in Wyoming was this?

She kept walking, lost in thought, not paying any attention to where she was going. When she looked around, there were more a lot more pine trees and a few small houses. She wondered who would want to live out here?

As she was about to turn around and go back, a man came up behind her and asked her if she was lost.

Startled, she replied, "Yeah, I guess I am. Where is this?" Amy asked, after her heart rate went back down.

"My name is Joe," he said, "and this is where I live. Do you want to come and see?" he asked.

4

She thought *what could it hurt* and besides, she was curious, so she said, "Sure, my name is Amy." *Anyway, he's kinda cute in a rough way,* she thought. He had dark brown wavy hair, a little long over his collar, brown almost black eyes, and he was a little tall for a kid. She had thought he was a kid at first because he sounded young.

They walked on for a few more minutes, past a couple of houses, to the very back of the area, where they came to a duplex. She asked him, "How many people live around here?"

He told her, "Only the ones that work here, my Dad is the mechanic."

"Oh, good, maybe he can fix our car," she said, excitedly, because she was ready to get of there.

"It will probably still take a while longer," Joe said, smiling at her. "Well, here we are, this is ours."

They went in through a garage, to a small kitchen with a washer and dryer by the door. She felt crowded.

She asked him, "How did you know it was me or my family who's having the car trouble?"

"I was watching you when you were sitting in your car and your Dad was asking my Dad about taking a look at it, then I followed you back here when I saw you," he said.

"Where do you go to school clear out here?" she asked him.

"Oh, some get bussed to town, about twenty miles to the east of here," he said, "but it's Christmas break now, so there's no school.

"Where you live?" he asked.

"Yeah, me too. We're on our way back to Boise, Idaho," she sighed. "I can't wait to get back to civilization."

Joe smiled and asked if she want a pop.

"A what?" she asked, looking confused.

Joe smiled, "You know, a pop. A coke, or 7-up,"

"Oh ya, sure, but we say soda," she said smiling.

"Well, you're in the country now," he said, trying to sound country drawl cool.

They sat down in the small living room area, with a brown plaid woven material on the couch and a matching chair that had half a wagon wheel design on the side rails. It was strange looking—-like something from another era.

Feeling nervous and thinking there was something else going on, she sat on the edge of the chair.

"So, what do you do here all day?" she asked, thinking there's not much here.

"I work with my Dad helping him pump gas and clean," he said. "But he told me I could take lunch now and when I saw you heading this way, I, well......" he stopped, as if not knowing what else to say and looking embarrassed. Then he asked, "What do you like to do, any hobbies?

She was puzzled by the question, and the only answer she could think of was, "I like to watch old movies, horror movies."

You like to be scared a lot, huh?" he asked, suddenly acting more interested.

"No, not really. I like watching zombies and all that weird, funny old stuff like that," Amy said shyly, not sure if she could trust him with her secrets either, yet sensing maybe he would understand.

Joe sighed deeply, nodding his head.

"Yeah, I think I know what you mean, I get it. Sometimes I find small animals in the prairie around here and bring them home to watch them and see how long they would live without food or water. You know, all penned up in a cage but alive for a while, just to watch them," he said, looking away from her.

"I wonder if animals have so-called souls like humans. Do you believe in those things?" he asked.

Amy thought she had better explain herself. "Well, my parents are both Professors of Theology in Boise, and for years I've been preached to about the theory and the origins of life. Maybe that's why I've always been curious about all that, also."

Joe didn't seem at all surprised or shocked by what she said and suddenly, a thought came to her about staying here, in this out of the way place, where no one would care enough to notice anything amiss. Amy wondered if she should broach the subject with Joe, or maybe plan to come back at the end of the school year.

"When do you graduate?" he asked, as if he were reading her mind.

"This year anytime, I could finish early if I wanted to," she said proudly.

"Yeah, me too. In fact, most of my classes have been at home anyway because we live so far away from town, it's easier for me and I've been able to get ahead that way. I don't really have many friends at school; they think I'm weird," he said, sadly.

Then she asked, "Do a lot of people pass through here and stop like we have?"

"Oh, yeah," he said, "this place is always busy with truckers who drive the highway all year. Other travelers are through here more often in the summer months. You know, on the way to or from Yellowstone. I-80 is the only route through Wyoming that takes you back to civilization, as you say."

What's the attraction here, and what's with the name Little America?" Amy asked, making small talk again to stay longer.

"Oh that, well, my Dad says the original business, back in the 30s, was on the old highway 30—US 30, by what is now Granger. The founder started it as a place for weary travelers to find food, gas, and a place to sleep, or just to get out of the weather. He was stranded out here on the prairie once, during a winter storm, a blizzard, and nearly froze to death.

He vowed to come back and build an oasis, you could say—for anyone needing help. They say there was a real penguin on site there and they had to bring ice blocks in during the summer months. And funny, too, was a picture I saw of the first building; it had palm trees planted out front. Weird, huh, in the Wyoming desert? Who would have thought?

Anyway, the name came from an Antarctic expedition 'Little America' with penguins and all that." As he explained all this, she wasn't really all that interested except for the fact that it's still in the middle of nowhere.

"What are your plans, then? Are you going to college somewhere?" he seemed curious about her.

"No, no plans for college, no matter what my parents say," she said. "That's not my thing."

"Ok, then, well I'll probably still be here, too. No plans yet either way. Better get you back before they send the cavalry out looking for you," he said, laughing.

"Ok, you have a Sheriff out here?" she wondered out loud.

"No, not that kind of law, but they stop in from town sometimes and the Wyoming Highway Patrol (WHP) also stops in to check on everything." Joe said, as if he were reading her mind again, as they started walking back to the restaurant.

They kept to their own thoughts as they walked because it wasn't very far. Joe had to get back to work anyway. His Dad was going to be pissed anyway, that he had taken a two-hour lunch.

"Thanks for the talk, have a good trip home," he told Amy.

"Sure, yeah, later." she said, as they went their separate ways at the main parking lot. *That was short and sweet,* she thought.

The car looked ready to go and Amy's parents were waiting inside the restaurant. They had begun to get worried, but not too concerned, knowing she could take care of herself.

When she found them inside, they asked her if she wanted anything for lunch or if she had already had something.

"Where would I have eaten anything, when I wasn't here?" she said, "And no, I'm not hungry, can we go now, please?"

She couldn't figure out why Joe abrupt with her after all they had talked about. Then when she got in the backseat of the car, she found a note with her name on it. Joe must have put it here while she was inside.

She read it: Amy, I wanted to say more about wishing you'd come back here, but I wasn't sure if you felt the same way. I was thinking we might have a lot in common. Anyway, here's my address if you'll write to me: Joe Turner, Box 1, Little America, WY. I hope you write, at least to let me know you made it home safely. Thanks again. JT

Amy looked up from reading the folded note, and saw Joe watching her from where he was sweeping the lot around the gas pumps and wiping them down. She waved good-bye as they pulled out to head home, and gave him a thumbs-up, for, "okay I will".

As they took the turnoff onto US 30 and Amy read the Granger exit sign, she remembered Joe had told her the first original Little America was on this road. The area didn't look any different than where they were. She couldn't imagine any palm trees anywhere along here, or any penguins, for that matter.

CHAPTER 3

After spending the night in Pocatello, to get an early to start on the road to Boise, Amy asked her Dad if she could drive, since the weather was nicer and no new snow was on the road. To tell the truth, driving scared her on the highways, especially in bad weather. She was going to have to learn sooner or later though, if she wanted to live in Wyoming. There were always bad roads in the winter time there.

He agreed, at least until they got closer to home, where traffic would be heavier than out here on the highway.

The only thing about driving was that she had to pay closer attention, and couldn't let her mind wander back to Joe and their conversation.

She did, anyway, for a little while as it was so quiet; her parents didn't talk much so they wouldn't distract her, and that was good. Amy decided that, when they got home, she would sit right down and write to Joe, so he'd have her address, and she'd also include her phone number. That way maybe he'd call her, even though it was long distance.

She pulled off the highway once for gas, at a truck stop off I-84 at Twin Falls and wanted to eat, because now she was really hungry, since they had skimped on breakfast. That was when she had another weird feeling of someone watching her, so she stayed close to her Mom, looking all around. Her Dad took over driving, so Amy thought she'd nap till they got home.

As she had planned, Amy sat down right away to write Joe a long letter. She didn't want to in the car because she didn't want her parents to see and ask a bunch of questions. She wrote:

Hi Joe, we finally made it home, all the same boring stuff here. Do you think maybe you could get me a job there if I show up this summer? Exploring all my options you know—check it out. Well, anyway, you'll have my address now and if it's possible for you to call long distance, my number is at the bottom here. If not, send me yours and your schedule of a good time to call, and I can try to call you, too. Thanks, catch you later, Amy.

For the next few months, all Amy could think about was driving back to Wyoming after graduation. She'd be eighteen then and could do whatever and go wherever she wanted. She had been dropping hints that she'd like to drive around the country a little before deciding on any future college commitments.

Her parents were like, that's cool honey, be careful and keep in touch. They bought her a little VW Beetle to drive and set up a savings account that she could access from anywhere. That was awesome; maybe they did listen to her sometimes.

Joe had written back a few times over the last few months before graduation and they talked on the phone, as summer got closer.

CHAPTER 4

Joe had arranged for Amy to be a waitress, as they were always looking for more in the summer. She was interviewed by Patty, a tall thin brunette, who was nice, but a little standoffish. Like her position there was not good enough for her status, whatever that was.

Patty told her she could start the next day. Once that was settled, Amy went to the administration office to find Jean, the secretary, in order to sign all her documents, and to pick up the keys to her housing.

She signed all the paperwork for employment and housing, the monthly rent of $80, to be deducted from her checks. Jean, gave her the keys, explained where to park her car, and wished her, "Good luck."

Now she was off toward her new life, not that she was looking forward to working. She had heard that waitressing was harder than it looked, but as Patty had told her, she's young and cute, and she figures it would be a good gig for awhile.

She pulled her little purple VW around in back of the restaurant, then around another corner to find Apt.18. Sure enough they were small one room, kitchen, and bath apartments. She didn't need much though. She had only brought a few personal items assuming the place was furnished, which it was.

After unloading her car and putting stuff away, she went in search of Joe. They needed to make a plan and she needed to find out where to go to buy a few kitchen items, towels, sheets, etc.

"Hey, how'd it go?" he asked her.

"Great, I guess. I'm all set. I've got a job, and a place to live, now all I need are a few things for the place to make it my home. Where would I go to get that, you got a K-Mart or a mall around here?" she asked sarcastically.

"Yeah, sure we do, but it's 35 miles that way," he answered, hooking his thumb eastward.

"Okay then, let's go. We can check out the lay of the land on the way," she said.

"You want to take my truck, or that little thing you call a car?" he asked smiling.

"Let's take your truck. That way we can tool around on the prairie on the way back here—do some 4-wheeling," she said, a twinkle in her eye.

On the way to town, Joe asked her when she would start work and what shift she'd gotten stuck with.

"I start training tomorrow morning at 6 a.m. with some Karen chick for a week. After that, I'll be on the afternoon shift I guess the 3-11, is that good?"

"Yeah, that sounds real good for starters, at least you didn't get the graves, 11-7 shift. You'd be bored to death with that until 5 am when it gets busy. You clean a lot on night shift too."

"Well it's okay then; we'll see how it goes, if there's more opportunity on nights, I could always ask for that shift later, right?" she asked.

"Speaking of that,..... no, wait, we'll talk about that on the way back when we have more time. We're almost to Rock Springs now where most of the shopping is, unless it's only food you need. There are a couple of grocery stores in Green River too," he added casually.

Amy wondered exactly what the plan was going to be. Would they both agree on everything?They still needed someplace to conduct her research without anyone being suspicious. Maybe he had that in mind after all our conversations the last few months, now we need to finalize, she thought, as she saw the exit signs for Rock Springs.

Amy and Joe went into K-Mart like any other normal young couple setting up a home. She went in search of the kitchen aisle, and the sheets and towels. While Joe went in search of heavy duty rope, duct tape and a hunting knife. All the comforts of home

"Another thing we have to be careful of is letting people get too far out here. We can't be doing this during any of the local hunting seasons. There are too many yahoos out here running around, someone could see something for sure." he explained, as he drove, "and that's coming up in another month."

"So you have someplace in mind to do this research?" she asked him.

"I found an old tool shed I'm pretty sure no one uses anymore. It's back off the property fence line a little ways. If not that, then maybe I can build something farther away; but there are no trees to hide anything away from the property. It's all a lot of sagebrush and prairie dog hills," he said laughing.

"How are we going to find people for this, the right people?" Amy wondered out loud.

"We have to keep our eyes and ears open, pay attention to everyone. Someone who might wander off alone, or someone who might be a runaway. Let's plan, get all ready now, before hunting season and winter set in and then in the spring, we'll get started. Okay? Sound good?" he asked, thinking practically.

"I have to learn to have a lot of patience, I guess. You're right, we can't rush the process. Too many from this same area here will be suspicious to others," she said.

They drove over back roads extending quite far away from Little America, finding a good one that took them back to the rear of the property where Joe thought the shed was.

It was a little worn out and dilapidated. No window though, that was good. Had a tin roof too, so that would mean it would get hot inside pretty quick in the summer and stay frigid in the winter. But the walls were crumbling. They'll need to be fixed from the inside, so no one will observe anything different going on from the outside, she thought.

They made plans while looking it over and considered planting another tree in front to obscure the entry from anyone coming and going. What was one more pine tree anyway?

While they were making notes about what to do first, Joe asked, what, exactly, she had in mind for the questions she wanted to ask these people for her research project.

"How long you think we're gonna need to use this place?" he asked her.

Amy had done some reading before she left home, and looked in all the journals she could find that had belonged to her parents and said,

"I don't have any idea, every person should be different. That's the whole idea, right? I mean it's not like we're going to kill anyone. Seriously, Joe, let's just say this is a little fun 'experiment'. I'll keep a journal of everything also, time of day, amount of light, hot or cold. That way at the end we'll have all sorts of data to compare." As she explained her process, she was hoping nothing would go wrong.

CHAPTER 5

The next day was Amy's first day of training, and she was supposed to follow Karen around all day, helping her out.

The thing was, Karen was a very friendly person, and all she did was talk, and visit. She knew everyone's first name, and not only that, she asked about the family, the Mrs, their Mom or Dad, or especially about their babies. Don't get her started when the pictures came out to show them babies off.

Even though she had at least three or four tables to take care of, as well as the counter, she made her way around to everyone, coffee pot in hand ready to refill half empty cups. All Amy could do was stay out of her way, yet try to follow and do whatever she was told to do to help her out.

Karen was also young like Amy, probably 19-20, and she already had a four-year-old daughter at home to take care of. She would be ready for school the next year, so that meant Karen was ready for another baby. She told Amy all about it, all day long.

Should see her face light up when her little girl's baby pictures come out. Amy wondered how she did it all. There was no way she'd want to be a mother this young. She had too many other plans, but right now, she had to get through the next few days.

After eight hours on her feet—literally running, she was beat. She wanted a hot shower so bad, then a nap.

Karen told her, "You did a good job, today, so come back and be ready for tomorrow. It's going to be another hard day."

"Yeah, okay," she said. She wasn't sure she wanted to, but after she saw how many tips Karen put in her pocket and kept to herself after tipping out the busboy, she thought this might be a good gig after all. She could be extra friendly, remember their names, give them special attention along with their meal, and make everyone happy. They'd be glad to tip well and see you the next time, too. How hard could it be, right?

After two more days of training with the best on day shift, Amy was able to tackle her 3-11 shift on her own. Again, she was only partially training, to get to know the ropes on this shift, so they only gave her two tables to start with. She had taken the menu home with her to try and memorize the dinner differences from the lunch, but they served breakfast all day—so that stayed the same.

Amy thought she was happy and perky enough, so all she needed to do was be more friendly, but not too much. There was a fine line to walk there—you especially don't want truckers to think you're willing to ride off into the sunset with them. Bring them their dinner, and refill their ice tea glasses or whiskey from the bar, always with a smile.

Jillian, her afternoon supervisor told her it slows down by October, then picks up a little more before the holidays. After that, she said, the only time it's real busy is in the winter when the highways close and everyone parks the trucks and stays put until I-80 is reopened again; and that could take anywhere from one or two days to a week, depending on the amount of snow or wrecks that needed to be cleared off the road.

Amy was not looking forward to that at all. Being snowed in here did not sound like fun to her. Then again, she lived here, so she'd probably get to work more double shifts and make a lot more money too. That might be okay. She'd worry about that when the time came. Right now it was hot and sunny and she was bone tired.

How many ice cream cones can I possibly make in an afternoon for those crying brats, she thought. The cones were only ten cents, but you'd think they were free, with thousands she made all day. Soft ice cream was vanilla, chocolate or twist and it was pretty good—until it was your turn to clean the machine late at night when no one was around to want one. That was a pain she found out.

She had heard someone comment that the price was going to go to fifteen cents by next summer. Yeah, well that's not going to reduce the line any I bet. Maybe they'll go out of business in the next ten years, she thought.

Joe and Amy only had one day off together, but it was enough time to get started with their plans. The rest of the summer they were both so busy working.

In the beginning, they made a pact to never take little kids, only teenagers like themselves, and never try it alone—always stay together. As they got older it would be drifters, runaways, parking lot whores, people not much missed or who would ask many questions.

Amy was great. She had the looks, of course, to get the boys to follow her anywhere. Then, when Joe showed up, it was two against one, the one always lost. They would first get them alone, begin asking some preliminary questions and walk back to the shed to the 'experiment'.

They would never be in a big hurry to get more and more. Instead they'd be patient and watch for the right person. Maybe one or two a year, hoping that wouldn't cause the local law enforcement to think anything was suspicious.

She wondered how much trouble they would get into if they were found out by someone in law enforcement, like the WHP's she saw coming into the restaurant a few times. One in particular she thought was too cute to be an officer of the law, but he told her he was a patrolman visting from another district.

CHAPTER 6

M att Gannett sat in the Flying J truck stop off I-80, outisde Rawlins, Wyoming sipping his coffee and contemplating his career as a Wyoming Highway Patrol Trooper.

This divison in south-central Wyoming is where I work, however, I always thought there would be oppportunities to move around the state and go farther west, toward Evanston. He had coffee a while back with some HP friends at that truck stop in the middle of nowhere—literally nothing around it for miles. Little America, I think it's called, and that would be a good place for some bad things to happen; drug trafficing, prositution, child pornography, any number of criminals could come and go in that part of I-80 and they wouldn't find out for a long time. For now, I'll stay close to home where I'm needed.

Matt remembered he had wanted to be a Wyoming Highway Patrol Trooper, ever since he was in high school. A local officer had come to the high school to talk with students about the dangers of drinking and driving and plain carelessness. He showed them films of the consequences of those decisions. He always thought saying that word, trooper out loud was cool—Trooper Gannett—has a nice ring to it, he thought.

One of his friends had lost his life in a car accident that year. Leon had been a shy guy and others sometimes made fun of him because his name—when spelled backward, was Noel. He was trying to fit into the cool group to overcome all the bullying, so was hanging out with the wrong crowd. When the car one of them was driving had flipped over, Leon was killed. The driver had been drinking, but the only fatality was Leon, who, of course, had not been drinking.

Matt had decided right then and there, that he was going to try and change lives and become a Highway Patrol Trooper. His mom, Donna had not approved of his entering this field so young, but she didn't stand in his way.

He came from a farming/ranching family, who after three generations still own and live off their land in southern Wyoming. It wasn't nearly as large as the bison ranch to the northwest of them, but big enough.

Matt learned young how to work hard for everything he had; which wasn't all that much material-wise, but happened to be very much in the love department, because family was everything to him.

Family included his two brothers, Zach, the oldest, and Drew the youngest. They also had a baby sister, Hope, who had been lovingly referred to as "oops", when she was younger because she had come along ten years after Drew.

He had worked many long hours on the highways of Wyoming along I-80 as far east as Laramie and west to Rawlins, and along the state highways south to Saratoga or north to Hanna. Through the rough winters and beautiful summers, he had enjoyed having his patrol car as his office.

Driving along these highways and byways, backroads, side roads in his patrol car, Matt wanted to help those in need. He looked for stranded motorists; wrecked vehicles, injured passengers and drivers ranging in ages from two-to-eighty years old. All had been grateful, of course. Although the pay wasn't bad, he didn't do it for the money, rather for the citizens of Wyoming, whom he could help by saving a life. A lot of his time was spent educating others on the dangers of driving on Wyoming roads, depending on the weather: snow, hail, heavy rain, and tornadoes. Yes, even Wyoming, has a few tornadoes in late spring, early summer, becoming more frequent each year.

Wyoming drivers also face the dangers of wildlife on open roads, and more than a few antelope, deer, and elk are killed by trucks and cars every day. The damage to vehicles and injuries of the persons can be extensive, and the death of wildlife unnecessary at times. If only motorists would pay more attention, and read the posted deer crossing signs, as it's their migratory route, not ours.

The majority of highway accidents and fatalities resulted from poor driving conditions, and poor drivers in those conditions. Many were driving too fast, impaired, under the influence, or falling asleep. State Troopers tried to minimize that by closing the highways during heavy winter snow conditions, which could also happen in the spring, when least expected. Wyoming weather can change from one minute to the next.

Learning how to drive in and handle those situations takes skill and years of experience most people do not have. A vehicle is a lethal weapon at times, traveling at high speeds, weighing a ton or more if it's a semi-truck. It's a well-known fact that high winds are frequent along Wyoming's highways, and yes, semis can blow over. Sometimes, if the driver can control it for a short while, he can try to have his rig fall over in the median or along the shoulder out of traffic. At other times, they fall over on top of cars, or into each other, causing huge pile ups. The driver has no control with 80 mph crosswise winds. These are the reasons highways may close in the winter and spring months. Proving that more semi accidents happen every year was one thing; getting anyone to listen to reason is another.

Matt knew, however, that educating drivers was one area they could help with. The more people knew and learned about these highway dangers, the fewer fatal accidents would occur, especially those of teenage drivers and their passengers. Coming up on that type of accident with fatalities was the worst part of his job. The scene is unforgettable, and so is having to inform the teens' parents.

If only there were better ways to show these kids how dangerous driving a car is in good weather, let alone on snowy, icy roads. That was why WHP Troopers taught at high schools, visited elementary and middle schools, offered driving safety courses, and provided public information via radio broadcasts.

The most rewarding part of his job had always been helping the local communities in times of need with essential things like; repairing and boarding up homes after a massive baseball-size hail storm, or rebuilding after flood damage or tornado damage. A close second to this would be delivering a baby, in a stranded car, in the middle of a blizzard. There was something about bringing a new life into the world that he found unforgettable—yet, at the same time, terrifying. While he had only had the pleasure of doing this a couple of times, he'd heard many stories from veterans on the job.

He had a few thoughts regarding matters concerning every citizen of Wyoming, be they young or old. He knew he would continue to serve the people of Wyoming on the roadways and highways that he patrolled every day and night that he patrols, in order to protect and help save a life or two.

There was always the possiblity of being caught in a car chase, or gunfight with someone along the highway, but that was remote. Those things didn't often happen on the open roadways of Wyoming, at least not in Matt's experiences. His radio suddenly beebed, alerting him that he had a call to respond to. Ah-ha, maybe it was a high speed car chase.

CHAPTER 7

This evening Amy stopped by Joe's little building on her way to work to ask him if anyone stopped in with car trouble, thinking she'd like to get a jump on things that they planned before fall or winter set in. Yes, she was getting impatient—but what could it hurt to try for one now, and that could be their prototype to scale all the others off of.

"Well, there was this one guy asking about tires because his spare was no good. So I told him to go inside and I'd take a look to see if we had the same size to fit it or not," he told her. "Are you really sure you want to do this now".

"Yeah, we're ready aren't we? I mean we're all set to try our first 'experiment', right?" she asked.

This lone traveler seemed the right type, not too old or too young. It would be interesting to see what worked and what didn't for him.

So they made a plan to get him alone after her shift and he'd follow her of course, because she'd be able to be real friendly with him during the dinner hour in the restaurant.

Once an actual plan was in motion, Amy was a little nervous, but not so much that she stumbled over words. She tried to think of something to say as she went inside to get to work. As luck would have it, according to Joe's description, he was setting down in her section. Hopefully he wasn't looking around in the gift shop first, that meant he has someone to buy for—-but not always.

"Hi, I'm Amy, how are you today? What'll ya have to drink?" she asked as she walked to his table.

"Uhm, Hi, yeah I'll have a Pepsi," he said.

"Okay I'll be right back," she smiled.

Amy got that for him and being as friendly as possible asked him,

"What'll you have something off the menu, or are you waiting," she asked as she gave him as menu.

"Yeah, not sure how long it will be, so I'll have the soda for now, thanks," he said smiling.

Amy smiled back asking his name then and where he's from.

"My name is Peter, I'm from Kansas, but I'm headed to anywhere but there," he answered.

"Oh really, why's that Peter?" she asked sweetly.

Shaking his head, "No way, not going down that road again, let's say there's nothing to go back to."

"Okay that sounds good, I'll check back in a few. If you change your mind to eat something, have a look at the menu." She said while going to check on another new table of three elderly people.

Great this is going to be a long night, she thought. Maybe it will be rewarding in the end—looking over at Peter.

After about a half an hour later, she saw Joe come in looking for her customer. He sat down next to Peter at the his table and proceeded to tell him some bad news. Amy stayed close by so she could overhear their conversation.

"Hey there, well Peter, we don't have another tire that size that you need, in a retread. But I made some phone calls to Green River and Lyman both as these are our closest towns in either direction," Joe explained.

"Okay, so what now, they have anything there?" Peter asked him.

"I'm still waiting to hear back from my buddy in Lyman, but the guy in Green River doesn't have any either. The thing is, I'm gonna have to go get it and bring it back if he does have one in Lyman, because he doesn't have a way to get it here, his tow truck driver is out on a job that could take another three or four hours," Joe said.

"Yeah and it's already what 5:00 now, so I guess I'm stuck here a while either way, uh?" Peter asked.

"At least we have real good food here and nice people. I'll let you know as soon as I hear back from my buddy in Lyman, okay," Joe said.

"Yeah, okay, Thanks, Joe," Peter said shaking his hand as Joe got to leave.

He made slight eye contact with Amy and winked at her as he left out the back door, that was her cue that it's up to her now to convince him to stay and may as well eat dinner too.

Amy only had two other tables as it wasn't the busy dinner hour yet, these few older people who like to eat early and get to bed early.

She walked over to Peter then, asking him, "So are ya having any dinner yet or are ya still gonna wait a while?"

"I may as well order now I guess looks like I'm stuck here for a bit longer. What's good on the menu or do you have a special tonight?" he asked.

Smiling, Amy suggested that yes, the special is pretty good. "Tonight it's pot roast slices, with potatoes and gravy, and carrots for the vegetable, everything is homemade."

"Okay sold, make sure you save me a piece of that blueberry pie right there assuming that's homemade too," Peter said grinning.

"Of course it is, and it's especially delicious warmed with ice cream on top. Would you like a salad with that first?" she asked.

With dinner ordered and Peter waiting to get a new tire, her first step was accomplished.

After serving Peter his dinner platter and refilling his soda, her other tables were leaving. She asked to step out back real quick before it got too busy.

Amy found Joe outside also and they talked about how long they could delay him or not before he got and left with a low tire and a flat spare to take his chances somewhere down the road to not get a flat.

Amy said, "I'll keep him talking and entertained another hour or two with dessert and all if he could come back and tell him then that you'll go get the tire and fix him. By then it should be close to nine or ten o'clock, and then delay the mounting with a few problems with the machine or something might work," she suggested.

Amy went back in to get to work, while Joe waited a little longer to go and inform Peter that it would still be a while before he could go to Lyman to get the tire he needs as planned.

Amy got back in time for a new table, as she walked by Peter smiling, "How you doing, okay?"

"All good here, the food is too," he said smiling.

As she got drinks for her table, another one was being seated. Now it was going to get a little busy, she thought when she needed to keep a conversation going with Peter. Well, she'll stop by and see if he's ready for that dessert yet in a few, or if he wants coffee first.

Peter said, "No, I'm good for now, not ready yet. I'm still full from that meal."

"Okay, I'll get you coffee then and you can let that dinner settle some." She said as she went by to her other table.

A little while later, she saw Joe sitting next to Peter probably explaining another delay, that's good she thought.

"So, yeah my boss is on his dinner break right now and he goes to his house out back here to eat. When he gets back, I'll take off to Lyman to pick up that tire. My buddy there finally called me back to let me know that he does have one left and he'll leave it outside the shop for me. I told him I'd settle up with him tomorrow and he said that's fine, he knows where to find me." Joe explained all this to Peter.

"Yeah, that's pretty cool of him to do that." Peter said.

"Yeah, he's a cool dude, we been friends a long time." Joe said.

"How long will that take then, I got time for a piece of pie, uh?" he asked.

"Oh sure," Joe said, "no problem. I'll take off here in a half an hour or so and then be back here by say 9:00 at the latest, get that mounted right away. How's that sound?" Joe asked.

"Okay sounds great, I'll hang out here. Chat with this chick here Amy, she's pretty nice." Peter told him.

"Yeah, she's real nice," winking Joe said, "Okay catch you later man, when I get back."

"Yeah okay, see ya, thanks," Peter said as Joe was leaving.

Amy stopped back by Peter saying, "How about more coffee, then get you that blueberry pie a'la mode?"

"Coffee for now, I'm hanging out a little longer if that's okay with you. Unless you'd rather I moved to the counter, so you can have a table for more than one to sit here?" he asked her.

"Sure, that'd be great if you don't mind. I'll take your cup and refill it over there then and get you another water also," she told him.

For the next hour, she was a little busy, so she only stopped to refill his a couple of times.

Then the next time around he stopped her and said, "I'll have that pie now, when you have time, no hurry still."

"Sure thing," Amy said, "Sorry I was a little busy there for a while, but I'll get that ready for you, be a few."

"That's okay take your time, like I said no hurry. I'm not going anywhere—still waiting." Peter said.

Realizing Amy had caught his eye finally, she kept busy behind the counter bending way down for something, then reaching over the other side for something else. GIving him a real good view, front or back.

Warming the piece of pie and getting the hard ice cream out to put on top took a little while also, so she stretched out the time as long as she could for that also.

She also had to check on her other three tables as more were being seated. Dropping off his dessert while going by, "Here you go, enjoy, it's delicious." She said smiling real big.

"I am....uhm I will," Peter said.

Two more new tables were seated and her other ones had left already, so that's about right. Amy had a little time to stop and talk in between.

"How is it?" she asked topping off his coffee cup.

"Everything you said and more." Peter grinned.

"Good, well don't rush the experience, savor the goodness, that's what dessert is for, right?" she said winking at him.

He said, "Oh yeah, I'm in no hurry what so ever, I could sit here all night."

So he wasn't watching the clock, that's good Amy thought, let him watch me instead that's what I want.

When Joe got back, it was closer to 9:30 and he stopped by to reassure Peter that he'll get that mounted, he needed to find out if he wanted the better one on the car now and the less flat one as a spare, he could trade that out.

"It wouldn't take that much longer and you'd be sure the better one is on the road." Joe explained.

"Okay sure, whatever you think is best man, I'm good here—take your time." Peter said.

"Okay, cool," Joe said. "I'll look for you when I'm all done."

Yes, Amy thought, he's pretty happy and I didn't have to do much, smile, wink, and bend over a few times.

That was easy, as she looked around to the other customers at the counter to make sure they didn't have any ideas of their own for her. Because she only had one thing on her mind as it got closer to end of her shift.

Amy felt the hair on the back of her neck rise and she looked around to see who really was watching her besides Peter, but didn't see anyone, A few new faces, but then she'd only been on this shift for a couple of months. Maybe she'll stop and ask Peter to walk her home if he would, because she felt uneasy, which wasn't really a lie.

Finishing her side work so that when all her customers were gone, except Peter, she'd be able to get out quickly that way. She stopped to ask him to settle up his ticket, so she could get her check out done by the end of her shift.

"So you're still here, uh?" she asked him.

"Yeah, Joe said it wouldn't take too much longer. I'm sure he'll be here soon," Peter said.

I'm sure he'll call soon or bring it over here when he's done." Amy then asked, "If it's okay with you when I'm done here in a little while, would you mind walking me home?"

"You live here too?" Peter asked.

"Yeah, in a little apartment out back of here, but I got this weird strange feeling earlier that someone was watching me, and not in a very friendly way." She explained.

"Sure, no problem," Peter said smiling.

"I'll call over to the station and tell Joe where you'll be, in case he's looking for you. Okay, thanks." Amy said obviously feeling better.

"You know Joe, does he live here too, that's helpful?" Peter asked her.

"Oh sure, everyone here knows everyone else, but we're just friends. He helped me get this job," she said being friendly again. "Well, I'll be back in a few when I get all done with my work to get ready to go," she said thanking him.

In another half an hour later when her relief person got there, Amy was ready to go. As they were walking out the door to go around the side towards the back, Joe saw them and said that he was finished.

"Hey guys, glad I caught you, you wanna have a beer before you take off Peter?" he asked as they all were walking along. "Yeah, I'm off now, we all can go to my place if you want."

Amy volunteered, "But then yours would be better, since you have the beer and I don't. We're not old enough, but no one cares about that out here." She said to Peter, pleading with him to go too—with her eyes. "I need to stop at my place first though to get a jacket."

"Yeah sure, I'm in no hurry now," Peter said. "Actually, I was going to ask if I could crash somewhere here or in my car and leave early in the morning, it's a little late now. You think that'd be alright?" he asked.

Joe and Amy smiled said, "Sure we have lots of room, no problem, man. Come on let's get a beer first," Joe said walking to the back of the property.

They all got to Joe's place, or his Dad's place, and he explained that his Dad must be next door, if it's poker night. He handed out a beer all around as Amy said, "Let's take these out back, it's a nice night."

CHAPTER 8

They were all hanging outside drinking the beer and Peter couldn't help but wonder what they were doing here in the middle of nowhere, so he asked them, "What do you guys do for fun out here?"

Joe said, "Well as a matter of fact, we were going to show you—interested?"

"Sure, what the heck," he said curiosity getting the better of him.

Joe went inside got his flashlight saying, "Great, follow us." Walking his way back to the far corner of the lot to go through the fence.

Even with a bright moon, it was cloudy. Down a short path, Peter could see a small shed he thought looked like a good sized tree covering the doorway.

"What the heck is this for out here?" he asked feeling a little anxious.

Amy took his arm says, "It's like a little clubhouse."

"Yeah, come on in, let's have our beer inside," Joe said.

Unlocking the padlock and opening the door to let the others follow him inside as he sits down the flashlight to look for the lantern he put in here somewhere.

There's only one chair, so being as Peter was the guest, they offered him to sit down. Amy continued to explain that her and Joe came across this earlier in the summer and thought it would be fun to fix it a little and use it later when the weather cooled off, because it was so hot inside with no windows.

"Yeah cool, but what do you use it for?" Peter asked

"That's the thing Peter, you're our first visitor," Amy said.

Joe announced, "Yeah dude, you get to be the first."

"The first what?" Peter asked cautiously.

Amy said quietly, "Well, our first test subject."

"What are you testing for, if I may ask—if I like beer?" Peter asked laughing, trying to light the mood.

"No," she said shyly, "we're going to ask you a few questions is all, about your dreams. Have you ever been hypnotized?" she asked.

"No, I'm sure I'd remember that. Why, have you? You said I was the first—so you never tried this on anyone else I take it." Peter said getting more nervous now. "I'm not sure I like your idea of fun."

Amy touched his arm lightly, "It's okay, we're not going to leave you. I'm going to ask you a few questions with only the flashlight shining on the little crystal pendant. All you have to is listen to my voice as I speak softly to you to try and remember some of your dreams."

"But why you need to know that information? I mean my dreams are my private thoughts aren't they, it's like intruding in my head or something," Peter said, not wanting to be a part of this any longer.

"No, I'm not going to ask anything embarrassing, I promise. You trust me don't you. And I'll make sure you remember everything you told us, how's that?" Amy said to him calmly. "You see I have these premonition dreams and I need to know if anyone else does also—or if I'm the only one that's crazy."

Well when she put it that way, it didn't sound so bad. Peter said, "I'm still not sure about the whole set up you got going on here, why can't we do this at the house then?"

Joe said, "I don't want my Dad to see us, he'll take away what little privileges I have."

"Why's that, doesn't he agree with any of this, or does he know about it?" Peter asked.

Joe answered, "You're right, he doesn't agree with our methods I guess you could say, but he does know about all of it. I assure you."

Peter thought about it some more and asked, "What exactly do I have to do?"

Amy replied, "All you have to is sit there and listen to my voice looking at this crystal and answer a few questions, it will take seriously no longer than ten minutes total."

Peter had no idea what was about to happen next, as it was a completely new experience for him too, maybe that's why he agreed to try it.

Amy asked, "Are you ready to start?"

"As ready as I'll ever be, I suppose," Peter relied.

"Okay then, relax. We're not going to be in the dark all the way, we have this flashlight. Okay, so look at the hanging crystal concentrate on that and listen to my voice," Amy told him softly.

She started to take him into a trance, "I want you to go back into your last dream and tell me what it was about, anything you can remember. I want you to concentrate solely on the sound of my voice and close your eyes now and go further back in your memory."

She told him over and over to relax and calmly clear his mind from other memories, only those in his dreams.

"What do you see, anything at all?" Amy asked him.

Peter replied, "Yeah, I see a river that's flowing by pretty high and it looks like a dog is in there and he can't get out. I'm trying to save him, but I can't reach him. He's too far away now and it looks like he might drown. I don't want to stay here any longer. Please can I go now."

Amy said, "Yes, release that thought and come back fully awake now on three— 1..2..3."

"Wow, that was really weird. It was like I was right there but not, you know." Peter said.

"Had you dreamed of this before, I mean is it a recurring dream?" Amy asked him.

"Yes I think so, I've had it before, but not always," he told her. "What you think it means?"

"Not sure, is this dog yours or was it yours and you were trying to rescue him, is that it?" she asked.

"No, I don't think so. I never had a dog before, but my neighbors did, maybe it was theirs," he answered.

"Did this dog drown? Do you know where or if it's already happened, or if it's about to happen?" she asked.

"That I can't tell you for sure, I didn't recognize the area or the type of dog it was. I couldn't see it too clearly you know, it's a dream." Peter said confused. "You think I get the same dreams you do—what did you call them cognitive?"

"No, that means being able to get information from someone else through thoughts—-like mind reading, only that it's highly suggestive or intuitive." Amy said, "I think that's the way I interpret it anyways."

"No, what I get is premonition dreams—like flashes of what is about to happen, or what has already happened with parts of that past coming out to show me something relevant to my future or to someone close to me." Amy said trying to explain what it was like for her, "Do you want to try it again, or no?"

"Well, doesn't this work for people who want to find out something out themselves or their past, to discover a hidden thought or something. Cause I don't have anything that I need to discover, so I'm good," Peter replied. "Can we go now? I'd like to get on the road."

"I thought you wanted to crash here and stay the night, we could hang out some more, have a few more beers so you wouldn't have to worry about drinking and driving," Joe said.

"I'd rather not, if it's all the same to you guys. I'll settle with you now Joe and get going," Peter said.

Amy spoke, "Was it something I said, or something I did that set you."

"No, it was all good really, I just need to get going," Peter replied.

"Okay if you say so, but I think you're afraid of something—of finding out something that you don't want to find out about or anyone else for that matter," Amy said, prodding him further.

"I don't want to make you angry either Amy, and I'm sorry but this isn't for me. And no, I don't have anything to hide, you're being paranoid," Peter told her.

"I'm paranoid, sounds to me like you're the one who's running away, not me. I faced most of my fears," Amy said. "And I'm sorry you're upset with me, but I have to find out all I can and do more research for my data. You understand don't you, Peter?"

"Sure, and I'm not upset with you. You were great, really I understand and I wish you luck with this research that you're conducting. be careful who you stop next time, you might not like the answers you get," Peter said. "Now let's get going, okay."

Joe said, "Okay then if you're sure, it's really no problem dude we can forget all this," as they all walked back to the shop to get his bill.

Peter replied, "I'd rather not, thanks anyway. I'm good to drive now really, I'm pumped and ready to go."

"Okay man, here's your total, and good luck to ya," Joe told him as he got in his car to leave.

"Well, that went well," Amy said to Joe.

"Yeah, let's make better plans for next time, maybe with a different approach," Joe reasoned with her trying to cheer her up.

"Yeah, back to square one I guess or two. Next time let's do this with a woman, so it's a totally different perspective. Deal," Amy suggested

"Deal, now let's get some sleep, I'll walk you home, tomorrow's another day," Joe told her.

As they walked slowly toward her apartment, Amy felt someone was watching them, though she didn't see anyone close by or anywhere around.

You know how it is when you feel someone's eyes on you, but you don't know from where or who it is. That made her more nervous of what she couldn't see, unless it was in her dreams, then that was worse somehow.

CHAPTER 9

I like the darkness, the stranger thought. He would watch and follow and wait patiently, quietly observing until the right moment to make a move or not. All depended on who those two little twerps were talking to now and what was their deal anyway.

Why would they con someone to go with them after a few hours or less, to let them go—what's with that. He couldn't understand the point of it all.

That's because the stranger was evil, he only knew about the hunt, not anything about why people what they do.

He went so far as to follow that young man a little ways down the road, after leaving the side of the building from observing those other two.

The guy kept going toward Salt Lake City on I-80 without getting off anywhere to give him a chance to question him, like at a rest stop of something.

So he headed on down to Utah also and made his way to Ogden on I-84, he liked that area. There were many young girls, and he could wait for right opportunity to pounce.

He'd let that go for now in Wyoming, he was way more interested in any young girls that they might come across anyway, then he could do something with that. He could take that girl from right under their noses. He'd observe again at a later time when he'd let them half his job for him.

Well, little did they all know, he'd done this before. The waiting, watching, and hunting of people. He knew what he was looking for as he had that watchful eye, that keen eye for detail. As any good photographer would.

$\mathcal{C}$HAPTER 10

B oy be careful what you wish for, Amy thought, this has got to be the worst winter ever. The wind never stops blowing and the freezing air it must be -30 outside.

Already the highway closed down twice both ways and it was only January, beginning of a new year. She could hardly believe she'd been living here for about six years already. Now with this weather, she's had enough of this middle of nowhere Wyoming living. There truly was nothing here for her any longer and she only wished she knew what she wanted to do or where to go.

Of course, she's going to have to wait for spring or summer again anyway. No one in their right mind was going to pack in the middle of this weather.

So, she would spend the closed time researching where to go next. And she also had all her notes to put together in some order from over the years. Naturally she's going to have to talk to Joe about this also. However, with Joe's dad so sick, he's not going to want to leave. Maybe it will have to wait a little longer, something she really didn't want to do, unless she leaves without Joe. No, she couldn't that. Even though they're still young and had only known each other a short time, she felt she'd always known him, which was why they had connected right away and why she moved here right out of high school. Still maybe by summer, his dad will be better and they could still leave.

This winter, however, gave her another try to convince someone to be hypnotized again. She had plenty of data to go with, but there could always be more. Always have a chance to find someone out there like herself.

Amy had a lot more to think about before making a move on anyone else, and it seemed as though she was still being watched by someone, which bothered her more.

She was always careful whenever she walked to and from work. Though it wasn't far to go, she was nervous a lot of the time. Thinking someone was watching her all the time was scary, and she tried not to dwell on it but to try and focus on other stuff like the freezing weather, and Joe, or her research, as she headed to work.

Meanwhile, Joe was finishing his shift to head home and check on his dad before going to Amy's place. He was hoping that his pa would have at least eaten something today. He knew that no appetite was not a good sign. He had to hope against hope for a full recovery, but he didn't really think that was going to happen with the way things looked lately.

He also wished the damn weather would give him a break and the wind lighten up, since he worked outside most of the time. But no, this is Wyoming where the wind always blows worse in the snow storms, causing below zero temperatures and no visibility what so ever, therefore, the highway closes sometimes for days. Then the truckers sit here in the parking lot taking up space. Most not bothering him unless they needed a tire fixed or something else was wrong with their rig.

As he started his truck to warm up, he thought about Amy and how she seemed more restless this winter than any other. Probably because it's so much worse out and lasting longer. Everyday it was more of the same, snow and wind for almost two months now.

At least the pine trees around the hotel and the housing in back were growing bigger and offering somewhat more protection from the wind out here. More than when he was a kid anyways. He could remember running around in between the tall trees and they only seemed big because he was little. Now, it's a regular forest out here. With all the extra planting every year to replace the dead or dying ones, it to have grown together a lot more also.

There's only nothing around this cold concrete building for a shop though. Oh well, another year and we'll see what happens, he thought as he got back in his truck to drive to his dad's place. He decided for a quick stop at the back door of the restaurant to find Amy and tell her he'll be a while, and see her later when she got off.

He saw Amy smile when she saw him come around the corner, "Hey you," she said.

"Hi, how's it going, good lookin? You been busy much with these closed roads?" Joe asked her.

"No, not much going on yet. It's almost dinner hour though. People have been hanging around drinking coffee and asking about when the roads will open. Are you going to come back later for something to eat yourself?" she asked

Joe said, "Ya, maybe. I'm headed to check on Pa right now, I'll see you later then."

"Okay, ya I thought you'd head there first. So I'll see you whenever, bye," Amy waved.

When Joe left out the back, and Amy got back to work, neither one realized they were being eavesdropped on. The stranger in the corner booth listened to them talking whenever he could get close enough. Always wondering when he could follow them to their little hide out with someone who he needed to have.

He felt the time was coming up soon, maybe with this snow storm, or maybe the next—but soon. The last couple of years have not proved very productive around here; and if something didn't happen soon, he was going to have to move on and come back next month.

$\mathcal{C}$HAPTER *11*

The winter wore on as usual, wind and snow all through January and February. Maybe not as many below zero days, but the snow and the wind didn't let up.

One particular sunny day in early March, when you think Spring is around the corner, Mother Nature has more winter in mind with heavy wet snows now.

Amy trudged to work sick of all the white stuff and more of the wind. Not seeing an end to this and becoming more depressed.

Grumbling to Joe last night that she's sick of this and ready to move on soon when all this lets up and starts to thaw—yeah this year for sure. He told her, "It's still a long way off for any so called spring thaw and that with more heavy snow predicted there wasn't going to be a springs until summer started. Don't you remember Wyoming only has two seasons—winter and construction."

Ha, yeah she should have remembered that one especially after this winter that's never going to end.

As she came around the corner to turn off the sidewalk and head in the back door of the restaurant, a girl of about thirteen came running right at her crying and shaking, looking behind her as if someone was going to jump out and grab her.

"Whoa, whoa, what's wrong girl?" Amy grabbed her by the arm before she could run away.

"Let go of me," she yelled at Amy. Looking behind her, more scared now.

"Hey, I'm not going to hurt you, I'm only wondering if you're okay," she said quietly to her.

"Yeah, well I will be if everyone will leave me alone," she said hiding her tears.

"Sorry, but if you need help, we could go inside. I work here and we could at least get out of the cold, if you want," Amy said.

"What's your name?" she asked her while they walked inside the back door.

"Uh, um, okay my name is Hope," she told her.

"Hello Hope, My friends call me Amy. You can stay here in this restroom as long as you want to, okay?" Amy decided to take her directly to the ladies room inside the back door off the side hallway. She reassured her she was safe here as she took off her coat, hat and gloves.

"Um, okay, thanks. It is a lot warmer in here, but I don't want my Mom to know where I am okay—you promise." Hope pleaded with her.

"Okay, whatever you say. Can I at least let her know that you're fine, so they don't worry and send out a search party for you?" Amy asked softly so as not to set her again, "because you know they'll find you eventually."

"Well, okay I guess you can say you saw me, but not where I'm at right now. I need to be alone for a little while," Hope said shyly.

"Okay, I promise. I'll come back in a bit to check on you, that be okay? Do you need anything—hot cocoa, or anything?" she asked smiling at Hope.

"Maybe later, I don't know yet how I feel. Thanks though," she answered her.

"Okay, we'll talk later," Amy said.

Amy left her to figure out whatever was bothering her by herself and went downstairs to put her stuff away and get ready to start her shift, thinking this girl could be her next research subject—or she could be in real trouble.

When she came back to the dining room, she spotted who she

thought were Hope's parents standing near the front door and large windows in the gift shop area looking outside and looking very worried.

Amy approached them cautiously, listening to the conversation in case she was wrong, she didn't want to set anyone else unnecessarily.

"Hi, my name is Amy, I work here in the dining room. I couldn't help to overhear you mention Hope, and I wanted to let you know your daughter is safe and upset but doing well," she told the older couple.

"What, how you know Hope? Where is she? I want to know right now—what have you done with her?" the woman said crying.

"Calm down Donna, we'll find out." The man told the woman and then turned to Amy to ask her, "Now, where did you see our Hope? Oh, I'm sorry, my name is John and this is my wife, Donna we are her parents," he explained.

"I'm so sorry, I didn't mean to imply anything was wrong, only that you looked so worried and Hope told me she wanted to be left alone. And well I promised her that I would only tell you that she's inside out of the weather and that she's safe," Amy said trying to reassure them. "You see I ran into her—literally—out back as I was coming to work and she was crying, so I offered her to come inside out of the cold and asked her if I could help," as she further explained. Then the parents seem to calm down more and relax a little.

"Can you at least tell me where she is? I won't go to her right away, maybe she'll come to me," Donna asked her.

"Well, you see that's the thing, I said I wouldn't tell you that, but if you were to follow or watch where I go with a cup of hot cocoa; and if I didn't know you were going to follow me, then I wouldn't be telling anyone now would I?" she said with a wink.

"She's only a little set, so I'll give her another 15-20 minutes and then check and see if she wants to come to you first. How's that—so you won't be going into where she's at right away, okay?" she reasoned with them.

"Okay, I guess I can wait a little bit longer." Donna said as John patted her arm to keep her calm.

Amy started her shift then, had a couple of tables to take care of right away. Then about half an hour later, she took a cup of hot cocoa to the ladies room down the back hallway and saw that Donna was at the other end of that hallway, so she motioned for her to stay there and she did.

Amy opened the door to find that Hope had relaxed a little bit, but that she was still sullen looking sitting on the little bench in the foyer of the restroom.

She went over to her and sat down beside her, "How are you feeling?" Handing her the cup of hot cocoa.

"Okay, I guess." she said, "Did you talk to my Mom and Dad?" Hope asked her.

"Yes, I did. And they're real worried about you. They were so scared something bad happened to you that your Mom practically bit my head off trying to get me to tell her where you were," Amy told her.

"You didn't tell her, did you? You promised," Hope asked looking nervous.

"No, of course not, but you might want to think about coming out on your own to talk to them at least. I mean they are your parents and they're going to find you anyway. Even if they have to follow me around all night," Amy told her calmly.

"Yeah, well, she gets so mad at me for nothing. I never get to anything like my brothers do. Just because I'm the 'oops' baby that came along 10 years later, they all think I can't anything on my own. And that I'm a girl—so what I can ride a horse as well as any guy can, better than most at my school," She exclaimed.

Amy said, "Boy, do I ever know how that feels—only my nickname isn't 'oops', it's 'moonbeam'. Ha, yeah, I know you can laugh now."

"And I wouldn't want to take a bet against you on riding a horse, you look mighty strong and very capable to me. How old are you Hope?"

"I'm going on thirteen—by this summer," Hope said proudly.

"Great, well I have to get back to work now. I was only going to check on you so I better get going. Are you okay now?" Amy asked as she got up to leave. "And think about what I said, okay?"

"Yeah, okay. Bye, and thanks for the hot cocoa," Hope said smiling.

"No problem, you come on out when you're ready." Amy said and then left out the door to walk down the hallway where Donna was waiting.

"Okay, so, remember don't go in, she will come out soon I'm sure. We talked again for a few minutes and she's calmed down and thinking about stuff now. You know it's hard being a girl at almost thirteen. She's trying though." Amy explained how she saw it, yet trying not to butt in too much into family matters.

"Yeah, I know. I blew my temper a little and lost it. But she's my baby, and I can't let it go sometimes," Donna said.

Amy shrugged and said, "Well you might have to come to a compromise this time." Then she had to hurry to get back to work before Peggy fired her. Yeah, like that was going to happen in the worst winter/spring snow storm ever.

Donna had waited a bit, then went back to sit, not wanting to get caught spying.

After another ten minutes, Hope came out with the mug in her hand and walked down the hallway around the corner and sat the mug down on the counter. When she saw Amy, she shrugged and whispered, "Thanks."

She then turned around and saw both her parents sitting there watching her not saying anything yet, but looking anxiously at her.

Hope went to the booth and sat down next to her Dad feeling a little relieved herself and said, "Hi"

Donna was crying now and wanted to reach over and hug her so badly, but she said, "I'm sorry honey, and I love you."

And then her Dad said, "Me too," giving her a big hug.

At this Hope laughed and said, "I love you guys too, sorry to make you worry."

Donna stood and wiped her tears and said, "Let's go home, and don't ever that again."

They all got up then and hugged and as they walked toward the door, Hope turned to find Amy and wave good-bye.

Hope told her Mom as they got outside to get in the car, "You know that Amy girl. Her nickname is 'Moonbeam'. Isn't that funny? I hope I get to see her again. She's a nice lady. Did you like her Mom?" she asked.

"Yes, she seems nice dear. You ready to head home now? Maybe next year we'll be back this way again and you can look for her then. Okay, baby girl?" Donna asked.

"Aw, Mom don't call me that. I'm almost thirteen now," Hope sigh

Amy thought about the girl during the rest of her shift and remembered herself at that age and what it was like to be thirteen— and a girl struggling for identity.

It's a tough world out there, but she figured that Hope was tough enough. She was glad not to have put her through her hypnosis research questions.

CHAPTER 12

They made it through that winter and the next because of Joe's dad being so sick and him not wanting to leave him like that. He was taking care of him day and night, thinking he seemed to be getting better last summer, but never really was in full remission. So they waited, and Amy felt it was so sad—like waiting around to die.

During that year, she really did manage to accomplish more research data for her journals.

They managed to get two more young men and an older woman to cooperate—although they had to pay one of them $50.00. But it was honest answers anyway with no tricks this time—the facts.

It was funny thinking back, the older lady thought it was all hilarious as all get out during another bad winter blizzard.

She's like, "So this is what ya'll do for entertainment here in the middle of nowhere during the winter."

And I told her, "Yeah and in the summer too."

She told me, "You'd better get a life or write a book about it one way or the other, but most of all to be careful, it could be dangerous. You never know about people."

She'd been around these truck stops a lot being a co-op driver and said she'd seen weird stuff and talked to some weird dudes over the years, therefore, she knew first hand about the types of people who travel the highways.

Amy told her, "We never do anything alone that's why Joe and I were always together during all this."

She said, "Yeah that's good, because you have to take precautions."

She was a surly old goat, Amy remembered her name was Mildred and that she'd been around the block a few times and had some good advice.

Now that it was coming up on summer again and the weather was sure warmer, Amy was ready to get out of 'Dodge'. Joe had told her since his Pa was in hospice care the last six months, that it wouldn't be long now. He had finally take him to town for someone else to take over the 24/7 care because he could no longer that and work every day also. He seemed a little more relieved also not to have to watch him die slowly every day, she though

CHAPTER 13

The first few of times the stranger spied on them was to try and figure out what the deal was, he watched and listened trying not to get too close though, of course. He went so far as to follow another young boy to ask him what was, what happened in that shed, but that seemed to scare him more and he ran off screaming, "Get away from me you creep, you're as bad as they are."

After that he would watch and wait until someone he needed to have would come along. He was very patient.

He felt however, that the time was coming when he needed to stay close by this chic and watch her every day.

And little did she know that someone was watching her a little too closely, but that he'd be back to keep his eye on this one. Yeah that's for sure this little filly would be a good ride, he thought.

It would take him a while to figure out how that was going to happen, especially after he started following her around before and after her shifts. Whatever she was doing with that mechanic, he'd find out.

Then that summer, Amy saw Hope again in July. It was her birthday weekend and they were coming back from a trip to Salt Lake City.

Hope bounced into the restaurant and went to the ice cream counter to wait in line and looking for Amy right away.

She finally spotted her and waved her over. Amy was also glad to see her again, "Hey girl, how are you?" she asked Hope. "Boy, you've sure grown over the last year, look how tall you are."

She says, "No, it's my new cowboy boots, they're great, uh. Guess what, now that I'm 14, I get my very own horse. Isn't that fabulous?" Hope said excitedly.

Amy said, "Heck yeah, that's great I'm happy for you. Does this mean that I'm going to read all about you going on the HS Rodeo circuit as the best barrel racer in Wyoming?"

"Ah, shucks, Miss Amy, I don't think so for a while anyway," Hope said with her best country drawl.

"Well, okay I'll give you a few more years to be proficient," Amy winked at her.

"Do you want to see her now? I've got her in the trailer outside," Hope asked her.

"Sure I got a few minutes, I can run out with you," Amy told her.

Well, well, there's that little filly again talking to Amy. I wonder if I can get her alone this time, the stranger thought to himself. After that encounter the winter before last when she ran off calling me all kinds of names. I'm going to have to change my appearance a little more again, something more appealing and carry my camera out in the open to take pictures of people and pets.

Yeah, that's it, she'd come to me if I took a picture of a cute dog or something. He'd have to go scout it out. He followed them outside staying way back so they didn't notice him as he went to his truck to get the camera.

He watched them go over to the next parking area where bigger trucks and trailers parked and saw them stop at a horse trailer. The little one opened the side door to give a good view to Amy. While they stood talking, he got the idea then to take pictures of her and her horse. Yes, she'd like that, then he'd have his truck right there beside hers and shove her inside and take off. Have to wait and make sure that Miss Amy, or her parent's were not around anywhere.

He sat in his truck fixing on a fake moustache and adding his longer hair wig to look more natural. All the while keeping an eye on the prize in his rearview mirror.

He had first thought he could pull his truck around back as it was getting dark outside and grab her from the ladies room out the back door. He'd seen where it goes and could easily take her out that way.

Now with this horse picture idea, he'll wait for the right moment and approach her. Soon, he thought, very soon he'll have her and then the fun will begin, as he watched from across the parking lot making sure he wouldn't be noticed.

Amy said she had to get back to work, hugged Hope good-bye and left. Then Hope had stayed to feed her beautiful horse some of the hay in the back and maybe an apple treat for being so good. As she went around the other side to the back, she saw a beat up old truck that had stopped and this weird hippy dude got out with a camera.

"Would you like me to take your picture with your horse, it is yours right?" he asked her.

Hope thought for a minute that maybe it's getting too dark out and that wouldn't be a very good picture.

As if he read her mind he said, "I got these new special lenses and night filter light focus on my camera that I'd like to try out, if that's okay with you, I'll be quick, I promise."

Hope looked back at the restaurant and didn't see her parents yet, so she said, "Okay, I guess that'd be good, but we have to be fast about it; my parents are coming back soon and I have to feed her and be ready to go."

The stranger told her, "Oh, don't worry I'm fast alright." Then he got closer to her and reached out and took a hold of her arm real tight and his other hand over her mouth with a cloth of chloroform so she'd be easier to handle, and pulled her into the back of his truck.

His little pickup had a topper cover on the back so as to hide anyone he had back there, which happened to work out fine this time to stash this little filly. He had the duct tape all ready to put on her wrists, ankles, and mouth in case she woke before he got to where he was going.

In less than two minutes, she was all trussed like a calf, and he was on his way driving to the exit of the parking lot toward the highway headed west. Not too fast—no need to hurry.

He smiled and turned on the cassette player to listen to, 'Life's a Highway', by Tom Cochran, his favorite. While Hope slept the night away, he drove on further west, taking US 30 to the Idaho border thinking there is less traffic this way, therefore less hassles.

He kept driving and looking for a place to pull off the roadway on some little side road so as not to attract any attention. Soon enough he would find the right spot, patience had to be his strong suit. Afterall, perfection doesn't happen overnight.

CHAPTER 14

D onna saw Amy come in from outside as she was walking out from the ladies room.

"Hey there Amy, did you see Hope? She was looking for you," Donna asked.

"Yeah, she took me out to see her horse, she's a beauty alright," Amy said.

"Oh, yeah," said Donna, "We couldn't resist her either. Hey, I wanted to thank you after last winter when you helped out Hope. It's been so nice since then. I can't tell you the difference it's been between us."

"Oh great, glad to hear it. She sure is happy," said Amy as they hugged each other saying good-bye.

Donna went in search of John and Hope so they could get going, they still had a ways to drive across two mountain passes to get home. She found John checking out the life-size stuffed penguin in a case by the front registration desk.

"Hi, there cowboy, what'ya doing?" she smiled at him.

"I'm waiting on two beautiful girls to take me home with them— looks like I got one, where's the other?" John asked her with a wink.

"Probably out with her horse still, we better get going, it's getting late you know," Donna told him.

"Yeah, it's a ways to go still, I know. Hey, did you see this, it's a real penguin—well stuffed, but it used to be at the first Little America's original site over on US 30 by Granger, cool uh?" John told her as they walked out the side door to the parking lot where the truck and trailer were parked.

They both walked over to the truck and looked inside where it was empty, so John walked around to that back of the horse trailer and the back door was open but no one was there, only the horse that was still in the trailer.

He called out to Donna, "Did you see Hope come out here or had she gone back inside already?"

Donna walked back there saying, "No, I haven't seen her. But that Amy girl said she talked to her and came out here to see her horse. She was showing her off a few minutes ago."

"Let's go find them, Hope probably went back in the front door looking for us or something. I wonder why she would leave the back door to the trailer open like this though," he said as he closed it and locked it shut.

They both hurried to the front door, walked past the gift shop to the restaurant looking for Hope. Not seeing her right away, so they searched for Amy to ask her. John figured they were together talking again about her horse and eating ice cream as she waiting for them.

He saw Amy then talking to a few at the counter, so he went that way and sat down. As she came over to say hi, he asked her, "Have you seen Hope come back in since you went out with her a little bit ago?"

"No, I haven't, why?" she asked him.

"She's not out there or in here, we need to look around some more and search all the rooms—maybe the gift shops. Thanks," he told her as he hurried that way,

"Wait, I'll get you some help, and I'll go check the restrooms back here. Have Donna check the ones over by the front desk too," she yelled after him.

"Okay, we'll double check everywhere." He hollered back while he went to find Donna to tell her.

"No, Amy had not seen her come back in, she's looking also and checking the ladies room, let's look in the other one too."

Now Donna was really scared and crying, again saying, "I don't think this is like last time, it doesn't feel right. She's happy now, she wasn't upset with us at all. She has her own horse. Where is she John? Where could she have gone?"

"Okay, now Donna let's look around some more and ask questions. Be calm, we'll find her. And Amy's getting help for us to look all over the building," John told her trying to keep her calm.

"Okay yeah, let's look in all the gift shops here, she won't be too far from her horse either. She loves that filly, but to get started, ask the front desk to call around to other areas, okay John, for me?" Donna said as she tried to think of where her daughter would be.

CHAPTER 15

Little did they know, or would especially fear to know, she was already in the back of a pickup half way down toward the Granger exit, on US 30 headed to Idaho somewhere.

The stranger had acted fast. Now he had to think real fast about where he was going, but carefully consider his surroundings and pay attention to his speed, so as not to attract any undue attention. The last thing he needed was a WHP officer to stop him and ask a lot of questions.

Even as he saw one headed in the opposite direction, he could still turn around. Be careful, watch your speed, watch your driving, don't anything stupid or get too anxious or excited. No need to hurry now.

He took the wig and moustache off, as it itched and he didn't need it on any longer. He needed to look different anyway.

He listened to his favorite cassette mix as he drove along on the highway, thinking he'd stop off on a side road somewhere because it would be dark outside soon and he'd have to find something to be invisible when he could turn his lights out somewhere off the main road.

He figured if he took care of this business sooner rather than later he'd be free to move on. Probably into Idaho where he'd been scouting out places this last year. There were quite a few small towns between here and Pocatello to hunt along the rest areas and truck stops.

There were so many side roads and open spaces out here, but where they lead to. He didn't want to be on anyone's private land either where someone might be coming or going. He also didn't want to take one of these gas line roads where someone might be doing maintenance checks. Probably not at night, but you never know. So he drove one, looking for the right seclusion spot.

He knew there wasn't much of anything or anyone past Kemmerer, so he went on down at least that far. Sure enough about thirty miles more he found the right hillside with a dirt road to take him over the top of that.

He didn't see any lights from any houses that could be nearby or from any vehicles either. So when he pulled off and stopped turned out his lights and listened, nothing was heard—not any traffic noise.

There still wasn't any signs of movement from the back, so he wanted to wait it out and have her come around some more on her own. Won't be much longer he thought, as he planned out the rest of the kidnapping, thinking of all the fun he was going to have and the new pictures he would have also.

By now Donna was really getting agitated and scared. She finally convinced John to call their son Matt who was with the WHP (Wyoming Highway Patrol). If he was back home, he could still make calls to friends here and get them here quicker than the Sheriff's Office from Green River. Because nobody was doing anything right now, and Donna thought she might go mad with worry.

Matt assured us that he would call the Colonel of WHP personally, if that's what it took and ask for assistance in this part of the state to be on the lookout for anyone suspicious. Except without a possible vehicle description as yet, there still might be someone out there that would notice something out of the ordinary.

That's why Matt also appealed to the local media, his friend in Green River at the local office there knew the owners of the Radio Network, and he would have them put out an Amber alert, asap. The sooner the information got out about Hope the better.

Since she disappeared along an Interstate highway, it was the WHP departments' business to handle this anyway.

What they needed now was a break for anyone to produce some information. They asked and searched all around the property that they could find. However, there could be someone out there who might have seen any small unusual thing happen, who have since left the parking lot area and is on the highway. Therefore, if he could get it out on the radio fast, someone might remember or had seen something suspicious.

Donna and John prayed for anyone to come forward with any information. They also pleaded with the media when they went into town to get on the radio themselves, to please have Hope returned to them. In case whoever had taken her was listening to the radio. Because they were now convinced she was taken against her will. There was no way she would have taken off and run away on her own. No way-not now.

When Amy heard that Hope was missing and nowhere to be found, she was very concerned and frightened for her. Especially after she heard the radio pleas for help and information.

She sincerely felt somewhat responsible leaving Hope out there with her horse alone in the parking lot. Trying to rack her brain for anyone around who was not familiar to her, or maybe someone who she had seen hanging around before that had seemed creepy to her.

But for the life of her, she could not remember seeing that one guy who she felt was following her at one time or another, or more than once. By now, it was the next day and she truly felt that Hope was not going to be found—at least not alive.

CHAPTER 16

As it turns out, the stranger was going to have a little fun and then dispose of Hope as if she never existed. From dust to dust you shall return he thought as he smiled, thinking of the plans he had for this very lively young girl.

Finally, he heard her crying and hollering for help though he taped her mouth. When he stopped, he went around and opened the back tailgate making sure to be careful of those feet of hers to kick out at him though her ankles were taped, she's wearing those heavy cowboy boots and that would certainly hurt if she connected in the right spot. He's going to have to remove those first thing.

He had this pen light shining in to see where she was, and fortunately she had curled at the other end by the cab of the truck. He crawled in the back and pulled the tailgate shut and heard her whimpering.

"Well now, look what I have here," he said as he got closer. "It's okay, I'm just going to take some pictures and we had to be alone to that, you understand that don't you?" he said trying to calm her into submission.

"I'm going to cut off the tape from around your ankles first, okay now don't you kick me or it will be worse for you—got it," he said sharply.

Hope nodded her head slowly. He took out his pocket knife and cut the tape then holding her feet down and then he began to remove her boots, and she started shaking in fear.

"I have to do this so you don't hurt yourself, remain calm," he told her.

It was an unusually warm night and being all in a small enclosed space was warmer, therefore, he started removing all of her clothes and told her so that she would be more comfortable while he took the pictures.

He cut off her shirt and camisole undershirt so that he didn't have to remove the tape from around her wrists. By now Hope was crying uncontrollably and he had to ignore that.

What a disappointment this had turned out to be, he thought she'd have more fight in her, well maybe when we get down to the good part she'll be more lively. Being totally nude now, he posed her in several different positions as he took several pictures—taking his sweet time.

Then he sat the camera aside and began to lightly caress her body and feeling the tremors she couldn't control, which only aroused him more so much so that he also took his clothes off and started to stroke himself while also feeling her body all over. Knowing or at least suspecting she as a virgin was half the excitement, the other half, the better part, was watching the fear in her eyes become intense and real as she knew what was about to happen.

"Yes, baby, we're going to have a little fun now. You'll see, you're going to really like it," he said smiling.

Hope began to squirm and cross her legs to get away from him and curling into a ball. Whimpering, "Please...take...me back...I won't...tell...anyone…. I..promise."

"I know you won't, because you won't get the chance," he said. That's more like it, he thought as he grabbed her by the ankles and she kicked and tried to scream. He enjoyed that more and got on his knees forcing her legs apart and then he forced himself into her so hard that her eyes about bugged out of her head. He could see the pain all over her face and that only got him to go faster and harder into her, then he purposely slowed down the strokes so she would start to relax and think it's over---then that's when he started to go at it again harder and deeper as he moved her legs further apart and held onto her thighs.

After what seemed like forever, but was only a few minutes, he was almost done with that part. He sat back looking at her and stroking himself again and playing with her some more to get all her wetness around his fingers to the ass and put them in there to get her ready.

"Now, we're going to try something else for some real fun, little girl. That was so good wasn't it—wait til you get some of this." He said turning her over onto her belly still rubbing himself to get hard again. Sure enough, he entered her ass then and pumped hard as before if not more, and that made her scream so much she was hyperventilating and passed out.

Well damn, he thought as he finally came, that wasn't as nearly as good as I had hoped it would be. So he turned her over and removed the tape from on her mouth and slapped her face so she would breath deep and slower now that she could get more air.

Her eyes were still wide with fear and he couldn't resist but take a few more pictures to enjoy later.

"Well that was a first for me too---" he said sarcastically, "Never had anyone pass out before. Well now it might be time to be done with this what you think little one, you had enough, or you want some more?"

Hope shook her head and crying whimpered, "No, please, take me back."

"Can't do that, but we're almost done—there's one more thing we need to do before the end," he said almost thoughtfully.

Something in his voice had made Hope realize she's in more trouble now. Now thinking she'll never get out of this alive and see her family or her new horse again ever, caused her great pain and sorrow. There was no fight left in her at all, she resigned herself to the fact that she was going to die here like this and so she was not going to give him the satisfaction of fear any more or struggle.

He managed to find a long pretty red ribbon and tied it around her neck---not so tight yet though. But he did notice she was quiet and not moving, as he got ready to rape her one last time.

"Yes, by now I see you know what's going to happen next, don't you? Well, okay you got me figured out, that's fine don't fight me anymore, I don't really care. We're almost done now anyway," he said flatly.

Yeah, almost done he said to himself as he began to rape her again and took a hold of each end of the ribbon and pulled a little bit and then a little more harder while watching her face contort with pain knowing she was about to breathe in her last breath.

Then he relaxed on the ribbon a little as he continued to screw her, letting her get another big breath so he could take it away. He really wanted her to struggle more and show the fear again, but she didn't, so as he was about to cum, he pulled tight as he could on the ribbon and she gave in to death at the exact moment he came.

All he had left to now was to tie the remaining ribbon into a bow, trim off the ends, take a few more pictures, and dig a hole while it was still plenty dark out.

After that little chore was done, he was exhausted. So he pulled himself into the cab of the truck took a long drink of water and then a nap before the morning light would come over the hill. He still took the time to write down the exact location markers in his notebook for future reference. He was relaxed and calm with new memories of satisfaction.

CHAPTER 17

After a few of weeks with no word of finding Hope, Matt finally convinced Mom and Dad to come home. At least to pasture Hope's horse if nothing else. They had to take care of the animal, he reasoned with them.

I promised them I would continue searching and asking anyone who would still listen to me. No matter how long it would take, I would find the answers they needed.

Of course, Donna and John were like walking zombies themselves, only the shell of the parents he knew. The light was gone from them and he feared it was forever.

This was going to kill his Mom he thought, when he first saw them return to the ranch. She couldn't bear to let go of Hope's horse either. She'll need that when she comes home to help her heal from the trauma, she kept insisting. She never wanted to give up on finding their daughter.

As the weeks turned into months and then almost a year later I knew I had to go back to where it happened. To Little America to ask around again for anyone who might remember something else, and talk to that waitress his Mom told him about who had last seen Hope showing off her horse to her.

As soon as the weather got warmer again in late spring that year, so that he could travel the distance it took to get there. I took more personal days off from work and headed out. I wasn't going to show up in my patrol car and full uniform and scare off anyone I might need to talk to.

Three hours later, I pulled into the gas station and got out to stretch and look around at my surroundings. I wanted to get a feel for the layout. When I was here after Hope disappeared, I was too upset also to really look around at everything. I noticed how the place was surrounded by pine trees all the way back. Lord, I thought, anyone could hide around here with all these trees for hours, or days.

I asked the young man filling my gas tank,

"What's back there in all those trees near the rear of the property?"

The guys says, "That's employee housing back there. Some larger houses for the managers and others are like apartment complex style only spread out in a ranch 'L' shape—not the two story high type."

"Oh ya, must be nice, uh? Do you live back there also?" I asked him.

"Yeah, I used to anyway with my Pa, he was the shop mechanic; but he's in town now at a hospice," he told me.

"Sorry to hear that. What are these buildings here behind the restaurant?" I asked casually.

"Oh well, more housing for singles though—not big enough for families," Joe explained.

"It's all pretty close to this truckers parking lot—you ever get any trouble from that area back here?" Matt asked more curious now.

"Naw, the only thing I had to get used to was all the noise from those trucks coming and going at all hours of the night and day when you're trying to sleep," Joe said.

"Yeah, I can see that," I said, "Do I pay you here or inside?"

"Right here is good, if you need change I can get it for you here in this little building," Joe explained.

"That's alright, you keep the change," I smiled, "and thanks."

I drove back around to the front of the building to the restaurant entrance and went in to get a late lunch. I asked the hostess if I could sit at the counter, and she assured me that was fine.

I remembered the name of the waitress I needed to talk to was

Amy that my mom had told me, so when I sat down I looked at all the waitresses name tags and didn't see anyone with Amy on it.

However, Karen saw him sit down and she smiled at him asking, "What'd ya have, coffee or ice tea?"

"Ice tea, thanks," I answered.

"Sure, you need a menu for lunch also?" she asked.

"Yeah, I'll have lunch, but what's your special today?" I asked her.

"Oh yeah, it's a great one today, hot roast beef open face, with mashed potatoes, gravy and green beans," Karen informed me.

"Sounds great, I'll take that," I told her.

"Okay, good. I'll get that going and be right back in a few to check on you," she told me.

"No problem, I'm good here," I said.

As Karen walked away then to check on her other customers and put my order in I presumed, I looked around at the layout of the tables in relation to the front windows and the gift shops.

Then I started to study the other people in the restaurant while I was waiting. I noticed truck drivers who sometimes sat in pairs or fews, but also quite a few singles—those were the ones I watched. I was wondering if one of them had taken my sister.

When Karen came back around to check on me and refill my ice tea, I asked her, "Is there still an Amy who works here?"

"Yeah, she works the afternoon shift though, it doesn't start until 3:00," she said. "Why you know her?"

"No, I want to talk to her and ask her a few questions about last summer. You see the girl who disappeared from here was my sister," I said sadly.

"Oh dear, sweetie I'm so sorry. All of us here still can't believe something like that happened here." Karen said with sympathy, then asked "Can I tell her you're here and that you want to talk to her?"

"Sure, is she here now, or does she live here too?" I asked her, getting anxious now.

Karen says, "Yeah, she lives out back of here in those little white apartments."

"Does she work today anyway? I can talk to her then or if not, I'll need to go find her apartment," I said.

"Okay, let me go get your lunch, and I'll double check the schedule to make sure she's on for today, be right back," she told me, walking away in a hurry.

She came back out after a few minutes with a huge plate full of food---my lunch and said, "Yeah, she'll be here at three, but if you want, I can go get her here in a few and then you can talk to her after you eat and before she starts her shift. That way you won't be interrupted. I can save a booth for you guys in the back with more privacy."

I thought about that for a minute and said, "Okay, maybe that'd be best if you don't mind. Because I do need to talk to her with a little privacy, if it's not too much trouble. That's why I came back here."

"Okay then, let me finish here with these few folks and I'll go get her." Karen said as she refilled my ice tea and continued on over to check on her other two booths near by. He watched her bring out meals for them and then she told the other waitress something before she went out the back doorway.

Karen found Amy talking to Joe at the back door of the shop and told her about Hope's brother being here in the restaurant and wanting to talk to her.

"Okay, I'll be right there," Amy told her.

"We have to tell him what we think happened," Amy told Joe nervously. Talking about the guy Karen told her was waiting to talk to her.

"No, we don't. We can't get involved. He can't know that you had anything to with that girl," Joe said.

"He already knows that I talked to her last, that's why he's here. Donna probably gave him my name," Amy said.

"It's not our problem, you have to forget about her," Joe told her.

"I can't, I keep having more dreams. Don't you see, maybe I can help find out what really happened to Hope. Maybe if I say I saw a pickup truck that day. At the very least, help provide a timeline, I was the last one to see her—except the killer that is," Amy tried to explain.

"It's been almost a year ago, I don't remember much about that day. How could you describe anything to him now? Then he'll wonder why you didn't the first time," Joe asked her.

"I'll never forget, now that I know she went missing from here for sure that day and was never heard from again," Amy said sadly. "Besides there's that one weird guy that's been following me around that I told you about, you know I showed him to you again last week and I know I've seen him before then also."

"Well, then maybe we can get some real proof that's not connected to us being involved, but someone else like him before we contact anyone with this case," Joe said getting exasperated with her.

"But her brother is in there right now talking to Karen, and he already knows that I'm here today. He is the law from what I remember Donna telling me, he works for WHP and he knows that I was the last one to talk to her when she was showing me her horse," Amy reasoned with him.

"Then we leave the area, that's what we do. Maybe it's time to move on anyway. Go to Idaho or something, like we've talked about. To where we don't know anyone else, some other small town where we can blend in and lay low for a while. Postpone this silly research data questioning people of all ages, types and genres," Joe said.

"Silly, uh? It wasn't silly to you a few month's ago," she said angrily now.

"Look I'm upset too, I don't want to be connected to any of these disappearances at all. So let's go now, while we can," Joe suggested. "I have some money saved, I know you too. There's nothing for us here anyway."

"Yeah, I suppose so, since you're Dad is gone now, we don't have anyone else for us here," she agreed. "But I can't leave without talking to Hope's brother at least—then we'll see, okay. We have to try and find out what happened to her. You promised to help me also, because if I ever see that guy again when we move from here, then it's no coincidence," she said heatedly.

"Okay, okay, I promise, but we have to get away from here as soon as we can. Let's give our notices tomorrow and start packing our stuff. We'll go to town, close out our accounts and use cash from now on. Okay, sound good to you?" Joe said, looking more and more nervous.

"Okay, I suppose so. You might be right to get away from here. I'll let you know what I talk about with this guy." Amy told him, and then she walked toward the back door of the restaurant.

When Amy walked through the back door and saw Karen head her way—probably wandered what had took her so long, she asked her where this guy was.

"I told him I'd save you guys a booth toward the back here for more privacy, okay it's table 23," Karen told her. "I'll go tell him you're here and see if he's finished with his meal, wait here."

"Okay, I guess," Amy as she went to help herself to a cup of coffee. It's going to be a long night she thought.

Karen went to check on the guy waiting for Amy—dang it she thought, she forgot to ask his name. She went to the counter area and saw that he was almost finished with his lunch plate and asked him, "Are you going to make it through that, or you need me to take it away?"

"Yeah, you better get it away from me, that's a lot of food. I won't need to have dinner now anyway," he told her.

She said, "I didn't get your name before, but Amy's here now. I'll move you over to the booth since you're done with lunch now and tell her she can come and take a seat."

He told her, "Okay, thanks, and the names' Matt," moving to where she showed him.

Karen went to find Amy again then and tell her that Matt was waiting for her at that booth she was saving for them, as she was stopped by someone at her table for a refill. Boy, Karen thought, I'm losing my touch worrying about what's going on with Amy and this Matt guy.

Amy came from around the counter and saw Matt first. Oh my be still my heart, this guy takes tall, dark, and handsome to another stratosphere, Amy thought, as she sat down.

"Hi, I'm...um...Amy," she said stammering like an idiot, but trying to recover quickly with a smile.

"Hi, I'm Matt, Hope's brother, glad to finally meet you," he said in a very nice voice. "I was hoping to ask you some questions about that day you saw Hope when she took you out to the horse trailer to see her horse, is that right?" Matt asked

I hope I'm not blushing, but those startling blue eyes and the little wave of dark hair that keeps falling over his forehead is driving me crazy. I might be involved with Joe, but I'm not dead.

"Uh, yeah, she did, we talked for a few minutes and then I had to get back to work," she said, looking down at the table to hide her blush.

He said, "You're the last one of us to see her except whoever took her, of course."

"I guess so, yeah. What you need to know? I told the Sheriff all I could back then. I'm not sure why you need to talk to me now," Amy told him.

"I wanted to meet you and ask if there's anything else at all that you might have remembered since then that could help me," he said. "I thought you were a friend to Hope then, so I figured you might give me a little insight to that day."

"Okay, yeah I guess we were friends. I helped her out of a situation with her Mom the year before that I think it was. So what do you want to know?" she asked.

"Well, if you can remember what Hope was like, was she happy, anxious, or acting scared of anyone? Did she mention anyone following her around that day—or did you see anyone?" he asked her following up with other questions, that made her feel like an interrogation.

"I remember that day very well—like it was yesterday; but no, she wasn't scared of anyone that I know of, didn't act anxious or anything like that. She was very happy, wanting to show off her new horse," Amy explained.

"What about you, have you noticed anyone strange or different hanging around that day or afterwards coming in here? I'm sure you see a lot of people, I was wondering if anyone or anything at all seemed suspicious to you?" he asked her.

She cast her eyes downward again not wanting to look him in the eye as she thought about what to say.

"There's always weirdos coming in here, you know, off the highway; but no one that I can remember seeing that day as unusual," Amy honestly told him.

"Okay, well thanks Amy, I appreciate you talking to me anyway. It was worth a shot to see if you had, since then thought of something else. Here's my card, you can call me anytime day or night if you think of anything or hear anyone talking. I'd truly appreciate it," he told her sadly.

Amy said, "Okay, sure," as she got up to leave and get ready to start her shift.

I certainly felt she was not telling me the whole truth about something. Maybe someone had threatened her not to say anything to me or anyone else. And maybe she's scared of that someone. No, she didn't really seem frightened, evasive for some reason. He couldn't figure out why though, especially since she seemed eager to help out otherwise. What does she have to hide. She seemed young, but not that young to be a runaway herself.

Maybe if I hang around here some more—another day. Ask more questions to other employees about that day, maybe she'll come around and confide in me about what it is that's bothering her. Because he truly felt there was more to Miss Amy than what she's telling him.

CHAPTER 18

Amy managed to get through the next few hours, although she felt Matt watching her for a while before he left. She felt really bad and sad about Hope and yes, she should have confided more to him about her feelings of being watched herself over the last several years that she's lived here.

But he would think she was off her rocker, if he ever found out about her dreams. Why would someone watch and follow her around, but then not anything else. It's not like I've done anything wrong, certainly not anything illegal— a few research interviews.

Um, because he's trying to find out what I'm doing with some teenagers for his own purposes, I suppose. What if that creep did take one or two of the kids she had interviewed in that shed? What if he followed them to somewhere else from here and took one? She tried to remember if there were any more missing young girls close by here over the years.

All this was going through her head, asking herself as she worked on through her shift on autopilot. Finally, Joe came in for dinner and asked how it went earlier.

"Okay, I guess. He wanted to know if I had remembered anything strange or unusual from that day was all," she told him.

"Well, I still think we should leave as soon as we can, however, that might look suspicious for us too. We should give notice though and plan on the end of next week to be ready. How's that sound to you?" Joe asked her.

It seems he's thought this over for a while after they had talked earlier, she thought. "Yeah, that should be enough time to get everything in order and ready to go. I still feel bad not telling him that there's a creepy dude that hangs around here sometimes." She said looking around over her shoulder now, thinking someone was there listening.

"I know, me too. You want me to come back when you get off to walk you home?" Joe asked.

"Yeah, would you please. If you don't mind, I'd feel better, thanks." Amy said. "I'd better finish around here with my sidework then so I can get right out the door at 11:00—see you then."

"Okay, later then," Joe said walking out.

Amy thought about talking to Joe a little more while they were walking home. Maybe he'll listen to reason about telling Matt all she knows to help find out what happened to Hope.

For now, she had to get back to work and finish what she could of her side work, because she still had two hours to go before she could call it a night.

When Joe came back Amy was ready to go right on time. They went out the back door and Amy said to him, "Did you know that Hope's brother is a WHP? Yeah, he gave me his card to call him if I ever wanted to talk."

"Wow, no wonder he's obsessed, he's the law and can't find any answers to finding the bad guy," Joe said. "Well, it's not our problem, I still think we need to get going to Idaho maybe. You know all those towns along US 30, from when you used to go that way to Boise. We could stop anywhere along there and get a new place, new job, new life. That'd be good, right?"

"I'm not sure I want to go that way, after all there's not that much down that way you know," Amy said.

"I know, that's the whole idea. To be anonymous as much as possible right, blend in, start fresh," Joe said. He was surely getting more excited about the whole idea, she thought.

They walked back to the little apartment they now shared after

Joe's dad had passed. No one ever said anything though they were not married, but it was saving a lot on expenses and able to save more money in the long run. They were going to need it now.

Amy felt strange as she was about to open the door, as though she was being watched again. She felt that oddness of hair rising on the back of her neck. Looking around in the darkness, she thought she saw a shadow movement behind that tree, and she nudged Joe to get inside whispering to him, "I think I saw something or someone back there following us."

CHAPTER 19

The stranger had waited in the dark shadows, listening to them stop and talk and argue. Raising their voices a little so that he could hear them with no problem.

Those stupid little twerps had no idea what's going on, but if they get in the way again or start to go to that dumb cop hanging around, then something will have to be done.

A lot can happen in the middle of nowhere here in Wyoming, where people can disappear. He had been so careful and successful over the last 10-15 years—wasn't sure how long it had been, he lost track of time. But he had no intention of stopping or giving up his passion. The perfect cover of being a wildlife photographer and knowing the lay of the land always helped him out.

He thought of all the perfect young girls over the years. Most were only 14-15 years old, but only two were provided by his little unknown 'friends'. The others came along in different places at opportune times that he couldn't deny those that were meant to be.

He was thinking to himself earlier, when he heard Karen talking to that guy. That maybe he had taken his chances too far along the way somewhere and that he was looking for him, he had only stopped here a few times over the years to hunt that is. To eavesdrop was another matter.

Then when he heard what these two were talking about him being a WHP and all, he had to be looking for more answers on that one he took from here with her horse. He had to come back and find out if anyone had any ideas about him, and it was a good thing he did.

Maybe it's time he moved on also---try some new territory. Montana was always good to him, he had taken a few there, and the pictures were always great for a side business. The wildlife pictures that is.

If those two idiots were going to Idaho, maybe he'd shadow them and go to wherever they settle down and look around in bigger cities also—like Twin Falls, or Boise for a while. Then come back to find them, to take care of any problems they may have caused.

The stranger waited in the dark until the lights went out and then he made his way back to his truck to head out to parts unknown as yet.

He figured if he headed back to Utah, or Montana, he could always find out where they went by hanging around in those small towns that he overheard them talking about on US 30 in Idaho.

Oh, the fond memories of taking that route along the highway in Wyoming—not quite sure if he had any luck in Idaho or not. Must be losing my mind, they all seem to run together, good thing I've kept such meticulous notes on everyone. It's probably not that important to so any longer, but it seemed that it was absolutely necessary.

Now, all he cares about is having the pictures to look at. That he's provided the most enjoyment during the long winter nights.

$\mathcal{C}$HAPTER 20

They ended up in Soda Springs, Idaho. When they decided on one of the bigger towns on US 30, it provided more opportunities for employment. That is how Joe got his job with the Highway Department as a mechanic.

That was because Amy knew the area pretty good with her driving back and forth to Boise to visit her parents during the time they lived in Wyoming. She liked this route better, because it was less traffic and better views.

They wanted to stay in this area, as it provided access to both Wyoming and Utah, which were close by to take a day trip to the truck stops or rest areas. They were also not too far from Pocatello or Twin Falls. Staying within this 200 mile radius was the plan in order to have more choices of who they would come across to interview again. However, that was becoming less and less now as Amy decided she needed to track down the guy that never seemed to give up following her.

It had only been about six months now when Amy got that feeling again and she wondered if she was losing her mind, or going crazy. There could not possibly be anyone here who knows where they moved to.

She had landed a job pretty easy at the local diner doing what she knows. Joe also got a job as a mechanic because that's what he knows best and loves. He always wanted to open his own shop, so he did work on the side in the shop he set in the garage where they rented.

If someone knew that they could find them through their employment, then they were so screwed because they pretty much stayed with the same type of job they'd had before. But, no way. They were so far off the radar, always spent cash, didn't open any accounts; and yet she was always looking over her shoulder.

Well that's about to change, she was sick of feeling hunted, she was about to become the hunter. She had to find out who it was following them because she knew it had something to with the disappearance of Hope and probably the others she had read about recently also.

Since moving here, she had went to the local library and looked through some past newspaper articles of Wyoming, Idaho, Utah, and Montana for anything similar to what happened to Hope. Gone with no trace, never to be found or heard from ever again---all young girls. Now she knew there really was a pattern here maybe something to follow her instincts with.

Joe had tried to tell her to forget it and let it go so they could get on with their lives and build something together. She refused, how could she stop thinking about it. Not when it involved her peace of mind. She would never be able to 'move on' as he told her, if she still felt someone was out there watching her every move.

This time she was able to get a day shift so she'd be home in the evenings same as Joe, also because she felt safer getting home when it's still daylight instead of late at night.

When she got home that afternoon after her shift was over, she would have a long talk with Joe about turning the tables on this feeling. She finally was going to be proactive and not hide any longer.

During dinner that night she brought up the subject with Joe, "So what you think about me being the detective and finding out who this creep is that's been watching me? Because I felt it again today, I know he's here somewhere," she asked Joe casually.

"You know what I think, you better not push your luck on this. It could be dangerous if what you think is true, that it's the same guy as who took Hope. Why not call that WHP guy---Hope's brother.

You have his card still, I saw in on your dresser. I'm sure he'd be glad to help you out," Joe said sarcastically.

"Yeah, I thought about that too, but I think I need some proof first. He'll think I'm loony, that's why I didn't say anything last year when he came back to Little America and was asking me all those questions about Hope. Well that, and I didn't want him to find out why I thought someone was really following me and close by all the time, before Hope went missing. But now we're not involved in any of that research any more." Amy explained in length trying to get her point across.

"I know what you're thinking, you're going to go off on your own, all maverick and set some kind of a entrapment on this guy aren't you—right? Well I'm not going to let you get yourself into trouble and maybe killed. So I guess I'll have to help you, because I see you've made up your mind already," Joe told her.

"Yes, well I appreciate your offer to help, but I'm not going to get into any trouble, I'm only going to gather information and then pass it onto Matt."

"Maybe you're right, but trying to find out is going to be tricky. How you plan to start, when you have no idea who it is or what he looks like?"

"Well, I have some idea of what he looks like at least what he used to look like. I'll have to be more observant and try to find that same type of person that used to follow me, in case he's changed into some other disguise. I got an idea anyway, use that familiarity and feelings to get a bead on him without letting him know that I suspect anything is wrong," Amy said, going on to explain further. "In other words no more looking over my shoulder. I'm going to sit somewhere and watch and wait for him to come looking for me again. Remember when I told you before we left Wyoming, that if we moved here and I was sure that I was being followed again and you promised to help find out who he is." Amy tried to explain how strongly she felt about all this.

"This scares me too much, maybe I ought to buy a gun," Joe thought out loud.

"No way, please don't that. It would only cause more problems, okay promise me—no guns," she strongly pleaded with him.

"Okay, okay, I promise—for now, no guns."

So the plan was to be the watching and hunting. She could do it—had to start somewhere, right. The first step was to sell her VW for cash and get something more able to blend in like an old truck. Maybe she'll cut her hair shorter too and add highlights, so when he came around again she'd not be as noticeable.

Then as a last resort, change jobs to something less publicly visible, yet to be able to observe herself. What could that be she wondered. There were not a lot of choices around here, and Joe was getting his side work going and he was going to want to give that to move again. No, she was not going to be pushed around either, time to stick it out and get this done once and for all.

She drove to the local newspaper office to take out an ad to sell the VW and look in the classifieds to buy a truck. She could have Joe take her to work for a while, if she didn't find anything to buy right away.

What she hoped for was that someone would buy her car for their daughter as a graduation gift like she had gotten it for. It was only eight years old anyway, ought to be able to unload it, as there wasn't that many miles on it.

And then if it was a local family, she could keep an eye on it to see if someone was following it around. Of course, she wouldn't want any other young girl to be abducted because of her, so she'd better be careful who it was sold to. It was a place to start she thought.

While she was looking at vehicle classifieds, she may as well check on other jobs in the area also. What she needed was something not public yet provided her some way to travel around close by always looking and checking out truck stops. That seemed to be the most common place that the girls disappeared from.

Nothing much like that was in any employment ad, in fact

not much at all. Guess she was lucky to be working at all with the way things were around here. She'd have to pay more attention to her customers and listen to their conversations. Then that way, something might turn up.

The following weekend, she got a call on her VW that seemed like a serious inquiry, so she met with an older gentleman who wanted it for his granddaughter that was headed off to college in Boise.

She thought that was a good call, far enough away. Yet her parents worked at BSU, and she hadn't told them she was selling it and what if they thought it was her that had moved back to Boise to go to school. No, they wouldn't think that, she'd have to tell them anyway that someone else was driving her car. They might be set thinking she needed the money and sold it without their advice or help or knowledge.

She'll have to explain that she needed a truck instead. Yeah right, after s years in Wyoming during some of the worst winter weather conditions and now all of the sudden she needed a truck---like that was going to fly.

In the end it was her decision to make, and she was an adult now, so she could sell her car to anyone she chose to and for any reason.

The agreement was good and she took the cash and signed over the title. To make the deal sweeter after she talked to the buyer about why she was selling it, he told her he had a 1980 Chevy Silverado that he would be willing to sell her and for only about half the cash back that he had paid her for the 1988 VW Beetle.

By the end of the day a few of good trades had been made, and both parties were happy. She unloaded her car and got an older truck that ran great, and he got a really cute car for his granddaughter and rid of the truck that had been collecting dust for the last five years.

When Joe got a look at the truck, he shook his head at her, until he started it and then drove it around the block.

"Boy, this sure is sweet, listen to that engine purr and it only has 60,000 miles. You sure stole this you know that don't you, sweetheart," Joe said excitedly.

"Yeah, well it's still mine—you remember that. Maybe I'll let you borrow it sometime though, if you're nice," she told him.

They went for a drive then around a few back roads checking out the 4-wheel drive. Joe was smiling all the while driving, and then finally let her drive it back home.

Winter was coming soon and she was very happy to have a dependable 4-wheel drive truck to drive to work or into Pocatello and Boise whenever she wanted.

First step done, next was to look for another job at least to checking for the right one to come along. All opportunities had to be considered. She had to be patient, at least she hadn't felt weird for quite a long time now. She'll be able to get to the next step in her plans real soon.

Then she asked her friends at the diner who was a good hairdresser to get a haircut and color done. Amy told them she needed a change was all; and the woman who worked days with her, Tammy, told her that her sister-in-law had a salon in her home and had real reasonable rates. When Tammy offered to call her and ask if Amy could get in that day after work, she agreed before she had time to change her mind.

When she got home with a cute little pixie cut and darker reddish hair, Joe didn't hardly recognize her.

"Wow, that's quite a change. I think I like it. Can we fool around before dinner, so that it feels like I'm with a stranger?" he said winking at her.

"Ha, yeah right, in your dreams," she said.

"Yeah, exactly, you are my dream girl now and always," he told her pulling her in for a long kiss.

Guess I should have done this a long time ago, this is the most outward affection I've had in a long time, she thought as she kissed him back with passion. After they tangled up the sheets and had a light dinner, Amy asked him what he really thought.

"It changed you a lot for the better—not that what you had before wasn't good, but I like it, of course. If you want to know if I think it's enough though to fool someone who knows what you look like. Maybe not close if you're serving him his breakfast when people all around are talking about how different you look, but from a distance, yeah it's real good," Joe told her.

"Well, it's going to have to work for now. I think when he's watching, it's been from a distance anyway, not too close. Even back at Little America, I don't think I've ever served him—he's too cautious for that. And certainly not here, there hasn't been anyone but regulars since I started," she said confidently.

The next day was just as Joe had said, everyone at work commented on who the new girl was. It only lasted a few days though, after everyone had a chance to come in, so it died down pretty quickly.

Amy ended up staying there through that winter and anonymously, as she told Tammy she lost her name tag and didn't want another one. All the locals knew her anyway, so it didn't matter.

Except it mattered to her as there were a few times travelers came in on their way to or from somewhere in Idaho, whether it was Lava Hot Springs, or Pocatello, it still made her nervous to serve a single guy. Joe stayed busy with his own shop work as her started to fix farm equipment also and was getting more and more referrals.

In fact, he told Amy that he figured he could do this full time instead of a side work, and quit his regular job at the Highway Department.

"Yeah, maybe, but the Highway Department was dependable work that was hard to find, especially if you wanted to save for your own shop. That is yours—your own building and business, not this rented garage attached to this house here," she told him.

"Yeah, I hear ya," Joe said. "It's been long days lately."

"Probably be as long if not more, if it was your own. You know that also because you'd have to get a tow truck and then you'd be called out all the time in the winter when the idiots run off the road into a ditch," Amy said with a smile.

"Yeah, you're right. I know, I'll keep at it for now---but someday," he said sadly. She knew he wanted his own business, but now was not the time.

They were silent for a while because Amy was also thinking about how much longer it would be before she found the right job to start her investigating.

Come summer time, they both got their wishes. Joe's answer came by way of no other choice, as he was laid off. His savings, however, allowed him to find a building to use for his own shop. Although he couldn't buy it right away, he was able to lease it at a reasonable monthly rate, Amy found out later. She was proud of him just the same.

Since they didn't need the big garage any longer where they lived now, the decided to move to a smaller, cheaper little cottage house that was also closer to downtown.

Amy got a chance to check out a new program that was starting at the local Get-n-Go station. They called it mystery shopping. Seemed easy enough to part-time and still keep her job at the diner for now. All this other job entailed was to go into the gas station, buy something, and report back on how the service was and the condition of the premises, was it clean restrooms, were the employees helpful and courteous and greet you when you came in the door— that sort of thing.

She was also always sure to keep her hair trimmed and roots re-dyed over the last few months. Now with summer here she wouldn't go anywhere without large sunglasses on. She felt it was going to be soon now, real soon to be able to spy on anyone she thought might be passing through who gave her a creepy feeling.

As it turned out the mystery shopping gig did allow jobs to be a little further away to the Flying J truck stops in Cokeville, and as far away as Pocatello and Evanston.

This made Joe real nervous as he wasn't able to get away and go with her. He truly wished she would carry some protection with her when she went so far out of the area. It was a quick trip there and back, but she was able to ask questions about the last time someone disappeared from that exact truck stop. That could give someone ideas of their own, he feared.

All she had to was bring it up and start a conversation with an employee about who it was that went missing, then watch for their reactions. She stayed a little longer outside watching people and vehicles come and go. It felt good to be the one watching for once. Trying to get a sense of her surroundings and the people she was watching each place she went.

Thinking he wouldn't be brave enough to come back to the same place twice. No, the guy she was looking for was a coward. A psychopath coward, she was sure of that. So she left the area and drove home, stopping once to use the restroom and also watch people at little bit at this rest area near Monticello, Idaho.

At least the company pays extra for traveling farther away, helps pay for her gas that way. And this allows her to check out all the truck stops and rest areas that are close by, that's a good opportunity.

So it's not bad, she needed a break though, something to peak her intuitions. Then again she could still have another dream too— that would help show her some things. Too bad she can't control when that happens.

She was so sure she would know it immediately if she ever saw the creep in her memory again, before he found her that is— especially the 'new' Amy.

CHAPTER 21

As he thought over the past year and a half of going from place to place in Idaho, Utah, and one more time back to Wyoming, the killer had at last found those two who have been interfering in his business.

It's not like he had stopped or slowed down much in his hunting of them. It's more like he didn't care and he surely had no worries for they certainly didn't have a clue who he was or what he looked like.

Most of all he absolutely didn't stop his other passion, how could he, that is what he lived for. He was not successful in Utah, which is why he stayed on the outskirts of Ogden. Where he could go to Idaho or Wyoming either way and back quickly, or stay in Utah. He particularly liked the parking lot at Lagoon, the choices there were very public but also well worth the risk.

He went to campgrounds though because he could use his wildlife photography more openly as a way to lure the young and curious to come to him—rather than he aggressively stalking them.

On one of his travels shortly after leaving Wyoming, however, he spotted the young girs' car, a purple VW Beetle. How many could there be of those around here in the small town of Soda Springs, Idaho he wondered?

He was sure it was her when he later saw her get out of it and put in gas at the local Get-N-Go there. So he figured that's good to know where to find them now. He could come back around this way next time, I'll see what they're up to then. He had no worries, he had changed trucks by now also, a newer Toyota with a full size camper.

After that next winter, he went on to Twin Falls and discovered a hotbed of activity at one of the truck stops of I-84 that was called Garden of Eden. Apparently this was a popular spot to get off the highway and go to a tourist area that was Shoshone Falls—hey a picturesque place for a photographer.

Anywhere there are tourists is a good place to find young girls and take really good pictures too—bonus. He thought he'd better check it out and drove that way.

He followed a nice looking family from the parking lot area of the Falls down the path to take pictures of the actual Falls overlook. This is nice, he thought, not nearly as picturesque as Yellowstone Falls—that's where he has fond memories also of a fine little Indian girl who was quite a handful.

Back to business. The family of four; Mom, Dad, little brother probably two, and a daughter of maybe fourteen or fifteen, who was really very beautiful. Not that that really matters all that much to him, but it's a bonus when he does find one. It gets the old blood pumping faster.

The family was obviously enjoying the time together, but the parents were distracted by keeping a close eye on the toddler so he didn't run off and jump in the river or anything stupid. That left the little beauty queen on her own, she's big enough to take care of herself.

Sure enough, as he had always done before; when he began to take pictures, a lot of pictures that is, by moving around to get different angles, that would attract the curious ones.

After about half and hour of this, the parents were tired of chasing the toddler and were ready to go. The daughter, however, was interested in what the nice looking photographer was doing.

"Can we stay a little longer," she asked her Mom. "Dad can take Joey to the car for a nap and we can catch up later, please Mom."

"For a little while I suppose honey, you stay here while I go check and make sure Dad gets Joey all settled in and I'll be right back. Okay, dear?" her Mom told her.

Perfect, the stranger thought, now I can have a conversation with her without Mom or Dad close by. Um, we'll see where this goes, as it was the girls idea not his to pursue. Not that he was complaining, but that was something he would suggest to get someone alone—not the other way around.

After a few minutes she made her way over to where he was still clicking away with his camera.

"Hi, what are doing this for, are you a professional magazine photographer?" she asked him.

"No, not really I'm trying to put together a wildlife/scenic outdoor photo book or maybe use the extras for a calendar," he told her. "Do you like photography also?"

"Yeah, I like the idea I guess, it would be fun to travel all over. Do you get to travel a lot?" she asked.

"Sometimes, when I get paid to, but for this stuff it's on my own." He said, trying to be more friendly now as he moved closer so she could look at his camera and more so he could breath in her scent. The smell of youth and freshness was intoxicating.

He knew he didn't have much time before her Mom came back, so he asked her if she'd like him to take her picture with the Falls in the background would be amazing.

She seemed shy at first, then shrugged her shoulders saying, "Why not."

He only stepped back a little then and she turned to look at the lenses—like a natural. He wanted a close up of her, forget the fucking Falls he thought, as he zoomed in on her face.

"You're such a natural, this is great." He told her as he clicked off a few more shots of her. Then he heard her Mom coming up the trail as he leaned in to tell the girl, "Make sure you ask them to stop at the Garden of Eden on the way back to the highway so you can use the restroom, then I'll give you this roll of film of you and these

Falls. It might also have some of your family on here too—you can get copies made anywhere, how's that sound?" he asked her secretly.

"Really you'd give me the whole roll? Okay great, that's cool, yeah." She said when she saw her Mom and stepped away from him quickly.

"Come on honey, we got to go, your brother needs lunch or change his pants or both. Whichever will make him happier and less cranky." Her Mom told her in exasperation and taking her by the hand.

"How many times have I told you never talk to strangers, especially alone like that, who is he anyway?" She asked walking quickly down the path.

The girl looked over her shoulder and smiled with a thumbs up behind her back and said, "I don't know, some photographer taking pictures of the Falls, I guess."

The stranger smiled too thinking of what's to come in a short while. He waited until they left, so they wouldn't pay him any attention or to which vehicle he got into.

Then he went back down the road to I-84 and the truck stop at the Garden of Eden to look for an obscure place to park way out of sight. Since it was starting to get a little towards evening, the shadows were long and inviting that should provide somewhat of a cover.

He went in the side door to the the restroom himself and look for the little beauty. She was waiting casually by the door—probably watching for me, he thought. He motioned for her to go towards the back by the coolers, which were more out of sight.

"Do you have it? I have to get going," she said.

"Not with me. I have a few more pictures to take in order to finish the roll off. If I take it out now they will all be exposed and therefore no good," he explained. Then asked, "Are you staying to eat also, your family in the restaurant?"

"Yeah, well, they're over there at the fast food area getting something for everyone. I said I had to use the restroom, so I have to get back now." She said looking around more.

"Well, why don't we hurry then out to my truck, I can take the last of the roll of film of you at the sunset and finish it off and it's all yours. Should make great gifts." He said not wanting to cause her any alarm by touching her arm or anything like that.

They went out the side door without anyone noticing anything, and walked around the side towards the back parking lot. "I parked away from people because I have expensive equipment in the back that I don't want to get stolen." He explained while they hurried to his truck, that now had a full size camper with a back door.

He opened the back and got his camera out of the bag while he told her to stand to the side profile with the sunset behind her would be perfect. He took a few more pictures and turned to the camper door and was working on winding the roll of film in order to remove it from the camera. He deliberately took his time so sho would be anxious and come closer to watch him, since he had his back to her.

He looked around once real quick and then grabbed hold of her arm pulling her close to cover her mouth with the cloth of chloroform and push her inside the door. He already had the duct tape ready to put on her wrists, feet, and mouth as she fell into the camper. That was smooth as ice, he thought.

He casually—no need to be in a big hurry—closed the door and locked it. Walked around and got in the cab started the truck to drive out of the parking lot and drove for the highway exit. Trying to decide if he was going to go north towards Boise or south to Burley and Snowville where there was nothing in between but sagebrush.

Big city or open desert. He really wanted to spend some time with this one. If he found an isolated campground to park and stay awhile, it wouldn't be suspicious. Somewhere along the Snake River maybe and then dump her out when he was finished he thought, as he turned north on I-84, he answered his own dilemma.

He had driven for about an hour, past King Hill exit, when he saw the sign for Paradise Valley, then drove another thirty minutes or so to find a campground.

He did indeed find a small almost empty camp spot, paid the overnight fee in the drop box, pulled into the far back parking spot and shut off his truck.

He sat listening for a while, to the complete silence in the back. So he knew she was still out of it, all that time, he figured he'd better go back and check to make sure she wasn't in a coma or something.

He opened the camper door and went in to find her still on the floor passed out. He lifted her to the bed at the end and proceeded to remove her clothing. May as well it now while she's still knocked out, as it's easier than fighting with her struggling. Although, he liked it when they fought back a little.

After she was nude, he took out another camera and began taking pictures of her again until she started to wake.

As she opened her eyes and looked around unsure of where she was or why she said, "What's going on? Where am I?" Then she realized she didn't have any clothes on and started to scream and curl into a ball, so he had to put the tape back on her mouth.

"Well, we're just here to have a little fun and take some more pictures. We're going to camp out for a few nights that's all." He told her as he got on the bed now to straighten her out and caress her body.

"It's going to be okay, you'll see, we'll have lots of fun tonight and again tomorrow and into tomorrow night most likely," he said smiling at her. He could hardly wait to get started.

"You see first, you have to do exactly as I say okay, can you that?" he asked her firmly.

She nodded her head yes, with fear in her eyes.

"Great, we're going to get along fine, now come over here closer to me, I want to look at you better." He told her as he started to stroke her body and her beautiful soft pussy. She tried to squirm away crying and pleading with her eyes.

"Now, now, you have to behave or it will be a lot worse for you, I can promise you that," he said in a harsh tone.

Then he undressed himself and turned all but one little flashlight out and laid down next to the pretty little princess, and proceeded to enjoy the ing by taking whatever he wanted long into the night.

After pretty much more of the same all the next day. They slept a little and he had some water and a little food for her, so she'd stop crying hopefully.

Damn it anyway, why does he always have to get the cry babies. Where has all the fight gone out of young girls these days, he wondered. Especially the more beautiful ones, they've been pampered too much.

By now he was becoming bored anyway, so he got down to the business of ending the play time. He found his red ribbon and cut a long piece to wrap around her neck and back to the front to crossover the ends and have a good strong hold.

Of course, he knew she realized there is no going home or anywhere else now, and the fear and pain is clear on her face. He had to stop and click that one last picture of the fear in her eyes. When he had finished with her and tied the bow, trimmed the ends neatly, he took her and her clothes and wrapped in a large black heavy duty garbage bag for disposal.

After scouting out the area of the nearby woods and river bank, and determining no one was around, he went back and got his shovel to dig a hole to be done with this.

He had to hurry though, because this was a public camping spot here. He sure didn't want to be seen now as he got ready to take out the 'garbage' to throw away and bury.

He decided to continue to drive on to Boise, since he was this close to see what he could find there. He figured he could take a walk along the river's green belt and take a few more pictures. He did after all need to make a living somehow.

It was dark by the time he pulled into Boise, so he looked for a cheap motel, as he felt like a hot shower and a regular bed for a change. He looked for something nice near the campus of BSU and the river.

He was ready to go then the next day when he went for his walk along the green belt, he could also check out the campus for anything tempting. The girls didn't always have to be that young. Sometimes he could crave an older, curvy, experienced one—like the one he thought about in Wyoming that used to serve tables, who seemed to have a sixth sense about her.

As he was looking around, he spotted her VW Beetle, same style, same color. No way, couldn't be here, could she? That's only because I was thinking about her that I would then see her car. However, he did remember her saying something to the other waitress about being from Boise. Maybe she came back for a family visit, then why would she be at the BSU campus, he wondered.

He didn't really want to take all day to watch it, to see if it was her that came out to get in it or not. After he came back the other way from across the river, he would be closer to the parking lot to get a better look at it then.

He took his time though taking more pictures of the scenery not in a hurry. Walking to the other side of the river crossing a bridge to walk back to where he started from. When he got to BSU parking lot, he saw the VW still there and decided to check it out. It had Idaho plates, but then they did live in Idaho now for almost two years, so that made sense. He thought he remembered a bumper sticker about anti-government—and sure enough there it was, the same one he was sure.

He looked inside pretty quickly so as not to be seen, especially by her if is she came outside. There were quite a few boxes of books and stuff in the back seat, uhm, maybe she did move back here then. I wonder where the other guy is, what was his name. He could almost see his name patch on his mechanic uniform. Oh well, doesn't matter he decided, he's not important.

He figured he would come back, at least he knew she sen to school here probably and that he'd better not press his luck anymore by hanging around. She always seemed to be aware of him being close by watching her too. Well, next time she won't be aware, because she won't be expecting anyone to know she's here in Boise.

This one is not an opportunity for the taking, this one is a strategy to plan ahead. She was pretty allusive alright and tricky, but he was a planner when he had to be.

Now, it was time to plan and strategize. Just you wait little Miss Amy, I'm coming for you real soon.

CHAPTER 22

Amy had made four more trips to other areas where there were Flying J truck stops. She was still trying to find out more information on missing girls being absolutely sure that somewhere—someone knew something that would connect to Hope also. She thought more every day about calling Matt and telling him what she was doing and her progress.

However, that's it, she hadn't made any progress, and he's probably doing the same tracking as herself. He has more resources than she does anyway. How could she possibly think she could find this guy when no law enforcement agency could.

After getting home late from driving back from Evanston, Wyoming, she sat down on the couch to watch the news and unwind before going to bed, but she didn't want to disturb Joe. He probably had a long day.

The local news was always nothing, but around the state had her listening more intently as she saw a few on the screen with a little boy. They were asking for information on their daughter, Caitlyn. Showing a picture of this really beautiful fourteen-year-old girl.

Oh, now Amy thought, that's just his type. What happened to her, she wondered. The news story told of this young girl gone missing from Twin Falls area after the family was at Shoshone Falls and had stopped at this truck stop off I-84 called Garden of Eden. She turned it up to listen to the Mom's plea to return their daughter or for anyone to provide any information of seeing her two days ago.

She did mention that her daughter was talking to a strange man who was taking pictures at the Falls and the man was not seen again.

However, but only an hour later their daughter was not seen after she went to the restroom at the truck stop either.

She turned the volume back down after that there was a number on the screen to call if you had any information on this case. She hadn't noticed that Joe was there and standing in the doorway watching her because she had been crying with her face in her hands.

He walked over and sat down next to her and took her in his arms and let her cry it out on his shoulder.

"It has to stop Joe, when will he be stopped? I can't stand this anymore," she cried.

"I don't know, but you're making yourself crazy over this. Look at you—you don't eat right; you're stressed out all the time. You have to take better care of yourself Amy, please let this go. I'm worried about you," Joe pleaded with her hugging her.

"I know, I know, but don't you see now there's another missing girl and I have a clue. We have a place to start—I can't stop now. It could be this guy taking pictures, using his photography to get more young girls." She told him more awake now and excited. "In fact, I'm sure of it, call it instinct or whatever you want, but he would have offered to take a picture of Hope and her horse and she totally would have fell for that."

"Okay yeah, maybe, but you have to let the law handle it now. Please promise me you'll call that guy you talked to in Wyoming a few years ago, Hope's brother and talk to him about all this, okay?" Joe begged of her.

"Okay, yeah. I know you're right. I only hope he'll understand why we had to leave, and that he'll let me help," she said.

Joe rolled his eyes at her and hugged her again telling her, "You're hopeless, you know that?"

"Yeah, but I know what I know, and I know I can do this. He'll not be expecting anyone to track him down, let alone me," she said with conviction.

They got up then and went to bed. They both needed to sleep, she only hoped it didn't come with nightmares.

She awoke with more clarity now, because in her dream she saw a face of a person watching her. This face also had a camera around his neck and he's smiling at her with that creepy—I know you smile.

She knew it was the same man doing all these terrible things and young girls are disappearing all over the tri-state area on the premises of him being a famous photographer. What pretty young girl wouldn't fall for that?

Being absolutely sure of this, she jumped out of bed in search of Matt's card and reached for the phone to call him. If she had to leave an urgent message, which is exactly what she did. Hopefully he'll get that soon and call her back. Time is of the essence now, have to set a trap for him somehow, she thought or track him down somehow. Hunt him down like the dirty dog he is.

$\mathcal{C}$HAPTER 23

For the last two and a half years Matt tracked down every disappearance I could find out about, even if it wasn't in Wyoming. There had to be a common ground somewhere.

The victims were not always runaway teenagers, some were young adults who were drifting. Others were parking lot prostitutes who traveled from truck stop to truck stop servicing truck drivers.

Still these people were all missing and presumed dead, as was his sister, whom he could not forget, even though they were not that close. Hope was ten years younger and had other interests, she was still family.

My Mom and Dad never got over the guilt of her loss, because she was with them on their way back from Salt Lake City. My brothers, Zach and Drew were currently running the family ranch; because John and Donna had given up on everything, lost everything when they lost Hope.

Especially his Mom, who went through the motions of being alive, not really wanting to live any more. John would always call and stay in touch, asking every day if there were any news. If they could find her body somewhere I would think, they could have a funeral rather than a memorial service.

The only pattern I could figure out was that people were consistently missing every year from the mid '80's until now—that's over a ten year spread, and nothing before that. The first few were from Little America, then surrounding area truck stops next; and then back to Little America when it was Hope that went missing in 1993, but nothing similar from Wyoming since.

Maybe a truck driver who had the I-80 route every time this happened. However, there are literally thousands of companies and drivers who use I-80. Therefore, I began to reach out to surrounding state official in Utah, Idaho, and Montana to try to find more disappearances at truck stops, rest areas, or gas stations looking for any similarities.

Finally, after about a year of messaging other state authorities, a Sheriff in Twin Falls called me asking why I was so interested. I explained what had been happening in Wyoming over the previous few years, and why I was looking to other states for any help.

He identified himself as Sheriff Marvin Cole, "folks call me Marv," he said very interested.

"I've been following your messages also because we've had a few of unsolved disappearances from our local truck stop off I-84 called the Garden of Eden. The latest one was today and there are no witnesses," he explained.

"Do you have any ideas as to who might be doing this if it's the same person or how?" Marv asked.

"I don't, the only theory I have is a truck driver who had the I-80 run and now maybe has changed to I-84. We have no leads here either, no one saw anything out of the ordinary," I said. "All I know for sure is the starting point was Little America, Wyoming and I've been searching around there asking questions for two years since my little sister went missing."

Marv asked me, "Did anyone who worked there then, maybe take off suddenly after you were there last time asking questions and looking around—maybe you scared him off."

"I don't think so, I checked out all the employees after I got a warrant back in 1993. Since then I hadn't thought to recheck each one, no. That's a great place to start. I'll double check everyone, see if anyone has moved away and where to and why. I'll let you know if I find anything. Thanks a lot, another set of ears/eyes helps," I said excited to get to work now.

"Glad to help, I'll let you know also if anything else turns up in Idaho." He said as they said good-bye and hung up.

Back at the ranch in Wyoming, I fixed another cup of coffee, looking out the window and watching Zach train one of his mares. Contemplating my first move before making a few more phone calls. I didn't want to say anything yet to the family and set up any false hope of recovery.

Therefore, I thought I'd better take a drive over that way again to ask around in person to observe people. I still had friends in the department in Rock Springs and Evanston also, so while I reached out to them, I mentally was making preparations of what to tell the family.

I knew my parents were beyond help to reconcile the facts, but at least with my pursuing all leads maybe I could give them some comfort with a funeral to lay my sister's remains to rest.

Over the years and the many conversations it always bothered me that there was no consistencies, but what did I know about one crazy psycho from another.

After I exhausted myself from any and all leads—would I then ever stop. Not sure then, because I wasn't there yet. All I knew for sure was that I had to keep going forward, keep looking, keep asking the right questions until I got the right answers or least what I wanted to hear anyway. I need to pull the first thread to unravel the truth.

Once again I was back at Little America looking for anyone who may have suddenly moved away after I was here in '93.

I thought after I tracked down all the previous employees that were here back then, I'd have a place to start. It was time consuming if nothing else. At least I didn't think I was wasting my time though. I sat in the restaurant, sipping coffee, talking to Karen, who was always very talkative and helpful with lots of local gossip and information on anyone who has ever worked and/or lived around here. Thinking he may have found that little thread and he started to pull it.

"You know back six or eight years ago, I was a kid myself with a baby girl, and now that baby girl is almost fourteen years old, so I can relate to what you're saying and why you keep looking for answers," she said understandingly.

"Can you think of anyone who may have worked here awhile and was here when Hope disappeared and then suddenly left, after I was here the last time asking around about my sister?" I asked her.

"Well, when I think about it, there was a young waitress who had been working here for about five years anyway and she hooked up with the mechanics' son, Joe. You might remember her, that girl you talked to when you were here, Amy," she said.

"Anyway, they both moved away about that time yeah. Haven't thought anything was weird about it though, they both gave their notices and were talking about it months before you were here. She came from Boise, I think, so maybe they went to Idaho. I don't really know where for sure. I haven't seen or heard from either of them since," she said thoughtfully.

"I'll check anyway, what's her full name, or can I get more information from personnel?" I asked her.

"Yeah, maybe you can with a warrant I guess you could get all you want to know, but let me ask first. The head administrator, Jean is my mother-in-law," she volunteered.

"Okay, great thanks. What about Joe does his dad still work here then?" I asked.

"No, sorry he passed away the same year they moved, maybe that's why he never came back. And I think I heard his Dad call him by another name once like Skylar, yeah that's it. Maybe Joe is his middle name," Karen said.

Then she refilled my coffee and walked away down a hallway to talk to Jean he supposed. It might be a dead-end; but I didn't think so, or at least my gut told me to keep going with it, either way I was sticking with this lead to follow through. At least with more information on this waitress might help, since the boy's family is no longer here.

Meanwhile Karen was trying to convince her mother-in-law to do the right thing, but Jean wasn't being swayed no matter what Karen said, no way was she going beyond protocol and provide any information without a warrant. It would cost both of them their jobs and Jean had too many years invested and looking at retirement in the next ten years or sooner. Not going to risk that above all else she also had to think of the health insurance she had and with a husband who had heart problems, she had to consider that also—Karen knew all this.

As I thought over my options, which weren't very many, sipping my coffee and eyeing the homemade donuts in the case. I figured I'd make a few phone calls while I waited for Karen to return. In case I'd better get the ball rolling on a warrant all I needed was a full name at least then it was a waiting game after that.

His friend at the local division office in Rock Springs would at least start the inquires needed while he waited on that name.

I got to wondering why would Amy leave like that. If someone or something scared her away, she could have called me. I gave her my card to call for any reason.

When I got back and sat down, I saw Karen walking back to the counter where I was, by the look on her face it was a no go with Jean.

"Sorry, she won't budge without a warrant Matt, I tried," Karen said sadly.

"Well, at least if you had a name I could go on—to put on the official warrant I'm trying to get?" I asked hopefully.

"I think so, I know the first name is Amy, so when I asked Jean if she remembered that girl, she said, "Yeah that Amy Winters girl you mean?" That was before she knew why I wanted to know," Karen said winking at me.

Thank goodness for quick thinking. I thanked her and I went

back to making another phone call to my friend with a name to fill in that blank on the warrant request.

I also decided to check in on any messages from my office back home and was put on hold. This was taking longer than I thought, I should have had that apple fritter that was calling my name while I waited.

Finally, when the desk clerk in the Captain's office came back, she informed me that I did indeed have a new message that came in that morning. After I wrote it all down and reread it, I couldn't believe my good luck, or the timing of it all either.

It was from Amy, they had moved to Soda Springs, Idaho and she left a return phone number to call back. Saying she had important information and that she also wanted to explain why they left Wyoming three years ago. This certainly was a new development. Another thread to pull, he only hoped it would lead somewhere. One way or the other he would find out. First he had to call Amy back, to hear what she had to say for herself.

He told Karen thanks anyway, but that he got a message to call this Amy girl and that he had to make a trip to Soda Springs, he still had time to get there before dark.

CHAPTER 24

Amy had been hanging around all day, feeling anxious and tired all at the same time. She cleaned and did the laundry that had piled up, anything to keep her mind busy and not stare at the phone willing it to ring.

In the late afternoon it did and she ran for it, answering, "Hello".

"Hi, Amy, this is Matt returning your call, I just now got your message," I said.

"Yes, Matt hi, thanks for calling back so quickly. I thought I'd be waiting a few days. But listen I have ideas and made a few plans and I thought you should know about it," she said excitedly. Rambling on about something he had no idea what she was talking about.

"I'm making more notes, I called into work so I'd be home if you called me back today," she said.

"As a matter of fact, I'm at Little America right now asking around about you to talk to you some more and I get here and find out that you've left---shortly after we talked last time. So I'd like to talk to you about that also. I could be there in a few of hours, if that's okay with you?" Matt asked her with some authority in his voice.

"Yes, well that's another thing that I need to talk you about also. I'm calling now, so yes we need to make plans. I'll be here at home. When you get to town go through downtown at the second light, turn right, go two blocks, I'm the third little cottage on the left.

Okay, see you later Matt, thanks." Amy said as she hung up, not wanting to feel interrogated any longer.

When Joe got home later he asked Amy if she called this Matt dude like she promised.

"Yes, I did and you'll be glad to know he'll be here in about a half an hour or so. He called me back about an hour ago and said he was at Little America asking about me and that he'd like to come here right away. So I said okay, I'll be home," She told him looking a little scared now.

"Hey come here, I'm home now, so we'll face this together. What's important is that we catch this monster right. Everything else doesn't matter any more and he won't care either way," Joe said reassuringly.

"So what's for dinner, I'm starved. You want me to help you whip something real quick and eat first or you want to have something ready when he gets here and invite him to stay. Maybe if we feed him, it will be a relaxed visit." He said smiling, helping himself to a beer out of the fridge.

"Yeah, I have a roast in the oven should be ready by them. I'll make a light salad to go with it. Maybe you should take a shower first though, there's got an oil and grease smell going in here," she said.

"Yeah, yeah, always the same never happy with me. What's the matter with a little oil and grease anyway?" Joe said sticking out a finger with some on it to touch her nose.

"No way, mister, get away from me until you're all clean and soap smelling," she said swatting him with her dish towel.

Shaking his head as he went to the bathroom muttering something about---"no love, no love, what's a guy gotta do around here anyway."

Amy busied herself getting the dinner ready trying not to think about what Matt was going to say or how she was going to tell him why they left Wyoming.

CHAPTER 25

Matt was driving down US 30 towards Idaho thinking about this turn of events and what Amy had going on that seemed so important to her. Could it have anything to with Hope and these other missing girls, he wondered. He could hear it in her voice, all that pent up nervousness, something was up with that girl, he knew it. Could she have come across something that would make a difference in finding who's responsible for all this madness. He wondered how anyone could get away with taking so many young girls without anyone seeing anything. That stuff only happens in the movies, right—not real life, not here.

People always make mistakes, part of being human—only this monster isn't. But maybe this time the bad guy finally did mess up and Amy has some information on that.

He also wondered as he was almost there, passing through Monticello, Idaho now, if what he thought about Amy leaving had anything to with Hope missing and now she has a guilty conscious. But then you would have thought she would have come clean when he talked to her back in '93, then again she was hiding something then too. I remember back then that she wasn't telling me the whole truth, what it was about her—he had no clue.

Soon enough, I was going to find out and get to the bottom of whatever she was hiding and whatever this important information she had was. What did she mean by making plans and what plans was it; I kept wracking my brain trying to figure it out and all I had to was wait until I got there and ask her. Okay here we go, coming in to Soda Springs in 8 more miles is all.

I remembered her directions to her house, and so as soon as I pulled into town, I was looking for the right street to turn onto, and then the third 'cottage' on the left. This must be it, I thought, as I pulled to stop at the place she described. Two trucks were parked outside and lights were on inside, so I got out and walked up the sidewalk to knock on the front door.

When the door opened and a cute young woman with reddish short hair came out, I thought I had the wrong place for a minute.

"Um, Hi, are you Amy?" I asked shyly. "I'm Matt."

"Hi, yes, it's me. It's good to know that my hair cut and color changed me somewhat." She said smiling as I came through the doorway.

"Why would you need to change the way you look? You running from the law or something?" I asked sternly.

"No, nothing like that, thanks for coming and I can only hope you keep an open mind as we talk. First though, I fixed a pot roast for dinner and it's ready, would you care to join us?" she asked.

I followed her through the small boxy living room into the smaller kitchen. It sure did smell good and I was hungry since I skipped lunch to drive here.

"Yeah, sure thanks a lot. I didn't expect you to go to all this trouble though." I said, when I saw a young man come from the back room.

"Hi, I'm Joe," he said as he extended his hand to shake mine.

"Oh yeah. Hi, I'm Matt. You're the same one who also worked at Little America...a mechanic right with the real first name of Skylar, isn't that right?" I asked him. "You don't much look like Karen described you either—what's going on here?"

"Um, yeah, how'd you know that's my real name?" Joe asked.

"I was at Little America earlier today trying to get a warrant for all your personnel files and more information on where you were, and I was told your first name on your employment records in case

I needed to know that to track you guys down through your SS numbers," I explained.

"Oh," was all Joe could say.

Then Amy says, "Okay, then well this is not a big deal, since we had to eat anyway, you may as well too. Have a seat." Then to Joe she asked, "Will you please set the salad out on the table and get the salad dressing also."

"Would you like a beer Matt with dinner, or um, we have ice tea looks like?" Joe asked while he looked in the fridge for the salad.

"Tea is fine with me as I'm driving tonight, but you go ahead and have a beer if that's what you want Joe," I answered.

"Okay, what about you hon, ice tea or lemon water or you want a glass of wine with dinner?" Joe asked her.

"Ice tea is good for me too, thanks babe. Well let's eat then," she said looking a little nervous.

While Joe sliced the roast, Amy passed the salad around, and the potato, vegetable bowl also. Dinner was mostly ate in silence as no one had any small talk, only thing Matt asked about was what their jobs were now and if they liked it here.

"Joe worked for the Highway Department here as a mechanic until recently, he was laid off; so now he was able to get his own garage up and running like he always wanted," Amy explained, smiling at Joe.

"And I'm a waitress over at the local diner, and also some mystery shopping at the Get-n-Go and Flying J's," she added.

Joe said, "Yeah, it's been good here I guess. We've made a life of our own."

Of course, I couldn't help but notice what a cute couple they made. I hoped they were not in trouble, or not going to make any trouble for me. What could that be I thought as they were finishing dinner and putting dishes in the sink and leftovers in the fridge.

"I'll leave that for something to do tomorrow, let's go in here and get comfortable," Amy said to both of them.

"It's a little warm in here Joe would you open the window to get a breeze through here? I think that oven heated it up a little," she said lightly.

They sat on the small sofa holding hands for strength it seemed, while I took the only chair.

"Well now, I don't mean to seen rude, but I'm a little anxious to hear what's happened Amy; you made it seem pretty important on your message," I asked her.

"I'm also anxious and relieved to get this all out in the open. Yes, I should have told you back when you first talked to me the year after Hope went missing," Amy said clearing her throat, taking a sip of tea.

"Let me explain, first for a few years before that, I have been sure someone had been following me," Amy said squeezing Joe's hand for comfort I noticed.

"Why you think that is Amy? Why follow you and not take you too 'heaven forbid', sorry to say it that way—it's not what I meant to come out that way," I apologized.

"No, that's alright. That's exactly what I always wondered also. He was spying on me or us I'm sure. You see back then we---um, we would take teenagers, to a shed that we had set up in the back of the property line. We only asked them a few questions about dreams, and then tried to hypnotize them for them to remember their dreams, for my research," Amy said as she tried to explain.

Joe also saw the look on Matt's face so he said, "Yeah, it really was innocently set up to determine what they remembered of their dreams or not—nothing else."

They were all silent for a minute, because quite honestly I didn't know what to say.

Before I could though, Amy jumped in with more, "So yeah, anyways there was this guy I could only catch glimpses of him really in the shadows late at night following us after we were finished and had let these people go—we only tried this research on a few, okay maybe ten people all together over a period of what six years or so," as she looked over at Joe, "that's like less than two a year. And so this guy I think he followed us so he could maybe grab someone as they came back out of the shed, but we never had young girls only a few older women—one really older, and a few boys," Amy had explained in a hurry.

"So, alright, let me get this straight. You guys took kids----to a dark enclosed shed and then what asked them questions about their dreams and what they could remember about their dreams by hypnotizing them? Is that right? Did you ever leave anyone alone in this shed?" I asked trying to understand and get a complete picture of what was going on.

"And you think someone was following you, to what try and take away someone that you had taken first?" I further questioned them.

"I told you to keep an open mind. I knew you wouldn't understand." Amy said as she got up to pace around the small room and refill her tea glass for something else to do, he presumed.

Then Joe said, "Okay, listen the real problem we have is that Amy thinks it's the same guy abducting all these young girls—even Hope, and that he's going to come here looking for her too."

"Is that why you've changed the way you look, because he'll come to find you here?" he asked looking more concerned now.

"Yeah well, but before he does, I've got a plan to find him or track him down. You see I never saw his face clearly, but a few weeks ago, I had this dream (I get these premonition dreams) about all this and I saw someone—still not a face but an impression and I did see he had a camera strap around his neck and that he got into a beat old truck with a camper topper on the back. Don't you see it has to be him—my subconscious telling me so. Pointing me in the right direction," Amy said getting excited again.

I didn't say anything right away, because I didn't know what to say to that, so I know I must have had this dumbfounded look on my face.

"Look, I don't know what y'all think you're doing bringing me me all the way here with these cock-a-mamy stories and all, but it's a waste of my time. I thought you'd have information for me. It's against the law, you know to misrepresent yourselves to the law. And as for whatever happened, or didn't happen back in Wyoming, that's for your conscious to deal with—not me," I said exasperatedly. "I don't want to hear any more about that part of your story."

Amy got right up again yelling now, "No, wait you have to listen to me, it does make sense. I saw it on the news last night, that little fourteen-year-old girl taken over by Twin Falls at that truck stop, what was that name of it Joe?"

"Garden something," he said.

"Garden of Eden?" I asked, "What about it?"

"Yeah, yeah that's it. They said the family had been to that tourist place the Falls or something in that area earlier that day and that their daughter, this girl, was talking to a stranger who was taking pictures of the Falls," she said all excited.

"You see now don't you, I had this dream again about someone with a camera weeks ago—and now this comes on an actual sighting of someone taking pictures," Amy said.

"That's what you got to go on—that could be anyone really innocently taking pictures of the Shoshone Falls. It is a tourist attraction after all." Matt said not fully convinced yet.

"Oh man, no way. I thought you of all people would see this for what it is—a clue, a way to get him finally. He uses the perfect set up, who wouldn't want their picture taken. We're all a little vain right—Hope would have wanted her horses' picture taken, if not her own," Amy said pleading with Matt. This time he did take it all under consideration, as he thought on it for a few minutes.

Amy could see she had Matt's attention now somewhat, although she had to use Hopes' name in there to do it. She let him think on it for a little while and didn't add any more yet—waiting for him to voice his opinion of her theory.

"Okay, I'll grant you this, it's a theory—a working theory. In fact I got a call yesterday morning from the Sheriff there and he told me the same thing, that's why I came looking for you guys to see what your story was," Matt said.

Amy looking over at Joe with a sigh of relief and said, "Finally, thank goodness someone with authority will listen to me."

Joe said, "Yeah, wait until he gets a load of your plan—then your screwed. No way is he going for that crazy thought of yours to get this guy. I personally hope he talks some sense into that thick head of yours." Then looking over at Matt he said, "She's stubborn as a mule—good luck with step two."

"What'dya mean step two—what's he talking about Amy? I haven't agreed to anything here," Matt said raising his voice and tone.

"Well, yeah that was step one to get you to here and to listen to me—really listen. Step two is my plan for tracking this guy down, us being the hunters and setting a trap to finally catch this monster." Amy said with a smile that she was hoping he wouldn't be able to refuse.

"Whoa, whoa, back here a minute, what's this about a trap to catching him—and what's with 'us' anyway? I'm all for hunting him down, but that's as far as you go little lady, there's not going to be anyone setting a trap or baiting him," Matt said firmly.

"Well, you know as well as I do, that he's going to come looking for me tually, because I've seen him. But he doesn't know what I look like now, and he doesn't know what I'm driving, because I sold my VW bug and have that old Chevy out there now. I'm going to find him before he finds me—with or without your help." Amy said as she crossed her arms in front of her looking more determined than ever.

"See what I mean," Joe said. "Stubborn, isn't she?"

"Okay, okay, listen you guys, let's not get ahead of ourselves here. First of al,l what makes you think he hasn't been around here already and seen you recently. He might have followed you home before you changed your hair and sold your car. Have you thought of that?" Matt asked her.

"He hasn't, I'd know it if he was around lately. I haven't felt anyone watching me since a few months after we first moved here and we weren't living in this place then," she explained when she looked over at Joe.

"Then how you think he won't walk in that diner you work at and listen for someone to call you by name—have you changed your name too?" he asked her trying to be reasonable.

"That's easy, I'm giving my notice there anyway, this is my last week. I'm going to work with Joe, be his receptionist, make appointments and take care of the books. He's doing real good now and can't run the place by himself. And of course, I'll still run to the mystery shopping gig, because that takes me to gas stations and truck stops where I can watch people," she said looking triumphant.

"So what if he comes looking for a mechanic and finds Joe here or Skylar and figures who you two are that way. He has seen you with her in Wyoming, right Joe?" Matt asked.

"Yeah, probably so, but I'm using my real name at my business also and I've got this beard now too with longer hair—so I don't look like I used to either. However, I don't like the idea any more than you Matt, in fact I hate the idea of her poking her nose around in this. I did think that if you'd be close by though to help with the investigation, that you'd keep an eye on her," Joe told him.

"Oh man, you all think you've got this figured out—that you've thought of everything, don't ya. Well, you have any more surprises for me tonight?" I asked looking at Amy, as I wiped my hand over my face and sighing loudly.

Amy dropped her head down looking at her hands trembling and said, "No, sir, that's about it."

"Well, thanks for dinner, I have to get going now, I've got a lot to think about. And I've got to talk to the local Sheriff here and the guy in Twin Falls again who called me yesterday. I can't go off on my own either without getting in contact with the local authorities. So I hope for your sake young lady, you don't anything rash before I contact you again. Is that clear Miss Amy?" I asked sternly as I got to leave.

"Yes, sir, but don't you think we have to move on this more quickly—on this photographer angle anyway. I could ask around…." she started to say.

"Oh no, you don't any such thing, I'll all the asking and investigating from here on out. You stay close by in case I need to ask you anything else. Got it." I said to Amy, and to Joe I said, "You hogtie her if you have to until you hear from me again, Okay?"

"Yes sir, I'll try. Thank you, sir," Joe said.

Amy asked, "Are you driving back to Wyoming tonight or staying here?"

I answered, "No, not tonight. I'll get something close by, and check with the Sheriff tomorrow and then maybe drive to Twin Falls, as that to be the latest or most recent abduction. You guys go to work as usual. I'll be in touch tomorrow, we'll talk about this some more then. Okay?"

"There's a nice little B&B over on Main Street, the little blue, two-story house with white shutters. The owner is Joanne, tell her I sent you," Amy said.

I thanked her and went out to my car sat there trying to absorb all that was said tonight, then finally pulled away back downtown to Main Street to find this nice B&B Amy suggested.

Sure enough, couldn't have missed it—it was painted bright blue, white shutters, big wrap around porch and a sign that said 'Joanne's Place'. The lights were still on though it was after 9pm, so I went in to ask for a room for the night or maybe two nights depending on what happened tomorrow.

"Yes, I have a few of rooms left, you want up stairs or ground level?" she asked.

"Upstairs is fine with me, keep the ground floor open for whoever may need it, my knees aren't too bad yet." I said to her as I signed the old-fashioned registration book and paid her.

It had been a very long day I thought since I left home at 6am this morning, and I was bone tired. Still my mind was racing with all the new information. I dared not to hope this might be the right trail to finally get this guy one way or another. But letting Amy set a trap for him—NO WAY.

I figured I'd better call home and check in with one of my brothers or my Dad, whoever answered the phone.

"Hi, Dad, I hope I didn't wake you up," I said. "I'm in Soda Springs, Idaho, going to be a few more days."

Dad asked, "What for—what was going on?"

"Nothing yet Dad, I have to check out a few things that came up over this way. I found Amy finally and got to talk to her again," I explained. "Don't worry I'll call ya again tomorrow night. I hope my Captain will give me more time off if I need it."

After that conversation with Dad, I wondered if I'd be able to this investigation in a professional manner—that is as a WHP Officer, though I have crossed state lines. It might have helped that I was already in contact with our DCI Office in Cheyenne regarding all these disappearances over the years, as I reached out to them first off for help. Probably not, but something to pursue with the higher ups in my division, I thought. Even if I had to call in a favor to the Colonel again, I would whatever it took to help catch this guy and put him away. But in no way was I going to jeopardize the life of a civilian.

CHAPTER 26

With all this going on in my head, I still managed about five hours of sleep. Got up early, found the shower wasn't taken yet and took advantage of that. Made my way downstairs to the dining room by following the smell of coffee, helping myself to that on the side buffet.

Joanne came out then with a stack of pancakes for her guests. There were already fruit bowls and muffins set out and I was going to have that until I saw what she sat down next on that platter. Might as well, he thought—I'll leave a good sized tip for all this. It wasn't what I had expected when she said breakfast included at six am.

After indulging myself and another cup of coffee, I headed out to find the Sheriff's Office. Down the Main Street, I saw the building and parked out front. It was only a little after s am, so the Sheriff wasn't in yet. I then went to the corner Get-n-Go to fill up, as I was planing on the trip to Twin Falls, so I might as well do it now.

Then I saw the diner where Amy works and figured I'd go in and check it out to get another cup of coffee, since I had about 45 minutes to kill. I opened the door to the little diner, which rang with a bell attached to alert customers were entering, I supposed. I sat down at the counter, as I spied Amy coming out the side doorway with two plates full of biscuits and gravy for her customers a few seats away.

She said, "Hi, be right with you," as she went by to sit down the plates and refill their coffee cups.

117

"Hey there, you got an early start, uh." She said with a smile and a coffee pot in her hand. He couldn't get over how cute she is.

"Yep, I did. I've been up for a few of hours already had a huge breakfast, so I'll take a cup of coffee while I wait here for the Sheriff to get in his office, if that's okay?" I asked.

"Sure thing," getting him a cup to fill. "But that's him right over there in the booth by the window, if you want to go talk to him now." She said nodding her head in the direction of where the Sheriff was sitting.

I looked over my left shoulder and saw a large older man in a tan uniform sitting in the booth and said, "Yeah, maybe, but I'd like to keep it professional, you know one officer of the law to another."

"Well, it's pretty casual around here Matt, come on I'll introduce you. He's a regular in here every morning," she said. "Sits here and reads the daily paper with breakfast, ever since his wife passed away ten years ago they say."

They walked over to the booth together and stopped, "Hey, Bud, more coffee?" Amy asked as he looked at her and she said, "This is my friend Matt Gannet, he's a HP Trooper from Wyoming and he'd like to talk to ya here, if that's okay with you, since he was looking for you and you're not in your office yet."

"Hi, Bud, glad to meet you," I said shaking his hand.

"Well, since I'm all done with breakfast and the paper now too, I suppose I could sit here with another cup of coffee and have a chat. Mr. Gannet is it, what can I for you?" Bud asked politely.

Amy refilled both of their cups and walked away winking at Matt for good luck.

"Yes, sir, I'm in the area following up on an investigation involving missing young girls in the tri-state area and I had a few questions for you," I explained.

"Well, now I didn't know WHP was crossing state lines to investigate missing persons these days, isn't that a job for the FBI or the local divisions to take care of. What brings you to Idaho anyway Matt?" Bud asked.

"Actually, for me this has been my personal investigation so far, because of my sister being one who disappeared three years ago. And I think there's a connection to all these other young girls missing from Idaho, Utah, Montana, and Wyoming," I explained.

"Oh yeah, what connection, you got any proof or vehicle description we need to put out a BOLO for or anything like that?" Bud asked more interested now. "And what brings you to Soda Springs specifically, when the last I saw was up in Twin Falls that went missing?"

"Well yeah, that part is a long story, having to with Amy here; who was working at Little America, Wyoming, when my sister went missing from there also." I said, trying not to sound too vague. "But yes, I'll be headed to Twin Falls today to talk to Sheriff Marvin Cole for any further information he may have on this latest disappearance. And no, I don't have any vehicle description or a clear physical description—a hunch on his presumed profession as a scenic/wildlife photographer," I said, as he looked over at Amy.

Then Bud said, "It seems like I've been asking all the questions here, what you need from me then?"

"Actually, yes I need to know of any formal reports of missing girls in this area or close by, as I've been checking with other small towns or large cities like Salt Lake City and Boise for the same information. I'm trying to establish a timeline. I have a few in my notes from Utah, Wyoming and Montana that fit the parameters of the that I'm looking for.

I've been working in conjunction with our DCI—Department of Criminal Investigation Office in Cheyenne with this. I need more information. There are quite a few years in between that are not accounted for and I'm sure he was not taking that long of a break." I explained what I had so far, and what I was looking for and the years that needed to be filled in.

Bud then said, "Okay then, let's head over to the office and I'll make a few inquiries and get started on this, and you'll work on getting me that official request from the head of your division in Wyoming."

"Sounds great, thanks. Yes, I will," I said as we were leaving.

"No problem. If all these agencies and departments could work together, we might accomplish something. So you're saying you don't think you have any bodies with all these missing girls. It's not homicide as yet then?" he asked.

"Yeah, as far as I know of. A lot of abductions with nothing to go on, nothing ever turns as to where they are or where they were taken. Even years later, as with my sister," I told him.

"Well, how you know some are not runaways then and are lost somewhere out in New York or Los Angeles?" Bud asked.

I replied, "I don't know anything for sure, only that the few reports I have and followed on myself over the last few years have not turned up anything new."

Bud suggested they could cross reference missing persons with homicides to get a better idea with the timeline they were looking at. That was where he was going to start with his phone calls, he said.

We were at the office going over all these ideas when I checked in for messages of my own back home and was told that I had one phone call from Sheriff Marv Cole and a number to call him back at. I asked Bud if I could use his phone to make a call to Twin Falls.

"Yeah, Marv this is Matt, I got your message. What's up?" I asked.

"I think we got a break, if you'd like to drive here still, we could talk about it. Actually, I have a couple of detectives here anxious to talk to you also," Marv said.

"Detectives uh, what they want with me?" I asked.

"I'm not at liberty to discuss anything with you over the phone. But the other day when we talked you said you'd be coming here anyway, so that's why I called to make sure you still have that plan," he explained as much as he could.

"Sure, I'm in Soda Springs Sheriff's Office right now, I was about to leave here in a few hours anyway—I'll revise that and leave now.

See you in probably two or three hours," I said as I thanked him for calling.

"Well that's interesting," I told Bud. "That was the Sheriff in Twin Falls I told you about, Marv, he wants to see me as soon as I can get there. He says there are a couple of detectives that want to talk to me also."

"Oh yeah, I wonder what that's all about, unless they have found a body and now it is a homicide and those are actual homicide detectives," Bud said. That was ironic as they were just saying that Matt hadn't found any connection to missing girls and homicides.

"You best get going then, I'll have more on this when you get back later tonight—unless you stay the night there, then I'll see you tomorrow or fax you any information if it's important enough," Bud said as Matt started to leave.

"Yeah, I'm not sure how long this will take or what it's all about. I should probably stop to get my overnight bag in case. Thanks Bud, see ya," I said as I went out the door.

I did do that, and swung by the B&B to get my stuff and check out; then stopped by the diner to let Amy know what's going on and that I might be staying the night there in Twin Falls. That and I wanted to see her before I left, I couldn't believe the attraction to her—she's living with Joe for crying out loud, but they weren't married, so who knew.

On the drive to Twin, I sure had a lot to think about. What if there was a body now and it is homicide detectives—does that change things, I wondered. I couldn't help but think that I'm about to get kicked to the curb on these investigations. I hope not that's for sure.

I was going to have to make a call to my Captain to either get permission for more personal time off, or get assigned to work this professionally, at least from the Wyoming side of things. If there was only a way to figure out what this guy did with those girls, including Hope and tie her to what's happened.

Some burial site needs to be found in Wyoming to help my

quest---that's not right to think that way. If that's what this is over by Twin Falls, could it be the latest victim already and how could that be—unless he was in a real big hurry and didn't a very good job.

All of these questions and possibilities were running through my mind all the way there. I had plenty of water to drink and a full tank of fuel, so I only had to stop once to use the restroom outside of Pocatello. From there it was another hour and a half maybe two hours at the most. I was making good time, I'd be there by before noon, he figured.

At least the scenery along this stretch of I-84 was a lot better to enjoy with crossing the Snake River than it was driving through most of SE Wyoming along I-80, that was for sure. The traffic was a little heavy being as it's early summer now, but that made time go by quicker and for me to pay attention, so as not day dream or wonder what was waiting for me in Twin Falls.

At around 11:45, I pulled off I-84 at the Garden of Eden exit so that I could take a look around before heading into town, being as the actual downtown itself was a few miles back off the highway and I still had a little ways to go. The area did look a little isolated as I drove around. I didn't really take the extra time to drive down to the Shoshone Falls though, as I figured I needed to find out what was going on first. I did get the street address and directions I was going to, so I started to look for that as I came in closer to town, which were pretty good I thought as I drove right to the building I needed to be with no problems.

I parked, got out and went inside to ask for Sheriff Cole's office. The deputy asked for my name and called ahead to inform him that I was here, and that his office was right through the double doors, down the hallway to the end the last door on the right.

As I went down that hall, I saw someone come out the last doorway, and Sheriff few himself greeted me as I got there. A tall, stocky, bald guy who walked with a purpose.

"Hi Matt, Marv. Thanks for coming so quickly," he said shaking my hand.

I said, "No, thank you for calling me, now we can get down to business."

As we went into his office, Marv said, "Have a seat right here, can I get you anything; coffee, water, soda?"

"No thanks, I'm fine," I answered.

"Okay then, well first let me call the detectives in and they can fill you in on what we got." He said as he got on the intercom phone and asked for Jim and Faye to come in now.

After a few awkward minutes, the door opened and Marv stood and made introductions.

"Jim this is Matt Gannet—Matt this is Detective Jim Young and his partner, Detective Faye Olson," Marv said as they sat down.

"So you're an HP from Wyoming is that right?" Jim asked first.

"Yes sir, that's right. I'm on personal leave right now, however, so this is not official for me," I answered.

"I see, you have a personal agenda I understand from what Marv had told me, your sister went missing a few years ago?" Jim said.

"Yes, that's correct, three years now, and no sign of her since," I said.

Detective Olson jumped in with, "Well we have a development, as I'm sure you've guessed, yes we're from homicide."

Detective Jim Young sighed and said, "Yes, we found a body early this morning, over along the Snake River in Paradise Valley area," looking exasperated at his partner.

My assessment was, she obviously didn't care if this was the good ole' boys club or not, she had business to get to. She was rather striking herself, with red hair and beautiful blue eyes and younger by about ten years. She was not the senior partner, but she was not letting any grass grow under her feet either. That did not deter her, however, she kept quiet for the moment.

"Matt, we understand you've been asking around to most law enforcements agencies in the tri-state region following on missing girls, is that correct?" Detective Young asked.

"Yes, I've been trying to find some connection for almost three years, since Hope disappeared. This body you have, is it really the most recent victim that went missing from here—what it's been, two or three days ago is all?" I asked.

"Yes, we believe so. The parents of the girl recently identified her body, when we brought her here to the county morgue," Detective Young inform me.

"Well, yes this is definitely a new development for me that is, if they are from the same perpetrator. May I ask how she was found?" I asked very interested now.

Detective Young said, "Apparently, with the recent snow melt the river had risen to a much higher bank, with that and some animal digging—probably coyotes—the shallow grave was uncovered somewhat. Since it was close to a public campground also, it was discovered rather quickly."

"That explains a lot, he must have also been in a hurry, if it's by a public area rather than a desert remote site somewhere in the middle of nowhere," I said. "Do you think also this could have been the work of the guy who was taking pictures at the Falls, you have any evidence to that effect?" I asked more curiously.

"Unfortunately, I'm not authorized to share any evidence with you as you are here only because Sheriff few called you and by your own admission, not professionally. However, if we were to receive anything in writing as to an official request from say your WHP Colonel, then that may change things."

"Now let me ask you, why you think this has anything to with— uhm, 'the guy taking pictures' at the Falls?" Detective Young asked.

I looked at them all for a minute and revealed, "I have a source who says she feels strongly the person who took Hope had a camera and drove an old truck with a camper topper on the back, who may have been using this ruse on other girls the same way."

"You have a witness," Detective Olson said, "why didn't you say so?"

"It's not exactly an eye-witness, she can't provide any physical descriptions or anything definite for a BOLO on a vehicle either;

but I believe her when she says she's seen him following her before in Wyoming," I tried to explain.

"I'm puzzled, how does she know he had a camera and drove an old truck with a camper shell then, some of that is specific, isn't it?" Detective Young asked.

"All I can say is that she's positive and that she's also sure he'll come looking for her too, since she's seen him. That's why she moved out of Wyoming and changed her appearance and sold her vehicle that she had then." I tried to explain without saying that Amy had this dream or a vision or whatever it was.

Then I added by saying, "Humor me on this one thing okay, can we get a composite drawing of the guy at the Falls from the Mom maybe and reinterview anyone else at the other truck stops. Then I can ask my source if she's seen him the way he is now in case he's changed his appearance. What could it hurt?"

The detectives looked at each other, and finally the Sheriff said, "It's worth a try, I say we get the Mom back here. I'm sure she'd be willing to anything to help us at this point."

"Another thing, have you already released this information of finding a body since the family has been notified and identified her?" I asked.

"We've been talking about that before you got here, it's going to be hard to contain that from the news media. We could release a full statement now though, and shake things a little by putting out the composite drawing for seeking a person of interest." Detective Young further commented, "That might be the way to go. He'd be bound to make a mistake then—they all do. If nothing else, maybe this photographer person will come forward on his own and claim innocence, and we could eliminate him or investigate him."

"Okay then, that's it. I'll call Mrs. LeBloom back in here to talk to our sketch artist, and you two go talk to the LT, and get a press conference set up, hopefully for this afternoon. The sooner the better, or at least as soon as that artist is finished," Marv said to everyone.

"Uh, Marv, may I use your phone to call my Captain to put in for that request—officially?" I asked him.

"Sure, we'll leave you to that and get done what we have to do," Marv said as he went out the door and they left me alone in the office for some privacy.

First I called back home to check on any messages then asked to be transferred to Captain Bill Strong's office.

"Sir, it's Matt, yes sir, I'm in Twin Fall, Idaho. Well it's a long story, but suffice it to say I may have a real lead on that missing person's case, or abductions of young girls are related. And yes, this is related to my sister's disappearance. What I need from you sir, since I'm not sure how this works, but what I have to to get an official request to be included in this investigation? They cannot share any evidence or any further information related to the case without an official call from the Colonel or a faxed statement to that effect." I explained the situation to my Captain to best of my understanding. He then offered to extend the request to the Colonel, J.P. Ogden, personally.

"Thank you sir, I really appreciate it if you could relay the importance that time is crucial. Yes sir, I'll be in touch soon with any further dates," I told him.

When I hung up, I couldn't believe how fast it was moving now—it was making my head spin. For years I had searched and examined every single case I could find, and called in all the favors that I possibly could with nothing to show for it. And now in a matter of two days, I may finally get some much needed answers.

I sat for a minute, bowed my head and said a silent prayer for strength for what was about to come, as I feared it was not going to be anything good.

CHAPTER 27

After half an hour, Mrs. LeBloom, the mother of the young girl, who was Caitlyn LeBloom, came in to the sketch of the man she saw talking to her daughter at the Falls. She was crying still from earlier when she had to view her daughter's body. Her husband didn't want her to be involved in that part of it, but she had insisted that she needed to know for sure and the only way was to see for herself.

She told the detectives that she was not thinking at the time about the man. If only she had kept her daughter with her—right by her side the whole time they stopped to get dinner at the travel center. Who could have known that would be the last time she'd see her daughter alive though.

As I stood by and listened to her, I could only remember what it must have been like for my own Mom and Dad too who were there with Hope and then she was gone—like that never to be seen again.

Mrs. LeBloom finally calmed down enough to get started and listened to the young artist tell her to breath deep and close her eyes and try to visualize the man in general.

He told her, "Don't give me features yet, that will come later, let's start with hair length and color, and any facial hair."

The questions and answers went on for longer than anyone thought it would, with a few of breaks in there because she got a little set looking at the results of her descriptions, which were almost exactly as she remembered them to be.

Finally, by two pm, we all breathed a sigh of relief when the artist was satisfied that it wasn't going to get any better and went to make several copies of the sketch.

One was used during the press conference of course, to show the public who the local Sheriff's Office was in search of. They also said he was seen at the Shoshone Falls taking pictures and that he was a person of interest, if anyone knew this person or has seen him to call anonymously the number shown on the screen.

Another copy was given to me to show to my *source* in case she recognized anything about him or not. Other copies were faxed to several surrounding law enforcement offices from SLC to Boise, to Cheyenne to Helena, who were told to distribute statewide in each state.

Now that action was being taken, I felt a tremendous burden lifted from me. I had always thought I was in this search by myself, as I was sure Amy felt the same way. I wished I could call her now to tell her everything, but that would have to wait until I got to a hotel room later that night. After all that was personal, not like calling his Captain, which was business.

I stayed at the Sheriff's Office until the press conference was over so I could watch that from the inside looking out the window. They like to do these things on the steps of the local station or courthouse, just like on T.V.

I thought it was rather straightforward and the sketch provided a dramatic effect that the news people jumped all over with more questions for the officials. The PR department and the LT refused to go into any further details and pleaded with the public to please call with any information, thank you.

ℭHAPTER 28

When that was over, he stayed a little while to talk with Sheriff few and tell him that he left his name and number with his Colonel to call and talk to him regarding his position in this investigation. Now that the news report will probably go out statewide and then hopefully get picked by the wire services, or at least go to the surrounding states, which is exactly what they needed to happen. Marv said, "That's fine, I should hear by first thing tomorrow then. Why don't you go get a room and some dinner and we'll be in touch regardless anyways. "How's that sound—not much more we can now, but wait."

"Okay, yeah, I was headed out to do that. Any good recommendations for a place to get a good steak dinner, I haven't eaten since six am and I'm starved." I said hoping my belly wasn't growling by now.

"Oh yeah, sure head over to the Outback on Blue Lake Blvd., it's great," Marv said.

After finding that with no problems according to Marv's directions, I ordered this big 'ole T-bone that is what I needed. I managed to finish off that with a baked potato and had a nice red Merlot to wash it all down, since I wasn't on the job now.

Sort of felt like a celebration to be this close, I thought as I sipped the wine. Well, at least to have a good lead like this to follow up on. I could only hope that now I'd be included in the investigation by as early as tomorrow so that I can review the full evidence. I'll find out in the morning, all I can now is go find a hotel room and call home and then call Amy, I thought of her with a smile.

I saw down this same side of the Blvd was a Quality Inn, good enough for me as I drove there to get a room for the night. When I got to my room, I went right to the phone and called home and Zach answered,

"Hey, bro, what's up—where are you anyways?"

I answered, "I'm in Twin Falls, Idaho right now. Yeah, we've had some developments happen here. There was a body found, turns out to be the young girl who went missing only a few days ago. I'm going to stay here though and try to be involved in this case, even if it's not officially."

"So that's why Mom's set. I think she saw something on the news earlier today," Zach said.

"Damn, I had hoped to be able to call you before that came out in order to warn you guys, there wasn't any time. Things were moving really fast here," I told him. "How are they now, can I talk to Dad?" I asked.

"Sure, let me get him. Hold on," Zach said as he went to tell his Dad that Matt was on the phone for him.

"Hi, son, how are you doing? Were you there at that press conference?" Dad asked.

"Yes, Dad I was there, sorry you all had to hear that way. I'm still in Twin Falls and I'm going to stay awhile, until I hear back from Colonel Ogden," I said.

"Okay, son you stay at it. Do whatever you have to do, please be careful and come home safe. We love you," his Dad said.

"I love you all too, take care of Mom, okay. I'll be home soon and this will finally be all over," I said before hanging.

Oh my goodness, my poor Mom, she had to relive that all over again, I thought and I was worried about her. She hasn't been able to forgive herself for something of which she had no control over or any knowledge of.

Next, I still had to call Amy. That wasn't going to be any easier. "Hi Amy, it's Matt, how are you doing?" I asked.

"I'm doing good, how are you? That must have been a tough day, uh? I take it you're staying in Twin Falls then," she said.

"Yeah, yeah, it's been a really long, but satisfying day. Did you see the photo on the news? That's a sketch of the guy who was being a photographer, while talking to that little girl at the Shoshone Falls. Her Mom did the best as she could remember. Does that look at all like anyone you've seen before? Those detectives need to know as soon as possible," I asked her.

"It didn't really stay on the screen all that long, it was a close though. But you know it could be, or it could be anyone for that matter. I'm not really sure, the way he looks now could be a disguise or the way I'd seen him could have been the disguise, who knows," she said.

"Well I have a copy print of that, so I'll bring it with me, when I come back that way in a few days. I want to stay here at least to be able to review the evidence that was with or on the body. I need to know everything I can about that, if I can," I told her.

"Okay, I'll see you in a few days then. Hope you'll have more news by then or maybe I'll have a more revealing dream. Goodnight, Matt." Amy said. I thought as I hung up to go take a cold shower and get ready for bed. I couldn't help thinking of her.

I turned the T.V. on to watch the late news again before getting some sleep. I wondered if maybe this killer was out there somewhere watching it also. Would he go off and kill again to show us that he can. I certainly hoped it would not be the latter, as I turned off the T.V. to try to get some sleep.

CHAPTER 29

M eanwhile, in Boise, there was no sleep for the stranger in the dark night. For night was the best time to hunt, and he didn't really care who it was going to be, only that he could. He'll show them, ha---to think they had an idea who he was and what he was going to do next. They didn't have a clue as usual.

He was about to show them that he didn't need his camera or photographer set up to be able to take what and whoever he wanted. All he had to do was wait and watch and he'd find someone real soon, he could feel it.

Then he'd go follow that little Miss Amy in her VW Beetle at the BSU parking lot and scope all that out over the next few days so that he could take her too, when he was ready.

That stupid little press conference was not going to stop him any, he had a lot more disguises than that one to use—it's just that one worked very well every time. Well he'd find another that would work as well. You wait and see; dumb copers

He was walking along the green belt again, but this time he was limping and was watching for girls alone. Maybe a jogger that he could convince he was injured trying to make it back to his car. If that didn't work or if he didn't see anyone, he'd go back and drive around downtown and pick a prostitute—that'd be his second choice.

Sometimes you had to what you had to do, and take what you could get. That's what happened, he was forced to take choice number two.

So he got back in his truck and took off for the better parts of Boise. As he cruised the streets in the downtown area, then over to the less desirable parts of town also, he didn't see one hooker out trolling. What the hell was the matter with all these do-gooders that lived here. I know there has to be some prostitutes around here somewhere, he thought. Just not finding them. Well hell, I guess I'll try again tomorrow.

Then he had a great idea after seeing a guy run past him earlier, jogging with his black lab. That was a sure fire way to get noticed on a nice sunny day along the greenbelt—who could resist a cute little puppy. He'll find one at a pet store somewhere and take him for a walk So that's the plan for tomorrow, use a cute puppy for bait to catch the cute girl.

As he went back to his motel room, he needed to decide what kind of puppy he was going to get, because he had no clue which breed was any better than the next. Well as long as it's cute, it should do the trick. He'll have to rely on the people at the pet store, maybe he'll spot someone there looking at the pets with longing to have one of her own.

The next day, he didn't go to the one at the mall because that was too many people. Instead, after looking through the yellow pages (what a concept) they still have phone books in the motel rooms, he called around asking if they had any puppies. Then he found one pretty close to where he was now, and go down to the green belt along the Boise river right after that and get down to business real early too—my lucky day, he thought. In fact, he anticipated a good day, so that he could get back to the BSU campus and check on that little VW by later that day, or tomorrow at the latest.

FIrst, he had to show them and this time he considered not burying this one; but maybe leaving her out in the open somewhere, a public spot, all naked with a nice red ribbon tied around her neck like a package wrapped for display. Yeah, there's no sense in being hidden any longer. They all know what to look for, so he'll show them.

That's getting a little ahead of myself, he thought, still need to take the opportunity as it presents itself. At the pet store, he did find a really cute fluffy, white and brown puppy that he got along with a collar and a leash to take him for a walk right away—that's the plan.

This is bound to work, who can refuse something so cute. He had to have the right type of ruse to get the girl to follow him and the puppy back to his truck. He'll think of something when the situation arose, and he was confident as he got out and carried the puppy to the lane to put him down and start off down by the river.

For the first few hundred feet or so, all he heard was, "Oh, look how cute. How sweet is that. What's his name?

What kind of puppy is he? Is he going to get big, you think?" One after the other all sorts of people came up to him talking about the puppy. Sure enough he was a chick magnet—not a single chic yet. There were all in pairs or groups of kids, parents, students, all kinds; but no single women.

So, he kept going as the little puppy peed here and there and whined a lot. Maybe he's thirsty or hungry. He would go back and look in the truck in a few minutes, still needed to head over to the other side of the river to go back.

When he crossed the river at the underpass and came back to the other side, the little guy barked and started running off, nearly jerked the leash out of his hand as it was so unexpected. He finally spied what the puppy wanted—to chase a squirrel that had run a tree to get away from his high pitched barking noise.

This little cutie was seriously becoming a nuisance and not at all what I had wanted to happen was happening, at least no one that was alone approached him. He continued to walk along coming close to the campus parking again, wishing he could spot the purple VW and was getting so distracted that he didn't hear someone come behind him. But the puppy did, and let out a little yelp as a slender blonde jogger came to stop and bend down to pet him.

"Oh how sweet, what's his name?" she asked scratching his ears.

"Toby, I literally got him this morning, thought he'd like a nice walk outside after being locked in that cage all night and day," he said.

"That's so sweet of you, he looks a little thirsty though. You didn't bring any water along with you?" she asked being concerned.

"I didn't think it would take very long really. I'm on my way back now, I'm parked here in this lot by the end of the trail," he explained.

"Okay, that's good. Take care of him, he's cute," she said as she was about of jog away.

He called after her suddenly, "Would you be so kind as to help me get him back into his carrier. You know, keep him distracted so he doesn't think he's going to be locked in again, so I can give him some water?" And then he added smiling, "I'm having a little trouble controlling him, I guess little puppies can be rambunctious aren't they?"

"Well, okay I can that I suppose, to make sure you get him some water. Where are you parked—did you say?" she asked.

"I'm over here by the BSU lot, the last one in the closest spot to the path here." He motioned for her to follow him.

"So you teach here also?" she asked.

"Only part-time, my real passion is traveling," he said going around to the back to open the camper door. He looked around the lot quickly to make sure no one was out there coming or going on the pathway. He handed her the puppy asking her to hold him while he opened the carrier to get it ready, and to keep her hands busy with the puppy so as not to be able to fight back as much.

They stood at the very back inside of the doorway to his camper, and he leaned over to get something, which was the cloth with chloroform on it. He took her firmly by the arm and pulled her all the way inside and shut the door while covering her mouth with the cloth, so as no one could see them struggling. It only took a minute though and she was out.

He picked the puppy and put him in the carrier with a little water dish as promised. Then he picked the girl and put her on the bed and taped her wrists, feet and mouth. Next he was off to find a home for the puppy, as his deed was done for the day. Then on to the business of taking care of the girl and where to go with her.

He picked up the carrier and put it in the front seat next to him so he wouldn't have to open the back door of the camper again until he was away from the city and ready to go in there himself. He made a sign to put on the puppy carrier that said 'FREE TAKE ME HOME', then he looked for a fairly busy shopping center to put the carrier outside on the sidewalk for anyone to have and take home with them. Easier that way for everyone, no questions asked.

He drove away quickly, so as not to be seen as the one who put it there and went in search of his next disposal site. Driving around thinking he'd better wait for it to get darker, but he had to a while to go for that. In order to have a little fun with this one though he also needed more privacy than the hotel parking lot.

He checked on her to make sure she wouldn't wake up too soon, and got his bag from his room to check out and find an out of the way campground again. This time it didn't matter if she was found right away or not, as long as he couldn't be traced to her. They had one body already—so what was one more by today or the next day.

He figured he'd drive south there were sand dunes he's read about in the things to do pamphlet in his room. It was by Kuna, which didn't look too far to go, so he headed that way. Soon after he got on the highway he heard all sorts of commotion from the camper.

Well now, she might be a handful, finally someone with a little fight in her. But then again she was quite a bit older and stronger than the last one. He'd have to be real careful. This was going to be a fun day after all, he thought to himself as he kept driving.

When he go to where he thought he was going, he stopped to look around and make sure there was no one else out here within sight of him. It was the middle of nowhere, but with still plenty of daylight there could be others show with their sand buggies or ATV's. He sure didn't need his vehicle description to get out in connection with any of this. This was all he had in this camper, and he couldn't afford to replace it. He probably should have rented something to come out here in and left his outfit back at the hotel— too late now.

He took the side road further back off the exit and turned down another dirt road looking for somewhere to hide his truck. A clump of trees, or ditch, or something like that. Finally, over the next hill, he saw an old deserted barn out here with nothing else or anybody around. He was able to drive around to the other side and park away from the road out of sight— in case.

As soon as he stopped and turned off the engine, he sat and listened for a few minutes. Thinking he might be opening a hornets nest when he walked back to the camper door, he stepped aside after unlocking it in case she was waiting to pounce on him or kick him in the nuts. Either way would not have been pleasant.

As it turned out. all was quiet inside so he stepped into the camper and shut the door and opened the window curtain to let in some light. He saw immediately the reason for the guiet. The beauty he thought was going to be a challenge, had given before the fight began.

There she was on the bed—still bleeding to death from the small cuts to her wrists, diagonally not across. She knew what she was doing that was for sure. All the noise must have been her looking for something sharp enough to the trick.

Well damn, he thought that took all the fun out of the rest of the day. He still wanted to tie a red ribbon bow around that beautiful neck, though pulling on it was no longer necessary or be her because of death. He needed to show those that would find her and examine her body that she was still his if it was only for a short time.

Maybe this would because everyone some confusion as it did for him also. He still could use this to his advantage that way he figured. As he watched her die, he took pictures anyway. Then left her bound with the red ribbon on, and took more pictures after that too. Then he wrapped her in an old sheet, so he wouldn't get any blood on himself, and got ready to take her out to the old barn to put her on display. Someone will find her anyway, because he saw several tracks of 4x4, dirt bikes, and ATV's close by this place. Must be a hang out. He'd sure like to see the face of the kids that would find her.

He went out and walked around first to make sure he didn't see anyone around, then came back to get her body and carried her inside. He decided to leave the barn door open, swinging in the breeze to attract more attention.

Boy, did he have a mess to clean inside the camper though. That's one of the reasons he never cut or shot anyone—what a mess. Going to have to stop and get some clorox and bag of shop rags or something to clean this and definitely some air freshener. Can't have the place smelling so bad for his next guest. He thought he saw a Walmart back off the highway before he took this exit.

The girl, whoever she was, or whatever her name was, must have decided to take the lesser of two evils and take matters into her own hands. That was her way of not letting him have any fun. Probably knew she wasn't coming out alive anyway, so this way she could throw it back in his face and have the last laugh, as they say.

We'll see about that he thought, but he is going to have to lay low somewhere for awhile to make sure no one saw his truck out that way though he never saw anyone else—you never knew.

Besides he still had to some spying on Miss Amy with the purple VW to make sure it was her and then wait for a good time to grab that bitch. Then the fun would really begin.

After he got the cleaning supplies at Walmart, he went in search of a KOA Campground to stay a few nights or a week depending on the outcome of today. At least he could get this mess all cleaned up in the camper tonight.

After he got it all done to the best as he could and bagged it all in a large garbage bag that he would leave in some commercial dumpster far away from here, he went to take a long shower and then maybe a swim at the KOA's pool. He sure needed to destress after the day he had. All that trouble for nothing—no release or satisfaction of the kill. But soon, he thought, it was coming soon.

The suspense of that was what got him through the night, but the results of the day he had were going to be eventful to say the least.

CHAPTER 30

Matt awoke early again wanting to check in with his captain and then head over to the Sheriff's Office. He called in, checked his messages first, then was transferred to Captain Strong's extension.

"Hey there Captain, sir, what's the verdict? Do I get to be in on this investigation going on in Idaho or not?" I asked him.

"Well, the thing is, the Colonel says in order to make it official business on our part, we have to be invited. In other words you have to have some information or proof that they need and then they can ask for your help to be involved in their investigation." Captain Strong explained. And then he asked, "So, you have anything to offer them, besides your extensive research on this matter?"

"Actually yes, Amy Winters is my witness. Even though she lives in Idaho now, she used to live in Wyoming and she contacted me first with what later proved to be valuable information," I said.

"Did you mention any of this to the detectives yesterday when you met with them?" he asked.

I replied, "Yes, of course I did. I told them all but her name, and how she believes what she knows to be true, of course. Which comes through to her by way of premonition dreams or visions. I don't really know or understand any of it myself how it works, but I believe her.

"Well, I'm not sure if you have to reveal all these facts about her to them first, however, the direct investigators have to request you for your help and insight into this case. So; I suggest you prove yourself invaluable to them somehow today, then we will sport you and authorize your involvement at that time." Captain Strong informed me of this decision and then said he had to go and would like to hear from me later that day.

Well, that was something anyway, he had to think about how he was going to breach this subject with the detectives. Maybe he should go get Amy and bring her here and let her tell them herself. No, that would be his last resort he decided. No use getting her involved any more than she has already inserted herself in all this.

Okay, he'll give them her name and where she lives. If they want to call to get her story, that's to them, he figured. I was going to head over there right after he got some coffee and breakfast. I needed a little more time to think it all over.

The conversation in my head sounded good to me, but what would they think, and what questions would they have to ask in order to let me in on the case, I wondered. Best get it over with, because I was going to find out one way or another what the autopsy results were and what the evidence is that they have.

I pulled into the parking lot a half an hour later and went in search of Sheriff few first. I was thinking he more sympathetic to my because to be involved and interagency cooperation makes more sense.

The deputy at the front desk had to make a call, then told me to head down the hallway again where I was the day before. Marv met me outside his door with a handshake and said, "Good morning."

"Morning," I said, then asked, "Are the detectives going to join us again, or can we talk first?"

"Come on in, have a seat Matt. What's on your mind?" Marv asked.

"I heard back from my Colonel this morning and the only official way I can be involved in this investigation is if I'm invited by the department here and then he would authorize it," I explained. "I was hoping you would put in that request for me, if the detectives didn't feel it was necessary," I added.

Marv thought it over for a minute and said, "You know I'm on your side here in this, I totally agree the more eyes and ears on this the better, however, it's not all to me. I have higher s to answer to, you understand. And technically, this is their case.

I answered, "Yes, I do, but with your recommendation, it would go far to push the process along. I need to review that evidence today Marv before I head back to Wyoming."

I was pleading now, but I didn't care how it sounded, I was going to whatever it took— if I had to beg.

"Let's see what Jim and Faye have to say and go from there, okay Matt?" he said as he picked the phone to ask them to come in.

"Okay, Marv thanks. My Captain and Colonel both will authorize anything you need with one phone call," I said as the door opened and Detective Young stepped in.

"Hey Marv. Hi again, Matt. Sorry Faye's tied up with phone calls still. We're swamped checking out all the tips coming in from that photo and they all have to be verified as legit or not," he explained.

"That's good to know, Matt here was telling me his Colonel will authorize anything Matt does here or provides for us officially. All we need to is put in writing that he's been invited by this department to be fully included in this investigation and any other that might arise pertaining to this case," Marv said firmly as to show his strong sport.

"Okay, well that's good then, simple enough right Marv. I'll run it by the LT and see what he says, but I don't anticipate a problem you? I mean we all agree that the more help the better, right. What about your source, would she be willing to come here for an interview with us?" he asked.

"I'm sure I can persuade her that's in all our best interest. I'll call her right now also and drive there to get her today if that's required before your decision is final," I said to Jim reassuringly.

"Sounds good, let's plan on that then and get this paperwork nonsense done so we can all get back to work. How's that sound to you? We have all your fax information right, Matt to get this going?" Jim asked to make sure.

"I'll be sure and write it all down and leave it here before I go, yes." I said, "May I use your phone again, Marv?"

"Sure thing, I'll get us a cup of coffee," he said leaving the room.

I dialed Amy's number, but then realized she might already be at the diner by now, so I had to call information to get the diner's number to call for her there.

When I finally got a hold of her and told her what was going on, and that I needed to come back and pick her to bring her to Twin for an interview with the detectives, she was more than glad to be able to be doing something productive.

She said, "I was getting very restless, but I'd rather drive there on my own if that would save you some time."

"That would save some time, yes Amy, but I would feel better if you didn't take the risk of driving alone. Besides I may have to get my patrol car anyway if someone could bring it to at least Kemmerer for me to trade vehicles, then I'll be headed that way as it is. I'll let you know if that's the case, okay. Shouldn't be but the next hour or so, as to what I'm going to be doing. Call you soon." I explained everything to her and hung up, so she didn't have the time to argue with me about it.

I sure wished I had one of those new mobile phone gadgets starting to come out everywhere, however, it cost way too much for my budget. There was no way the department was going to authorize us lowly patrolmen to have one yet. Only the Governor could probably get one, then it would be only as needed with a state government requisition.

Maybe in the next five to ten years they'll be more affordable for everyone, or it could be a fad and not amount to too much of anything at all. That would make his life a whole lot easier though. No use wasting a few thousand now, that's for sure.

I thought about all this, as I waited for the authorization faxes to come back from Colonel Ogden, because after explaining that I was going to go pick Miss Winters today, they seemed to agree that we were necessary. I also still needed to arrange for my patrol car to be transported as close as they could meet me to the Wyoming/Idaho border.

I didn't have to wait very much longer as it turns out, the authorizations came back as promised from Wyoming, as Colonel J.D. Ogden is as good as his word. But then I didn't have any doubts about that.

My next step was to call my Captain and find out if he was required to get his patrol car, since I was on official business now. And if so, if there was someone who could meet with me at the state line or Kemmerer and trade vehicles. It would still take about five hours to drive across Wyoming from the other end of I-80. If I had to wait that long, I'd rather drive back to Soda Springs and wait there at Amy's. Then it would only be an hour from there to meet someone.

One way or the other, I was going to head that way, either to pick her up and come back, or go get my patrol car and then get her on the way back. By then I'd have to stay the night there, as it would already make for a very long day.

If we left to come back to Twin after that it would be after 11pm getting back, so I would leave that to Amy to decide if she was to it or not. Because one way or another, we had to get back here as soon as we could.

CHAPTER 31

It's still early now though, only nine am, so I had all day. I was able to get through to Captain Strong, and "Yes," he said, "I already have someone on their way with your car and that he'd meet you at the state line in five hours."

Good to know, now I could be on my way to Soda Springs, and be there before lunch to go to the diner first thing. Even with that I'd still have to hang out for about two more hours before heading to the state line to meet with transferring to his patrol car. That's okay—gives me more time to talk to Amy.

I stopped by the hotel as it was on my way to the highway to make sure I can have my same room for another night and to reserve another one for Amy, either next door or across the hall, so it's close by.

I called her then from my room to tell her my plans and if she could get the next few of days off. She said that she'd already planned on quitting remember, so a day or two early was not problem.

I did make it back to Soda Springs by 11:30, so I went straight to the diner to get lunch and see Amy. When Amy saw him walk in right about the time for lunch rush, she smiled real friendly and when I sat down at the counter, she asked, "Hey cowboy what'll ya have?" in her best western drawl.

I smiled back and said, "What'da got for your blue plate special, because I'm purdy hungry as a bear," playing along with my best accent too.

Laughing she said, "Well now, mister we got this here homemade meat loaf with some Idaho taters and gravy."

"Okay, then little lady. That's what'll I have," I said, "and some of that there ice tea," as she hollered in it.

She filled a glass with ice tea, sat it down in front of me, leaned over and whispered, "I like your cowboy drawl." Then went to get his plate in the pick-up window.

When she came back, I said, "I like yours too."

Amy had a few more customers to get to and more coming in the door by this time. She couldn't for the life of her concentrate very well with looking at Matt and realizing she had flirted with him. Where did that come from, she wondered.

Well, I'd better get over this little crush I got for him, as I'm living with Joe for crying out loud. I do can't that to him after all we been through, she thought to herself.

She hadn't done anything—a few of fantasies and one dream— that's all. But who could blame her, he's so dreamy with those blue eyes so clear you could drown in them. She was still thinking about all this as she went about the rest of the afternoon and on to each table almost on autopilot now.

As she went by to check on Matt and refilled his tea glass and take his plate away, she asked, "Is there anything else you need?"

He said, "No, I'm good, if you don't mind me hanging out here for the afternoon until you get off that is."

"It'll be another hour and half," she said, "before we slow down so that I can leave. I could give you the key to the house. You could watch T.V. or something, if you want."

"You're sure you don't mind? Maybe that would be more comfortable, since I have two more hours before I have to leave here to meet with my friend to trade cars," he told her.

"No, not at all. I'm gonna be pretty busy here for a while anyway.

Hang on a sec, let me get you the keys, okay?" She said in a hurry as she turned to get plates out of the pick-up window.

She came back a little later after refilling drinks, taking two more orders to put in, she reached under the counter close by where I was sitting and got her purse out to give me the house key off her key ring.

"This is the key to the front door, go on in and make yourself at home. I'll see you when I get done here, okay," she said with a smile.

I didn't really want to leave, as I had a pretty good view sitting here watching her work, but I didn't want her to think I was like all the others that ogle at pretty waitresses. "Yeah, okay. Thanks, see ya later then," I said as I paid the ticket and left.

I parked in front of her house and went inside to relax, feeling a little weird in someone else's house with them not home. I figured I may as well watch a little T.V., maybe catch the news or something. After only half an hour with nothing good on, I had a fallen asleep on the little sofa.

That's where Amy found him still an hour later when she got home.

Oh my, be still my heart, he does sleep, she thought. And look at those long dark eyelashes—should be a sin to have those on a guy. With that little wave of dark hair that had fallen over on his forehead, she wanted so badly to touch it and put it back in place. But was so afraid that if she did that, she wouldn't be able to stop there and then he'd wake up, and then what would happen. No, not going to go there, she told herself.

Just go about your afternoon, and don't disturb him act like he's not here—yeah right. He's fine right where he is—SO FINE. So she did, she went to her bedroom and undressed to take a shower to get the smell of fried food off her and change clothes.

The little house didn't have a bathroom right off her bedroom, so she had to use the only one that was in the hallway. When she finished her shower and came out with only her bathrobe on, she practically ran right into Matt who was awake now obviously, and also looking for the bathroom.

"Oh dear, you scared me. Hi," she started to say, knowing she was blushing.

"Uhm, yeah hi. I was looking for the, uh restroom. I didn't know you were in here. I mean I didn't know you were home either." I said with a very dry mouth as my foot was stuck in it. Oh man, you jerk—that's all you can say, I thought to myself.

"Okay, yeah well here it is. I'll go and get dressed, be right out," she said going toward her bedroom.

I threw a little cold water on my face before I came back out hoping that would help clear my head. Amy also came out after a few minutes and was towel drying her hair.

"When do you have to leave? I didn't want to wake you when I came home, at least I tried not to because I thought you'd need a little rest with the drive there to get your car and then drive back to Twin Falls still tonight, I figured it's going to be along day for you," she said thoughtfully.

"Yeah well, thanks. It was an early morning, I must have dozed off a little, but yeah, it's getting about that time for me to take off here in a few. Do you still want to come back with me or follow me there? I've already booked you a room in the same hotel I'm at— across the hall. I hope that's okay? I should have asked first," I asked her a little sheepishly looking down at the floor.

With that look alone, she was ready to anything he wanted and forgive anything he ever did—even if it was a little presumptuous of him, she thought.

"Yes, I definitely want to go back with you, but maybe I should follow you in my truck. I mean, I don't know your policies, if I'm allowed in your patrol car as a passenger," she said.

"Well, you are my witness, so technically this is official business. Can you be ready when I get back here in a few hours?" he asked.

"Sure, no problem. Do you have that picture of the suspect I could take a closer look at?" she asked.

"Yeah sure, I'll got it out in my car, you can keep it to study as long as you want," he told her.

"Okay good, Joe should be home by that time, but if not I can give him a call to let him know that I'll be leaving with you to go talk to the detectives in Twin, and that I'd be a few of days maybe, right?" she asked to make sure how long they'd be gone.

"I don't know for sure. It shouldn't be any longer than that unless there are any new developments when we get back there tonight or tomorrow," he said.

"Alright then, it's a plan. I'll be ready to go, pack lightly for a few of days and see you later. You better get going—so your partner, whoever, won't have to wait for you," she said.

"Okay, yeah. I better get going you're right. I'll see you in a few hours or so," he said as he walked out the door.

I thought I was in big trouble if I kept thinking about her in any other way than a witness or more than a friend as this point. No way was I going to let my feelings interfere with this investigation. I'd put in too much time and emotional effort to get this far. But I wasn't going to let anything happen to Amy either, not if I can help it.

I drove on down US 30 to the state line and only had to wait another fifteen minutes for my fellow officer to trade cars with me.

"Hey, Buck, how's the drive?" I asked him.

"Long, but I'm glad it's summer time and not the middle of winter that makes that I-80 drive so miserable," he said.

"I hear you. Hey, thanks again. You can leave my car there in Laramie if you want. I'll have my Dad or one of my brothers come to get it. If that's okay with you?" I asked him to make sure.

"Sure thing, Matt. See you when you get back. Good luck," Buck Johnson said.

"Okay, thanks and drive carefully." I told him. Then I got in my patrol car and put everything back to normal to drove back to Soda

Springs. Another hour to get there, then two more after that to Twin Falls. It will be getting late by then, going to make for a long day.

When I got back to Amy's and parked in front of her house, I saw that Joe was getting out of his Jeep also. I waved at him then, "Hey, Joe." I hollered.

"Hi ya, Matt," Joe said as they both walked in the house at the same time. I could tell by the tension between them that Amy had told Joe she was going to Twin with me, and that's why Joe had come home early.

Amy was packed and ready to go like she promised, so I said I'd wait for her in the car. No doubt they needed to talk this over.

"So you're going anyway?" Joe asked, "Even after what I told you earlier?"

"I have to Joe, you know that. I can't walk away from this—not now," she said trying to reason with him.

"Yes, you can," Joe said sounding more angry now. "We can move again, I told you that—this shop of mine can be rebuilt anywhere. Don't you see that you're more important to me than all of that?"

"Okay yeah, I know that Joe, but it's my conscious I have to live with not you. I can't stand by and let this guy keep killing and then come looking for me too, not if I can help in any way to stop it," Amy pleaded. "I'm going now and that's that. Matt is waiting for me." Then she picked up her bag and headed for the door.

"Wait," Joe said almost in a whisper, "come back safe, you promise. I can't stand that you're leaving it like this, please let's not be angry." Then he walked over to her to give her a big hug and kiss. "I'll walk you out."

When they both went outside to where Matt was waiting by his car, he was standing on the driver's side and then he came around and put Amy's bag in the backseat for her and started to open the passenger side door, when Joe called him over.

"Matt," as he shook his hand, "keep her safe please, I'm putting her life in your hands buddy. I trust you'll bring her back safely to me."

"Don't worry, she's not going anywhere without me. I won't let her out of my sight, I promise you that Joe," he told him.

With that said, I went around to get in my car and started it to leave, then I saw Amy and Joe hug good-bye. Something about the way they looked, made me sorry she was coming with me. That she should stay here and mind her own business. I wasn't exactly sure that she'd be any safer here. If this guy really did come looking for her, this town would be the first place he'd look, he was as sure of that as she was.

The two hour drive to Twin Falls was quiet, as they each were lost in their own thoughts. I asked as we pulled into town if she was hungry. "We could stop and eat first if you want, or head on over to the station?"

"No, not so much hungry, a little anxious to get this started and over with so that it might lead to something," she said. "I also can't wait to see the evidence the police have on this guy or from the scene anyways."

"Yeah, I haven't reviewed any of that yet either, so I am too, obviously. I had left right away to get my car and then pick you up. I didn't hang around to ask, but now I definitely need to know everything," I told her.

I pulled into the Sheriff's Office parking lot, since we both decided that was to be our first stop. We went inside and asked to see Sheriff Cole, and again the deputy on duty recognized me, but asked to see the ID for Amy. By then, I saw the Sheriff come down the hallway after the deputy had called him.

"Hey, Marv, this is Amy Winters," I introduced them. "Amy, this is Sheriff Marv Cole, I told you about."

"Glad to meet you Amy, come on back," Marv said.

"I wasn't sure you'd still be here, but we wanted to see you first," I told him.

"I figured you'd stop in when you got back to town, and I was getting all these calls to help verify anyways, so I waited around," Marv said.

"Thanks for that. Well, Marv, we'd like to review the evidence and autopsy reports now, if that's okay with you and the detectives?" I asked him.

"Sure, no problem, let me call Detective Young. He has all that, and you guys can go in the conference room to do that if you want. I'll show you where that is and have Jim meet you in there." He said as they started to leave and head down the other long hallway.

Both detectives and Marv came back to the conference room soon after that, and they all were introduced to Amy.

"So, let me be the first to ask you this Amy, what exactly do you know about our suspect?" Can you offer any more information for us—from that picture perhaps?" Detective Faye Olson asked her.

"I don't know anything more than you specifically. The only other help I can be, is because I've seen him. Probably in a disguise, but I would know if he was close by me again," Amy answered.

"And how do you know this, if you can't identify him positively?" Det. Olson asked more curiously.

Amy looked at Matt for some help here—not sure how to answer without sounding crazy.

"Let's say, it's a combination of intuition and premonitions in my dreams. I'm not sure how to explain it any further," she said.

I interjected my thoughts before detective could object and kick her out, as he noticed they looked at each other and Faye rolled her eyes as Amy had said that.

"Let me say this before you guys prejudge her, I've researched this phenomena and I truly believe Amy has a lot to offer us; and she also has excellent insight that we might miss otherwise," I told them.

"And to answer the other part of your question," Amy said. "Yes, I have studied that picture and the eyes are the most familiar, that is one thing for sure. That stands out the most to me as being very similar if not exactly like one of the regular customers where I worked in Wyoming. I haven't seen him since then—that was three years ago," she offered as more information.

"So that artist rendering that Mrs. LeBloom did was pretty close to our suspect, what about anything else, hair color or facial hair?" Det. Young asked as he became more interested in the 'eye-witness' part of her explanation.

"Not the same, but any of that can be changed, the eyes can't really be changed, other than the color with the use of contacts. The shape, however, that and the coldness is hard to disguise, and that's the part that I recognize," Amy said.

"Okay then, I'm convinced. Let's get started. Here are the latest victim's photos, the autopsy photos you don't have to view if you prefer. Matt can go over the written results with you. In this box is all the physical evidence, we have found from the burial site. Any questions?" Det. Young asked.

"I think we got it from here, thanks a lot. We appreciate your confidence in us," I said.

"Don't thanks us yet, let's all get to work on this to get this monster, okay. So you guys want anything for dinner? Have you eaten yet? We were about to order take out for delivery in here," Marv asked.

I looked at Amy, she nodded. "Yeah sounds great, we could eat; because no, we didn't stop for any dinner. We came straight to the station," I said.

"All right then, what's your preference? We can get Chinese, Thai, pr pizzas, that's our top three choices around here." Marv asked.

"Whatever you guys are having is fine, any of those are good for me, you Amy?" I asked her, looking over at her.

"Yeah, whichever, I'm partial to the Thai, but I'll take anything at this point," she said anxious to look the evidence over.

"Okay, I'll bring it in when it's delivered," Marv told us going out and shut the door behind him.

"Great, let's see what we got here, are you okay with looking at these photos? I've seen some before, but this stuff still gets to me," I told her.

"Sure yeah, let's take a look," Amy answered.

So, I opened the folder and passed some to her and I kept the rest, then we would trade I told her. When Amy looked at the very first photo of the young girl, she was so shocked and gasped, "Oh my, she was so young and very beautiful. This image with the red ribbon, I've seen this before. I must have dreamed it, but it's very familiar." She said then closing her eyes trying to remember the 'vision'.

"Really, that's good, it means we're on the right track. Anything else familiar?" I asked.

"Not with this one, but let me look at the rest of these," She said and kept looking at more, "I'm not sure, maybe the river, but it's more like a canyon with a river at the bottom."

"Good, because that's the Snake River, area and it does flow through a large gorge with high cliffs, like a canyon, all through. Let's trade, you can look at these now."

"Have you had any more of these dreams recently that you haven't told me about?" I asked her. "Cause you sound like you've described this whole crime scene in your head, without looking at the rest of these photos."

"Well, I don't know about these particular images as familiar, but yes, I can't be sure how long ago I've had them though. Probably at least a week, no more than two for sure," Amy told me.

"As for anything more recent, something about the red ribbon keeps coming back from last night. I almost mentioned it on the way here, but I didn't know how to interpret it, until I saw these photos," she explained further.

"Let's try this, close your eyes again and envision the red ribbon as a bow like this one. Only focus on that and see if it helps you remember anything more specific, okay?" I said.

Then the door opened and Marv came in with a few containers of Thai food. "Dinner is served," he said, "Any luck with all this stuff?"

"Yeah, maybe, Amy here is remembering images of seeing the red ribbon tied in a bow from one of her dreams," I told him. "She was trying to remember more from a more recent premonition."

"If the photos helped, then look through here. This is the box of physical evidence where we have the actual ribbon that was used, here you go—look at that now," Marv suggested as he got excited by her 'visions'.

Amy held the baggie with the ribbon in it. It was still tied in a bow as they found it around her neck, they had cut it off of her in the back. She closed her eyes trying so hard to concentrate on this exact bow for a minute.

"The only other image I get with this from my dream is an old barn, that's it," she said when she opened her eyes to look at Matt.

"Well now, that could be something to with a new victim, right, someone we haven't found yet." I was excited now as I asked Marv, "Did you also send any of these descriptions out to all law enforcement agencies in the areas of Idaho, Utah, Montana when you sent out the photo of the suspect?"

"You mean the crime scene details, not specifically, no. Why?" Marv asked.

"If we could get any more other recent crimes with these similar details, red ribbon, strangulation. It would point us in the direction of where to look next," I explained.

"Yeah, I know that's why we've been trying to set up a network of databases with like M.O.'s to follow suspects paths of destruction, so to speak, but that's a lot of information to go through and enter in the computers. Let me get this all emailed to all the agencies that we sent the picture to, and ask them to notify us if anything similar happened there. Thanks again for your help," Marv said and then he left.

"Well, let's eat then look at these written details next, okay?" I told Amy.

"Yes, it smells so good. I didn't realize I was so hungry." Amy said when she opened a container to dig in.

"Well, I knew I was getting hungry. I hope my growling belly didn't offend you," I told her smiling.

Amy smiled back thinking she was in big trouble this close to him, if she didn't pay attention to the case instead of looking into these blue eyes. He has to know how irresistible he is, with a day's growth of stubble on his face and a grin that says it all. Yeah, she's got it bad for admiring the 'eye candy'.

CHAPTER 32

After dinner we again looked through all the physical evidence, and then he read over some of the autopsy report also. Then while she was reading the accounts of events, statements from the parents, she realized they didn't have a witness of the vehicle description he may have used. They recalled all the other vehicles in the lot at the time they left the Shoshone Falls, which were two cars and one truck with a full size step-up camper on the back.

The kind described was dark blue truck, with a white full size camper that had a red stripe on the side. They recalled clearly because it was red, white and blue. This description also ringed true as to a small memory for Amy.

"Hey, Matt does this truck description sound familiar to you at all?" she asked him reading it out loud.

"No, I can't say that it does. Why you remember seeing that in Wyoming or somewhere?" he asked her.

"No, not exactly. Not this specific color or style, but remember when I told you when Hope disappeared, I saw an older truck with a camper topper on the back. Well, what if he's been using that method still, only now he has a newer model is all, to take these girls away in," she said.

"Oh my, Amy you're right. It only makes sense. No one is going to look twice at a camper truck in a campground either, which is where this girl was found close to," he said.

Then he got up to go look for Marv to make sure he also had

this vehicle description out on a BOLO (be on the lookout), and to make sure they double check at all campgrounds and KOA's in and around the cities.

When he came back, he had both detectives with him again to sit down and go over all they had come up with that directly related to the evidence. First, he listed all the important details, the red ribbon tied in a bow, strangulation as the cause of death, vehicle description most likely a blue truck with a full size step-up white camper that has a red stripe.

"These are all good leads to list in specific details to be going out to every law enforcement agency within the tri-state area—asap. This information, of course, will never go out to any members of the media, so as not to alert the suspect to hightail it to Canada or somewhere," he said.

The detectives seemed impressed that Amy could put these specific details into context with her premonition dreams, and her insight into the way this guy thinks.

"Okay, let's call it a night and see where all this leads us tomorrow, folks," Marv said to everyone.

We cleaned the room from the dinner to go containers and gathered our personal belongings. The detectives took the evidence to put back in the locked room and thanked us both for coming in. The only thing left to was head to the hotel, and get some sleep and wait to see what may develop tomorrow.

Matt drove to the hotel and got her room key for her, then they took the elevator to the second floor rooms.

"This is yours here, and I'm right across the hall if you need anything, holler, okay? See ya in the morning, good-night Amy," he told her turning to go into his room.

"Good-night, sleep well," she said.

He looked back at her and smiled saying, "You too."

Amy took a long hot shower to try and relax herself and clear her head of all the details. She couldn't get the poor young girls photos with the red ribbon tied around her neck and the perfect size bow out of her head. That's a meticulous detail of a photographer would use to be so precise. She finally got to sleep a few hours later only to be awakened by another frightening dream. This time she saw herself running away or toward someone, not sure, but definitely running scared. Joe and Matt were there too, she didn't quite know how that fit in with regards to her or to whatever might happen to her. Oh man, if this truly was a premonition dream though, she better be more prepared. She better get herself a gun for protection. Maybe she should mention it to Matt over breakfast, see what he thought about it.

She tried laying there to go back to sleep, since it was barely 2:30 in the morning and had a ways to go yet till daylight. No way was she going to wake Matt over a dream at this hour, no matter how upsetting it was. So she did her deep breathing exercises and some yoga stretches to relax and then tried laying down again.

Seemed like she barely dozed off, after an hour or so later when the phone was ringing by her bed. Who could that be at this hour, she had already talked to Joe when she first got to the hotel and then again to tell him good-night, so she answered cautiously, "Hello."

"Amy, it's Matt," he said. Of course it was, dummy no one else knew she was here. "Sorry to wake you, but we have news. Do you want to go with me back to the station or stay here to get some more rest and I'll come get you later?" he asked.

"I haven't slept much anyway, might as well get up. What's going on anyways?" she asked yawning.

"There's been another victim found in Boise," he told her.

"Okay, I'll get dressed be ready in five minutes," she said.

Amy thought he looked far too good this early in the morning, she could only imagine how he would be every morning.

We headed back downtown, it was four am and they needed coffee in a bad way. Matt drove through a Starbucks on the way and asked for two large double mocha espressos.

When we got there, and met with both detectives and Marv,

they were looking over the pictures that had come through on both their faxes and their office emails. They were more clear printed off their email of course, so they studied those. They all agreed it had to be the same unsub.

"Look at this red ribbon tied in another perfect bow," Det. Young said.

"Yeah, but what's with the slashes on her wrists, that changes the cause of death drastically," Det. Olson said.

"Yeah, but that's not him, she did that to herself," Amy said.

"How can you tell any different from a photo without an ME report?" Faye asked her.

"Look at the tape still on her wrists in relation to the cuts. There's no way in hell if I had something sharp enough to cut my arteries, that I wouldn't cut that tape first to get away," Amy said as a matter of factly. They all pretty much nodded in agreement with that.

"We need more information on this victim to establish any psychological theory," Matt said.

"You mean suicide and why?" Amy asked.

"Yeah, more to the point is why," he answered.

"And we need to get to Boise now," Amy said hurriedly.

"Whoa, what's this we part, you're not going anywhere near this guy" he said to her firmly.

"I go where you go—remember you're not going to let me out of your sight—I believe were your exact words," she said.

"Where was she found?" Amy asked the detectives.

"Inside an old barn near Kuna, Idaho, close to the sand dunes in that area," Det. Young told her.

Amy crossed her arms and looked at Matt as if to say, I told you so, but didn't say it. He looked at her like, I don't care you're not going, but didn't say it either.

This was also up to the detectives in Kuna and Boise to invite any of them there to take a look at it anyway.

"What was the time of death, and when did they find her?" I asked.

Detective Young looked at the email again said, "They found her early this morning at one am by some kids who were using the barn to 'hang out'. The estimated time of death was 12-15 hours prior to that. They'll know more after the ME examines her body."

"And you got this email what a half an hour ago?" I said shaking my head.

"Yeah the deputy called me when he got a call from a Detective Wilson in Boise asking for me and that I should check my email when I get here. I called him back when I got in right away and he said he got our notices late yesterday and remembered the red ribbon detail, so he called as soon as he could. Took a little while to process the scene you know, then he emailed me what they have so far. He's got two other detectives on it, and all of Kuna deputies doing a search of the area," Marv explained.

"What about the BOLO on the vehicle we described?" I asked.

"Well, that's the other thing. Yes, they're checking all the campgrounds and KOA's in the area, and yesterday there was a truck and camper that matched that description in Eagle, Idaho KOA, but he's since left the area with no other sightings since. He may be anywhere in Idaho or Montana by now," Det. Young said.

"Crap a day late," I said disappointed. "When are you headed there? Have you called this Det. Wilson again to ask him if we are invited to help as yet."

"I was about to, I take it then you both want in on this also?" he asked looking at Amy also.

"Absolutely," they both answered in unison.

"Okay, I'll see what I can do, might not be until tomorrow though. If they don't have any further developments like finding that vehicle or making an arrest. Then they might call for our help on the case, when they don't find anything useful," Det. Young told them.

"Has the FBI been nosing around yet?" I wondered.

"Not here, but I imagine they'll be called in at Boise before we are," he answered.

I looked at Amy and shrugged, "Well, is it okay if we come back after grabbing breakfast and take another look at the evidence you have here? I hadn't read through the all the autopsy report," I asked.

"Sure thing, I'll have it brought out again and ready for you in the conference room," Marv said.

"Okay, thanks, see you guys later then," I said.

Then we left Marv's office and headed out to look for a quiet place, like an all night diner to eat and talk about all these new developments.

"You're always hungry, I'm fine with this coffee—it's got me so revved right now I could fly through all the evidence again," she said as they got outside.

"Yeah, that's why we need to eat something to slow down the caffeine rush and be able to concentrate calmly. And I'm not that hungry either, but I could use some fuel to get me by. Besides I want to talk by ourselves, away from the others," I told her.

"Okay then, I saw a cute little Mom and Pop place back towards the hotel. Then I could use a shower before we come back, if that's okay with you?" she asked.

"Sure, me too. Sounds like a plan," I grinned.

CHAPTER 33

I spotted the little diner from where Amy had told me it was, and pulled into the side parking lot. We walked in to get a seat at a booth in the back with a little more privacy. Sat down and turned our coffee cups over, to signal the waitress to bring the coffee pot with her when she came over to them. Not that we needed any more—a little more would be good—with breakfast.

"Morning, need any cream with your coffee? The special for breakfast is a small stack with bacon, eggs for $4.99," she announced as she filled our cups.

Amy looked at her name tag and said, "Thanks Julie, I'll have an english muffin with two eggs, over easy."

Julie said, "That's it for you miss, okay. What about you sir?"

I answered, "I'll have your special sounds good to me, with my eggs also over easy, and no cream for me—Amy. Thanks."

Amy shook her head, "Me neither,"

"Alright then I'll get it right out to ya, thanks," she said walking away.

We sipped our coffee slowly, each of us thinking what to say first.

"So why didn't you want to talk about any of this back at the station? Was it in front of the detectives or Marv that you didn't want to overhear? I thought he went to bat for us, I like him," she asked.

"I like him too. It's that I was thinking why couldn't we go there on our own first and poke around a little, you know unofficially," I told her.

"We couldn't take your patrol car then that's for sure, it kinda sticks out," she said smiling at me.

"Yeah, no kidding. I was going to get a rental car, for the day and run and check it out—the crime scene a little, and drive around get a feel for the city," I said.

"Great, sure then what will you do if we find out something or spot the truck/camper out of all the other 200,000 people there that drive trucks?" Amy asked.

"You're from there right, your folks still live in Boise then?" I answered with a question avoiding the truth of the matter—they haven't been asked to go there yet.

"Yes, I am, and yes they live there, why?" she asked.

Julie came back then with our plates, just in time to avoid answering her question and sat down everything asking, "If that's all?"

"I'll have a glass of water too, please," Amy answered her.

"This is great, I'm good," I said. After she went and brought Amy's water back and I dug into my pancakes, then I said to Amy, "Well, I was also thinking if I needed to come back here and get my patrol car and check us out of the hotel, you could stay with them and wait there—if need be."

We continued to eat and discuss that possibility. In the end though, I agreed it'd be better to wait and see what the detectives in Boise had to say. Even though I didn't want to, because I felt we were so close and I didn't want to back off now or be left out.

Amy finished her plate when Julie came to pick it up and refill her coffee cup. Then she sat and sipped it as she watched Matt devour the rest of his platefull, admiring his strong appetite and still be able to look the way he does, "Uhm," she sighed.

Then he looked at her and met her eyes saying, "What, I've got a fast metabolism all right, I need to fuel it daily—several times."

She smiled and said, "No, that's fine with me. Are you ready then? I'd better call Joe too, now that it's a reasonable hour of the morning, but before he goes to work."

"Okay yeah, I got to check in at home too. I'll pay for this then we're out of here," he said.

Amy left a cash tip for extra on the table, because she knows how it is to get through that kind of a long day, doing what Julie does. We went to the hotel then and to our respective rooms, and he told her to call his room when she was ready. Amy called Joe then to bring him up to date on everything and told him not to worry, she wasn't going to Boise with what's happened there yesterday.

"Yeah, but we both know you will eventually, if you think you need to; so be careful please and stay with Matt—at least he has a gun. Okay?" Joe told her that he had to get going to work, "Love you, bye."

Amy hung up feeling more depressed and anxious remembering her dream and the feeling that he was coming for her, which was the reason she wanted to have a gun too. She could ask her Dad for one of his she thought, if she hadn't time for anything else that is—keep that in mind.

She went to take a hot shower then to get ready for the long day ahead, all the while thinking. I'll have to call Mom and Dad soon anyway to fill them in too. I'll ask him then, she figured she had the time.

I also called home to tell my Dad what was going on and that the case was moving faster now, and that he was going to follow through to wherever it took him. My brothers had the ranch under control, my Dad told me, "Not to worry about them, do what you have to son, but be careful and come home safe."

"Okay Dad, take care of Mom let her know that it's going to be soon. I'll have Hope home for her to bury properly. I love you too," I told him, then hung up and sat there and thought about what I had promised. I have to find him, bring him in alive. I need to know where all the others are, especially Hope.

I'd better get in the shower and change to be ready when Amy calls, and I was of course ready and waiting on her. But what a woman to be waiting on—seemed worth it to me. I didn't want to keep thinking this way about her, wanting her so badly, I concluded. She's taken by a good guy too. Then again they were not married and she seemed interested also. Oh hell, get this investigation over with and let things fall where they may afterwards. Before I could get too much further into that line of thinking, she called and told me she was ready to go.

We headed back downtown to the Sheriff's Office then, both of us looking refreshed and ready to take on anything, especially the bad guys.

$\mathcal{C}$HAPTER 34

As promised, all the evidence and files were back in the conference room again when we went in a sat down. Amy brought water with her from the hotel fridge, and I of course forgot, so she offered me her other one.

"Thanks," I said, "let's get started here."

"Do you want to look over the ME report also or you want me to highlight it for you?" I asked her.

"You go ahead, I'm going to look over the rest of this box here. If there's anything important in it, you'll let me know," she said already distracted.

So, of course, as I read the report, I expected the strangulation with the petechial hemorrhaging in the eyes. What I wasn't ready for was the obvious signs of rape, severe damage to the vaginal and anal areas both. She was a virgin and violently raped and choked to death, while she probably was forced to watch how much the bastard liked it.

Oh man, I sighed, as I realized this is also going to read like Hope's autopsy report when I find her, and that made me angry all over again.

"What's wrong?" Amy asked when she looked over at me, noticing I was upset.

"All this hits home when I least expect it to, you know, thinking of Hope," I told her. "But hey, that's why we're here right? To find something to end all this. What did you find?" I asked.

"Oh yeah, well there's this really large heavy duty garbage bag he must have used to carry her out in to bury her—like throwing out the trash," she said, looking as sad as I felt inside.

"I wonder if you have to get those through a commercial supplier or if you can pick these kind up at any Walmart," I thought out loud.

"Well, let's see, I'll call them and find out. Walmart that is first, then if not, I'll call around to the restaurant supply stores also," Amy said and went in search of a phone book.

"What you suppose this size is, 50 gallon or more?" she asked me.

"Yeah, I'd say at least that maybe more. I guess just ask them for their strongest, largest size and go from there," I told her as she sat down to look up the number.

"That would probably be too easy, along with this duct tape, it's most likely been bought at any hardware store too—that bag might be in the lawn and garden section," I said.

"I'll ask and see," she said.

While she was tracking down those possibilities, I went in search of the detectives to see if there were any updates on the latest victim information. It would be nice to know who she was and what she was doing yesterday morning when he found her with the hunt he was on, I thought.

I went down the hall to Marv's office to see if he was in there. I knocked first, heard him say, "Come in."

"Hey Marv, any more news yet from Boise?" I asked.

"Come on in, have a seat," he said. "I got off the phone with Detective Young, he heard from his buddy in the local FBI Office there," he explained as I waited for the other shoe to drop.

"Yeah, what's the verdict for us, are they sharing or taking over?" I asked trying to be patient.

"Yes, they're convinced it's the same unsub, using the same MO with the red ribbon. What they want is all of our evidence and information, in order to determine that inconclusively, so that it can be labeled as a serial killing or not," Marv said.

"Did Jim tell him they can only have all this, if we all come with it?" I asked sarcastically, knowing they'll come and get it anyway and take over the investigation.

Marv chuckled, "Ha, no, not exactly. He did mention your names however, and the importance of both of you in relation to the case."

I asked him, "Then what—we wait here?"

"That is still to be determined unfortunately, you won't know that until someone shows up here to gather our evidence and maybe interview you both at that time," Marv said. "Sorry buddy, that's all I got," he added.

"I'd better get back to it then with Amy before they come and take it all away," I told him. "Thanks."

"Have you found anything useful to uhm, Amy's visions or dreams?" Marv asked politely.

"No, nothing like that, she's tracking down possibilities on that huge garbage bag," I answered.

"Yeah, we tried that also—dead end," he said. "You never know, let her call around, maybe she'll get lucky."

"Couldn't hurt right? Talk to you later, thanks," I said to him and then walked out the door.

I went back to the conference room to see how Amy was doing and give her the bad news.

"Hey there, I talked to Marv, he said the FBI wants all this evidence to tie both cases together 'inconclusively' and confirm it's a serial killer on the loose in Idaho." I told her when I sat down, then asked, "Any more luck in here with you?"

"Not so far, no. Well, I suppose you think that idea you had earlier sounds pretty good about now, don't you?" Amy asked me with a long look.

"Yeah, it does more and more. I wonder how much trouble we'd get into," I said sheepishly.

"It's less that two hours to Boise from here, I could call my Mom and tell her we're coming and why." She said tempting me in more ways than one. If she only knew how flipping cute she is, but she don't act vain at all. So, I'm sure she has no idea what those hazel eyes do to me when they change colors subtlety with her moods.

We were like frozen in time staring at each other, when she finally looked away. "So what's the answer, call my Mom or not?" she asked when she cleared her throat.

I don't know for sure what she was thinking in that moment, but I really wanted to know what color her eyes would be in the throws of passion. Then I replied,

"Uhm yeah, let's do this, get out of here and on the road. I'll call a car rental place and we'll go with that—sound good?" I said to her to make myself sound more assured of what we were about to do.

"Okay good, I'll call my Mom then. We'll both stay there don't worry they have a huge old house down by BSU and don't use half of it." She said, picking up the phone to call, "If you're sure?"

I answered with a smile, "Oh yeah, more than sure. I'll be right back. I'm going to tell Marv we're headed out to lunch or something, and that we're done with the evidence."

Oh hell, Amy thought when he left the room, he's gonna drive me to drinking. He really has no idea that my insides melt when I look at him looking at me, like a cat with a bowl of milk ready to lap it up.

When he came back to tell her, "It's all set, let's go,"

She told him, "Cool, Mom said no problem, to let ourselves in if they are not home; which would be most likely as it's only 10:30 now, that makes us getting there around 12:30."

"All right then, I got a car all ready to go for us at Enterprise. We'll go pick it up and leave my patrol car at the underground parking garage at the hotel," he said, adding, "Let's go be nosey."

They drove to Enterprise so she could follow him to the hotel. He parked and locked his car in the prepaid parking garage and then went to check us out of the hotel.

Heading north to Boise after that, and as she suspected, we got there by a little after noon—closer to 1:00 by the time we got my parents' place. He parked out front, and we went to the front door, and let us in with a hidden key by the step.

She asked, "So what's the plan now? Are we media reporters looking for a story, or no let me guess, we're a few of thrill seekers who get off on murder?"

"Haha, funny, no we are who we are. I don't plan on running into anyone who wants to check our ID's," Matt told her.

"Okay, whatever, you figure out a plan smarty pants, I'm going to raid the fridge for lunch. I can tell you need to recharge," she said with a smirk at him over her shoulder.

"This place really is super cool. I love old homes, or in this case, old mansions," he said following her to the kitchen.

"Yeah, it's cool, but a little creepy too; to grow up in, you know. As a kid, the tall cathedral ceilings and all the windows overlooking the river were not so fun then," she said.

Looking into the fridge she pulled out what looked to be a ham, "You want a ham and cheese sandwich, and let's see here, we got some watermelon, or grapes or what about artichoke hearts to go with it?"

"Sandwiches are fine thanks and fruit is good," he said looking out at the view of the river. "Wow," he mumbled.

"Yeah, it's an amazing view. I think that's why they still live here after all these years," she said.

"You said that they're Professors at BSU. What do they teach, if I may ask?" he asked.

Smiling she said, "They both have doctorates in psychology, physiology, and theology; so they teach anyone of these or all of them if they so choose to. Right now, this semester, it's Theology 101, I believe."

"I'm impressed. What kind of childhood did you have, Amy? Were you lonely?" he asked her.

"Ah-ha, the psychiatry comes out now—not that I remember much. I had friends though, everyone wanted to see the inside of my home, of course," she said with a wave of her hand around her. "Isn't this worthy of a lot of sleepovers?" she smiled sadly.

"Oh yes, I could definitely see that. But were you happy here? I wonder why you left so young right out of high school, you said the first time we talked," he asked her.

"The first time we talked was not a conversation, it was an interrogation, as I recall," she said smiling. "Here come sit down, lunch is served."

"Thank you, my lady," he said as like bowing to the lady of the manor.

"Your welcome, kind sir," she said, ignoring his questions altogether. She had had enough of all that growing up.

CHAPTER 35

After lunch we took a drive down to Kuna, it wasn't too far to go or out of the way as I thought it was going to be. With Amy's help, I found the right turn off to the dirt road that led to the old barn.

"How is it you know about this place? Had you come here too in high school to 'hang out'?" I asked her.

"I may have been curious to see what it was all about. Turns out it was a bunch of jocks with their 'ho's who put out to anyone having drunk, falling down, stupid-ass parties, so I left. End of story," she said proudly

"Good for you," I said, "not to succumb to peer pressure."

She gave me one of those looks that says yeah right, and rolled her eyes at me. We drove to the barn finally with all the yellow police tape, 'do not cross' all around it to keep looky loos like us out.

I parked a little ways away though to get a look around first. There were a few people who drove by still see where 'the murder' happened.

"It doesn't look like we're going to be able to get a real look inside until it's dark," I told her.

"You want to come back here after dark, that's only asking for trouble, you know that don't you," she said.

"Well, how else do you propose we see what's inside there?" I asked her.

"Why do we have to see what's inside? Nothing is there, they took everything away and locked it up as evidence somewhere," she emphasized *'locked'*.

"I got a better idea, let's go back down the highway to the closest Walmart and ask if anyone bought a bunch of shop rags or towels, clorox, and an air freshener. I bet you he had a mess to clean that he wasn't exactly counting on," she said with logic.

So, that's exactly what we did. I found the Walmart right off I-84 and we went in to the service desk and asked them to ask their clerks if they remembered the guy in the picture we had. If he had came in to buy a large amount of shop rags, clorox, and an air freshener, as this would be an unusual purchase we thought.

The service desk manager asked us, "What for, are you guys looking for the killer of that girl?"

"Yes, as a matter of fact, we are." As I pulled out my badge quickly flashed it and put it back away before she could tell what badge it is or where I'm from.

"Well, okay officer, it's about time someone came in. I called you guys yesterday, right after I saw that on the news," she said. "I thought it was unusual also and that picture looked a little familiar."

"We been pretty busy ma'am," I said with my best drawl and smile.

"I bet you are. Anyway, yes I did. Someone similar to that came in for almost those exact same items. How'd you know that?" she asked me curiously.

"Sorry, ma'am. We can't divulge any information. What did the man look like that you saw here?" I asked with a side glance at Amy, who turned away from me to look around.

"Well, he didn't have long hair or a moustache. He had grayish temples, medium length hair that fell over his collar. He was real polite, but always looking around. It was those eyes that got me," she explained.

"What was he wearing?" I asked her.

"Uhm, let's see, plaid shirt, short sleeve but with a sweater vest.

He looked hot too, and I wondered why he had on that vest," she said.

"Okay, great. Thank you very much, you've been a great help ma'am," I said, then we walked out to the car.

We sat for a few minutes thinking about all that lady had said, then I asked Amy, "Did you get all that, I have to write it down so I don't forget?"

Amy replied, "No, I got it. Don't worry, I had a feeling he would change it up some. He had to, you know, look far older and more trusting."

I looked at her with awe, and asked. "What made you think of the rags and clorox and stuff anyway, have you had another vision you're not telling me about?"

"No," she answered, looking away. "It's what I would have done. Wouldn't you want to clean your camper if that happened with all that blood in there?" she asked reasonably.

"Well, we have a new description now, what do I with it? I can't exactly call it in to the Det. Wilson here, as I just impersonated a Boise Police Detective," I said.

"Let's go back to the house and write it all down and think about it, maybe we could call it in anonymously," she suggested with a smile.

"Don't look at me that way," I told her. "I know I'm in big trouble. I have to call Marv."

"Yep, you're gonna be in trouble I think," she said.

It was getting to be late afternoon when we got back to the house. Amy turned on the radio saying she thinks better with music and wanted to catch the latest updates on the news also.

"I have to tell them—someone. About this description to get it out to the public, so we could get a new sighting before he changes disguises again," I told Amy, who was pacing again.

She said calmly, "He already has anyway by now, most likely."

"I'm going to call Marv like I said, I trust him. I'm going to tell him everything we did, how we found out the information. What he decides to with that then is up to him. If we get a visitors from the FBI tonight; well, I'm sorry," I told Amy.

"Okay, but you may not have to tell him exactly how we know. You could tell him I had another vision on the way here and he can explain it that way—or not," she said like no big deal.

"After the new picture gets out, maybe someone will call with more sightings from today or yesterday, I guess it was. Then he'll forgive you," Amy said looking tired.

"Why don't I do that then we can call it a night, stay in and watch an old movie or something to get our minds off all this," I suggested, since we didn't get much sleep last night.

"Yeah and tomorrow we can go find his truck too, okay that's a plan. I have to go call Joe and let him know where we are. You call Marv and we'll meet in the kitchen to decide dinner." She said as she went into the den, I think it was a den or maybe a library. There are too many rooms in this house.

I found a phone in one of the livingrooms and called Marv. "Hey Marv, it's Matt, yeah Hi." I told him, "We're in Boise."

"Yeah, I figured that's where you guys took off to when you never came back from your so called lunch. I called your hotel and they informed me that you both had checked out at around 11:00, which was right after you left here. A little heads up would have been nice," Marv said, sounding disappointed. "So what'd ya got for me Matt?" he asked, because he knows I only called for help now.

"Well, okay yeah, you got me. First I want to apologize for doing that to ya. I have something for you though, a new description that I can't really tell you how I got it or call anyone here to give it to you, because we're not supposed to be here," I explained.

"So you're not going to tell me how you got it for real, you're going to give me some other reason, I suppose," he said.

"Well, that's another thing, you guys are the only ones beside me who know about and believe in Amy's premonitions," I started to explain.

"You're saying she had another vision of this guy and can provide a vivid description of him. She was always so vague before Matt," he said not really believing my story.

"I don't know how this all works either for sure Marv, this is what she told me. So can you adjust that picture we have to this? No moustache, no long hair—more medium collar-length with grayish temples, a preppy look with a blue plaid short sleeve shirt and a sweater vest. I called as soon as I could, so you could get it out there right away in case someone has seen him yesterday or today," I told him pleadingly.

"No problem Matt, you guys stay out of trouble now you hear me?" Marv said.

I told him, "Loud and clear Marv, you got it, thanks."

That's out of the way, I thought, as I went in search of Amy in the kitchen.

"Well, I talked to Marv, and he's not too happy with us skipping town on him, but he'll get the new picture out there anyway. I don't think he believed me about you having another vision of him either," I told her.

"Do you think he would have liked to hear the real story on how we got it—no, me neither," she pointed out to me. "What d'ya feel like for dinner? Mom called said they're going to be late, a meeting or something she said, so it's only us."

"In that case, why don't I order a hot pizza for delivery? That way you don't have to cook and I don't have to go pick up something either," I asked her.

"That works for me, oh, but no black olives—yuck, and thick crust, oh, and add jalapenos," she rattled off.

"Is that all?" I asked jokingly. "Okay then, I'll call it in. Give me the address for the delivery," I said and she wrote it down for me. Then she brought out a bottle of wine, and asked if I wanted a glass.

"Sure, I'll have some. After pizza, we can get relaxed and head to bed early, I'm beat—how 'bout you?" I asked her.

As she poured us a glass of wine she said, "Yeah, me too. It was an early morning uh, and with very little sleep before that."

I asked her, "So why didn't you sleep so much, well before the three am call that is?" Wondering what could have kept her awake most of the night.

"I, um, was restless I guess. Not very comfortable when it's not my own bed, you know." She said looking down and into her glass instead of at me. I let it go at that for now.

"Well, while we're waiting for the pizza, care to show me my room and the restroom, I need to use that." I suggested in order to change the subject, for which she looked relieved.

"Oh, sure yeah, sorry. Grab your bag, it's at the top of the stairs here on the right. And you have your own restroom." She said shyly remembering the encounter yesterday at her place.

"Great thanks, oh here take this to pay for the pizza in case it comes before I get back downstairs, oka," he told her handing her a twenty.

Shaking her head saying, "No way, you don't have to keep paying for everything you know. You checked me out of my hotel room before I had a chance to pay for my own. This is on me."

"Yeah, and look at all this great hospitality you got for me here tonight. We're even then—so take it," he insisted.

"Okay, okay." She said going back down the stairs as the doorbell rang.

Hearing that, I hurried and put my bag on the end of the bed, used the restroom and went down to the kitchen.

"I started without you," Amy said with a mouthful of pizza.

"Of course you did," sitting down; I asked, "How is it?"

"Great, hot, spicy, wonderful," she said smiling with another bite. I almost said what I was thinking, which was, yummy like you, but I kept my big mouth shut and helped myself to some and stuffed the pizza into it instead.

After we literally stuffed ourselves, we took another glass of wine into the living room/family room to watch some T.V.

Sitting on the sofa, Amy found the remote to look for the classic movie channel. Then she asked,

"So why haven't you gotten married Matt? Wondering why a nice guy like yourself isn't taken yet?"

That was out of left field, but I answered, "The usual answer I guess, would be the job, long hours on the road away from home, called away at all hours of the day or night. The truth would be more like a cliche', I haven't found the right woman for me, as yet," I told her sipping my wine, and thinking then again maybe I have.

"Um, okay. Sounds reasonable, but unlikely. Seems to me you like the bachelor lifestyle," she said.

"No, I don't at all, that's more like my little brothers' area of expertise right now. My life is a little lonely at times, working by myself in my patrol car, living alone gets old too. Even though my family only lives a few miles away from me, it's not the same as your very own family, you know. And until all this gets resolved with Hopes' remains and a killer out there, I couldn't get involved with anyone—it wouldn't be fair," I explained.

"That's the more honest answer right there," she said sounding satisfied.

"Okay then, why haven't you and Joe gotten married since we're being so honest here?" I asked her.

"Yeah, boy that's a good one—-you got me." She said running her fingers through her hair being distracted, but thinking about it.

"You know, I'm not really sure. Oh, he's asked me like a dozen times that's for sure. And I love him, but not enough I guess to spend the rest of my whole life with him. So we live together to wait and see what happens next," she said.

"What you're saying sounds a little carefree. But you don't seem that way to me—not deep down," I told her what I thought.

"Goes to show what you know. My nickname is moonbeam. If

that's not carefree enough for you, I don't know what is," she said laughing at herself.

I chuckled, "Yeah, but what's in a name really, your parents are the ones that named you, and they're the carefree hippy types—not you."

"Maybe, that's a debate for another time. Let's watch this movie, tomorrow will come earlier that we want, I think," she said seeming intent on changing the subject.

After about an hour, they were both asleep on the sofa. WIth the combination of a heavy dinner of pizza and then wine, it didn't take long. When her parents came home and found them asleep, her Mom shrugged her shoulders and touched Amy's arm waking her up saying,

"You'll both be more comfortable in a bed, let's go." Amy replied, "Okay Mom, thanks for waking me, it was a long day," reaching over to wake Matt.

"Matt let's go, come on, wake up sleepy head and get to bed," she said.

He woke slowing from a very nice dream of being asleep next to Amy. "Okay, lead the way," I said, yawning and dragging myself up the stairs barely remembering getting into the big bed by myself.

The next morning I woke to the sound of rain hitting the windows. Took me a minute to realize where I was as I looked around the bedroom, stretched in the huge oversized bed. This is pretty nice, I thought, too bad it was a dream with Amy here next to me sharing this bed it would have been nice for real. Wondering if she dreamt another vision last night or of us together like I did, as I made my way to the shower.

Amy was also waking up about then, but no she didn't dream of them together. She did however, have another vivid premonition dream though. It was very disturbing, visions of her other car; the

VW Beetle that she sold to the older gentleman back home for his granddaughter, who coincidently is in school here at BSU.

She saw someone trying to grab a girl, maybe this same one with her VW, because that was the most prominent part of the dream. Probably because it used to be hers. She had to tell Matt right away, because looking at the clock it was past 9am and classes have already started at BSU. He could be there now waiting to get to this girl. I don't know if she gets away or not, she wondered, because she had woken then before the ending of what happened to her. Better get in the shower fast and grab a cup of coffee to go. Hurry, hurry time is close, she can feel it.

$\mathcal{C}$HAPTER 36

The time is right for the taking as the stranger sat in his rental car looking at the little VW Beetle in the parking lot of BSU dorms. He left his truck in a rented storage garage and went to rent a car yesterday instead, in order to follow this cute little Amy around in her VW. But she only came out once from the dorms to get something out of it and right back inside. Must have been her though, but why would she stay at the dorms when her parents have a house here in town. He was sure of that, because he remembered her telling someone where she moved from and why. Maybe that's why she's not at home now, so as she could live away from them. He didn't get close enough to see her face, but it had to be her. It was the same hair color and length as he's seen her last.

It was late morning by now and he was being very patient. He thought of using an excuse to get inside to her dorm room, but there were too many others around. Maybe she was sick yesterday and didn't go to classes. Not today he felt this was it—had to be—so I can take her with me and get out of this town. Too many people and too many cops everywhere.

It was raining today though and he figured he could get a lot closer to her to be ready to make his move. Sure enough here she comes now with a rain coat on and hood up, but he could tell she came out of the same building heading toward the VW Beetle. This is his chance now without anyone else around, she must have later classes today than usual, he thought.

He pulled his car right next to hers—his driver's side to hers. She didn't see him at first, then she turned around when he got out. He was about to ask directions when he looked at her and thought, no way—how could this be.

He grabbed her anyway, yelling at her, "Where is she? Who are you?"

"What, who are you? What do you want? Let go of me," she was yelling now, "Help, someone please help"

"I need Amy, where is she? This is her car, tell me why you have her car?" he screamed at her, he was losing it now.

"No, let go of me, HELP," she screamed again, and kicked him in the shins and then his nuts with her heavy boot.

Then as he let go of her, he felt someone reach for the back of this shirt but he'd doubled over with pain and managed to twist away and get in his car to sped away.

"Are you okay?" her rescuer asked her to make sure.

"Yeah, I think so. That guy was really crazy, he kept yelling at me about someone named Amy, and then he grabbed me. I thought I was toast. Thanks so much," she said to the big looking jock that saved her.

"Sure thing, but I think you about had him with that last kick to his ball," he told her smiling at her impressively. "We better report this. What if it's that same guy who killed that girl over in Kuna?" he suggested. "May I at least walk you over to the admin office; or follow you in your car, since it's raining," he asked.

"Yeah, thanks a lot. I better tell someone, but I'll be late for my Theology class with Prof. Winters," she said as they left to go around to the main building entrance.

"Better late than not at all. Let's go, I'll testify to that," he told her. "By the way, my name is Max."

CHAPTER 37

O h man, that was dumb, you idiot — the killer thought to himself. You about got caught, but what the hell? He was sure that was Amy. That's her car, I know that for sure. Where could she be, he wondered. She has to be back in Soda Springs still—she must have sold her car to someone else to throw me off. How could she know I'd be coming for her. No way, that's crazy, she doesn't know anything about me—nobody does.

Well let's see about that, I got all I need here, he thought. Keep this car and leave the truck in storage to get it later when he's done with little Miss Smarty-Pants. So you think you can outsmart me and get away with it ya, we'll see where that gets you, he said to himself.

He got away pretty quickly from that parking lot, so nobody can really describe this car very good. It's kinda like everyone else's that's why he choose white. There are a lot of white cars on the road these days.

He made his way to I-84 quickly and headed south, going to be about four more hours to get there well before dark—enough time to scout it out. It wasn't not that big of a town, she had to be somewhere there. She had to be working at that little dioner he remembered. If he didn't see her, then he would listen to people talk—he was good at that. Maybe the mechanic boyfriend or whoever he is tossed her to the curb. That's it, I can track him down and get some answers that way from him, he figured. Just you wait and see, I'm coming for you and this time I won't miss, he said to himself.

Amy came knocking on my door as I got out of the shower, "Good morning," I said when I opened the door with a towel on.

She's all in a hurry though and didn't have a wisecrack about that for me saying, "Come on, we got to get going, hurry up. We'll grab coffee on the way—no wait, no time, I'll explain in the car. Get dressed, hurry."

"What, wait, I'm coming, I got to get my pants on and my wallet and my gun," I told her and went back inside to finish getting ready and grab my stuff.

"Yeah, be sure to bring your gun, you may need it," she hollered after me and ran down the stairs—not waiting for me. What the hell, as I ran down the stairs two at a time.

"Hold on, where we going in such an all fire hurry?" I asked her putting my holster and gun on.

"Can I drive? I know a shortcut and we have to hurry and get to BSU parking lot," she said.

"Okay, but you better talk and drive at the same time." I told her getting in the passenger side before she could drive away.

"So, I had another dream, remember I told you I sold my car, my little VW Beetle. Well, so happens she goes to school here at BSU. In my dream, I saw my old car—that car, with a girl standing beside it and someone in a white car trying to grab her arm. I never met her personally, I sold my car to her grandfather. He bought it for her to go to college here," she said as she drove fast around a corner.

"All right, go on—so what happened to her?" I asked holding onto the armrest and overhead handle.

"Not sure, I woke then, but we have to hurry. Maybe we could catch him still or save her at least," she said turning into the BSU dorms side lot. "I think it was a lot like this one, or maybe over in front of the dorms, I don't know. I'm driving around, be on the lookout for my old car a VW Beetle, it's purple and a white car also."

"There," I said pointing to the purple VW, "It's in front of the main building over there." Then she whipped the car around the other cars in the lot and parked close by the VW.

"Do you see a white car anywhere?" she asked looking all around.

"No, but let's go inside and find whoever it is that has this car here now," I said taking her hand and running up the stairs.

We ran into the main lobby and the lady at the desk asked us who we needed and how she may direct us.

"I'm not sure," I said, "we need to talk to a young girl who drives that purple VW parked outside."

"I saw someone run in about twenty minutes ago—looking to report an assault attempt or something," she said. "I directed her to one of our counselors."

"Okay good, which one, where do we go?" Amy asked in a hurry.

"Down this hallway to the end almost, room 110-B," she said pointing to the right.

We walked really fast down the hallway she told us to go and went into the room of 110-B looking for a young female, and found a receptionist at a desk and a young man, who was quite fit.

"May I help you?" the receptionist asked us.

"Did a young woman come in here to report an assault just now, we need to talk to her. Where is she?" I asked very authoritatively and flashing my badge quickly.

"Someone is in with our counselor now, she should be about done. Should I interrupt?" she asked.

"Yes please ask her to come out here, or if we can come in," I told her.

"And your names, please?" she asked.

"My name is Officer Gannett and this is Amy Winters, she sold her car to the young woman's grandfather for her and we have reason to believe she's in grave danger," I told her to please hurry.

Amy was pacing back and forth and the young man came over to her and he asked, "I couldn't help but overhear, your name is Amy is that right?"

"Yes, why?" Amy asked him.

"The girl who I helped or tried to help I guess, was attacked this morning at about an hour ago now, she's in there talking about it with her counselor. I decided to wait for her to make sure she got to class alright. I'm Max," he told her.

"Yeah, so what happened?" I asked him. Then the young woman came out of the other room.

"Are you Amy?" she asked.

"Yes, your grandfather bought my VW Beetle for you, is that right?" Amy asked her.

"Yes, yes, I'm Amanda, oh and I guess you met Max," she said, coming over to Amy. "I'm so glad to find you or you found me—by the car I guess, you must have found it first, right?" she was obviously still upset and rambling on and on.

"Please tell us what happened," I said to her.

"Okay, yeah. This crazy guy—um, in a white car—tried to grab me. I got away at the last second by kicking him in the nuts—oh sorry," She says looking at me shyly. "Anyway, it's what he said that's so crazy. He says to me 'where's Amy? You're not Amy. Where do I find Amy? What did you with her and where I find her?' He kept asking this over and over while I was screaming, help, help and then Max here shows up too. He was going to grab him and tackle him I think, but then the guy slipped through and took off in a white car."

She says this all really fast and shaking all over.

"Okay, Amanda have a seat, calm down. Can either if you tell us what he looked like?" I asked her calmly.

"You don't know him? He sure knows you. That's why when I turned around and he saw I wasn't you, he went berserk," she further explained.

"I'm not sure what he looks like now, he uses different disguises," Amy told her.

"Well, um let's see, he wasn't very tall, about a little less than Max here I guess. He has brown hair, shaggy, uncut. He had a long jacket on—it's brown like a trench coat style. And a cap, like a sports cap, but no team logo on it, plain black. That's all I can remember," she says.

"And you Max, anything else you remember about him, a beard or mustache or anything like that?" I asked him.

"No, nothing like that, a little reddish complexion though. Not zits like that, but an irritation of a shave like bumps, you know," he said.

"Yeah, I do, great kids thanks a lot. It's a big help," I told them.

"Hey, I heard your name on the phone when she buzzed into the counselor's room, is your last name Winters—like in Professor Winters?" Amanda asked.

"Yeah, they're my parents," Amy said.

"Cool, would you mind coming with me to my class? I'm late for Theology 101, with your Mom, maybe you could help explain what happened. Unless you don't want them to know, of course, then that's cool," Amanda asked.

"Sure, I was headed there next anyway? Oh by the way, you know what type of car he was driving, a make and model, something other than white?" Amy asked her.

Amanda looked at Max for help with that one, shrugging she said, "I'm not sure, you Max?

Max replied, "Um, I was going to say a Honda Accord or something similar to that, but I'm not a hundred percent, sorry."

Then he turned to Amanda saying, "I'd better take off, I got practice in an hour. Don't want to be late for that. I'm glad you're safe. See ya around, take care—bye."

"Bye and thanks Max," Amanda said giving him a big hug. "Okay, let's all go see Prof. Winters" she added walking out to her car. "Oh, by the way, I was so set that I called home and talked to my grandpa, and he might be calling your house looking for you too. When I said Amy was who the guy was looking for, he immediately thought of you too and was real worried."

"Okay, thanks a lot Amanda, let's get over to your class, because we need to get going," Amy told her, looking over her shoulder at Matt.

We all walked into the lecture hall together interrupting class.

I held myself back at the door while Amy and Amanda went to talk to her mom, Professor Winters. I could tell by the way things were being said and the hand gestures, that her Mom was not happy. After the three of them talked, Amy and her Mom came over to talk to me also before we left.

"Matt, this is my mom, Anne Winters. Mom this is Matt," Amy said introducing us.

I shook her hand, "It's a pleasure to meet you, Mrs. Winters. Thanks for letting me stay at your home."

"Yes, yes, you're welcome anytime. Now, what's this about a serial killer looking for my daughter?" she asked me matter of factly.

"I am—we are tracking him down, yes ma'am. I am going to keep your daughter safe, you have my word on that Mrs. Winters," I told her firmly.

"Mom, we really have to get going. I promise I'll be careful. Now, where's Dad at this time, I have to talk to him too?" Amy asked her mom.

"He's stairs in room 212-C now, it's his psychology class. Please dear, let us know when you get home, okay. Love you," she told Amy as they hugged good-bye.

"Love you too Mom, bye." Amy said. "Let's go Matt, I need to ask my Dad something, then back to the house to pack and get home. I need to warn Joe also," she said as we went upstairs to her Dad's room.

"Yes, and I need to call Marv and he can relay to the detectives here, while we get out of town, so we're not held up downtown being interrogated," I told her and she agreed.

After Amy had a talk with her Dad, he looked over at me but didn't come over to talk. I gathered he was busy. We then left the building. I got my keys back and we started back to the house. First though, was coffee and a croissanwich breakfast. Stopping at Mickey D's for two large Mocha Frappe and two sausage-egg breakfast sandwiches, through the drive-thru of course and on our way again.

We packed our bags and Amy had the luxury to pack clean

clothes, while I'll have to either stop to get a few T-shirts, socks, underwear, or my laundry in Soda Springs. I've spent one night in each town now and no time for laundry or to buy new clothes either one. Fortunately, I have one change of everything to put on this morning.

"Damn," Amy said mad at herself, "If only I hadn't taken the time to shower."

"You didn't know anything for sure, no timeline to go by, we were lucky to get the information we did and that Amanda is safe." I told her, "Quit beating yourself."

She went to go call Joe, and I went to call Marv and alert him on the new developments. My call didn't take long, because again Marv didn't ask a lot of questions, knowing what I'd say I suppose. He took down the information and said he'd pass it along. However, Amy was taking a while longer in the library, or den, or wherever she went. Probably trying to pacify Joe and telling him to be on the lookout for a white Honda car.

When Amy came out and we got in the car to leave, she seemed upset, so I let her sit quietly for a while. Until we got going on the highway again, and then I couldn't stand the silence any longer.

"Everything good at home?" I asked her calmly.

"Yeah, sure why wouldn't it be?" she answered a little sarcastically.

"You've been quiet, had to make sure is all," I said. "I was worried about you—you're not yourself."

"Why because some maniac is looking for me to kill me, but that because I'm a 'girl', I can't take care of myself. Are you worried you won't be able to protect me if I go off on some rampage to get this guy by myself? Well, relax I'm not stupid either," She said all that like it was my fault.

"Hey, don't go all ballistic on me. I'm the good guy here remember," I smiled at her to lighten the chilly mood in the car.

She shrugged and was still sullen and mad looking.

"Hey, what did I do?" I asked her.

"Don't worry, Mrs. Winters, I'll keep your daughter safe—yeah right. I'll keep my ownself safe, thank you very much. I've been doing it for quite a few years now fine. I don't need your help or Joe's help either for that matter," she said getting it all out now—that's good.

"Whoa, hey I was only trying to reassure your Mom and that maybe she'd like to know that her daughter wouldn't get murdered if I could anything to prt that. Not every Mother can have that, you know," I told her. Then we both were quiet for a while longer. With the radio turned down, I could hear her sniffling and saw her wipe her eyes a few times.

Then she said sadly, "I'm sorry, you didn't deserve that outburst, that Joe said some things too that got me going and I took it all out on you, that wasn't right. Forgive me? And thanks for making my Mom feel better."

"Sure, no problem. I like being a good sounding board, or wall to beat on, whichever you want," I told her still trying to lighten it a little. "So what else took so long in the library?" I asked.

"Nothing," she said rather quickly and guiltily. "I called Tammy at the diner too and told her to watch out for anyone asking for me, any stranger at all in a white car. That I'm not in town any more— that you thought I moved away, and not to mention Joe to anyone either," she explained.

"Okay yeah, that's a good idea. You think he'd find Joe too and use him to get to you?" I asked.

She shrugged, "I don't know, anything is possible, right?"

"We got about another hour to Twin and I told Marv we'd stop in to get dates. Besides, I need my car back and drop this one off at Enterprise, okay by you?" I told her my plan.

"Sure, he's got at least an hour or more head start on us anyway. He might drive around and wait until dark, so we got time," she said trying to convince herself more than me.

"Okay then, first stop, get my patrol car and then return this one. Oh, and I need a few things at Walmart too if that's okay with you for a quick stop there?" I asked to make sure ahead of time. I didn't want to piss her off again.

She shrugged again and looked out the window. I took that as either and okay or I don't care, and left it at that. Sometimes things are better left unsaid.

We arrived in Twin Falls before noon, picked up my car, and dropped off the rental as planned. Then I drove to the Sheriff's Office to check in with Marv. Even though I was bracing myself for a butt chewin'. I still had to know if he had any further information on our suspect.

The deputy on the desk let us in to talk to Sheriff Cole, and I met him at his office door.

"Hey Marv, before you go all ballistic, we're both fine. Our guy is probably on his way to Soda Springs, any word on that BOLO yet?" I asked.

"Funny, since I don't have much of a description, no plates remember, not sure of the make and model, a white car—no I don't have a have a BOLO out. Now since you asked, the most recent suspects' picture went out yesterday has had several hits in Boise. However, nothing concrete, still waiting on word back from Det. Wilcox on possible positive ID at the car rental for—yes a white Honda Accord. Then we can go from there on that BOLO," Marv answered. "Anything else?"

"How mad are the detectives in Boise for not reporting in or sharing information with them or the FBI?" I asked him calmly.

"Well, since you've relayed everything through me to them, I'm the one in this that is sitting on hot coals. However, at present they have verified your information, so I'm not as set with you as I should be," Marv answered.

"And you little missy, you be careful heading home, you hear me. You everything that Matt here tells you to do—GOT IT?" he told Amy.

"Yes, sir. Thank you for understanding my situation. We had

to get going on his trail, hopefully and not stuck in an office or interrogation room all day," she said.

"Speaking of which, you better get home then. Call when you get there to check in, please," he told us both.

We got back in the patrol car and I said, "Okay, one more quick stop at the Walmart that's on the way to the highway and we're outta here. You need anything?" I asked.

"No, I'm good. I'll wait here for you so no one vandalizes your car." Amy said smiling.

"That's my girl," I told her and hurried inside to get a few things.

Amy thought, yeah if only, as she watched him run inside. I could be your girl if only I didn't already have one pain in the ass waiting for me—who needs another one, she sure didn't. She leaned back her head to clear her mind a little and rest. then a flash came through her brain like a light or something, and with it a blinding headache. She sat quickly then and opened her eyes, looked around when that move happened before, what was that she thought to herself. Maybe if I close my eyes again I can recall what vision that was—if anything at all.

I guess it was a gun flash, but whose gun was it, mine, Matt's, Joe's or that guy we're after. Oh man, I don't know that's it, it's not clear of the type of gun it is. I could narrow it down that way, she figured. No such luck, damn I gotta get home. Hurry up Matt.

CHAPTER 38

Damn it to hell, I got to get rid of this car, the killer thought. He pulled into the Flying J off I-15 outside of Pocatello heading on US 30 and saw this little blue pickup sitting there idling and full of gas too. But no, that is too quick, I need to find something belongs to an employee maybe that won't get reported for hours.

He drove around back, came to know this particular truck stop pretty well also and from there he could watch them come out the back for a smoke or something and determine which cars are good to be able to take or not.

He didn't have to wait long, an old geezer came out the back door it for a smoke and wandered over to an old beater Ford pickup. Man, I don't think I could get ten miles down the road in that old thing, he thought. That was until the old guy started it up, and boy, did it hum rather sweetly. Sure didn't look like much, which might be the thing he needed to blend in. And he could hot wire it, and it runs great.

He waited for the guy to get out and go back to work, which he did after his fifteen minute break was up. Then the stranger parked next to that truck, getting his supplies he might still need, but leaving the keys in the ignition. Not a bad trade off, he figured.

He looked around to make sure the old guy wasn't coming back out and he snuck into the floorboard of the truck and hot wired it to life. He drove out of the parking lot like he owned it and got on US

30 headed south, smiling all the way. Only another hour or so, then he'll be in Soda Springs, then he'll see the real little Miss Amy again.

It was still going to be early when he got there, so he figured he'd drive around and check out the town. Stop in at that diner and listen to their conversations a while, maybe casually ask if Amy still worked there—like she's an old friend.

The lunch rush didn't seemed to be over yet when he got to Soda Springs, as it was very crowded at the diner. Therefore, he went there first, he was hungry anyways. He parked right out front—nothing to hide, and walks in and sits at the counter.

An older lady with dark hair that had gray roots showing walked over and said, "Good afternoon, what can I get ya to drink?" she asked.

He noticed her name tag said Tammy. "Well Tammy, since you don't have beer, I'll take a root beer," he chuckled thinking he was funny.

"Coming right up," Tammy said and giving him a menu and some silverware also.

"What's your special?" he asked rudely before she had a chance to tell him herself.

"We have a good size taco salad with either beef or chicken," she said.

"Naw, I don't want no rabbit food, give me a rueben with fries." He told her throwing the menu down on the counter at her.

"Okay, thanks," she said extra politely. She had always believed to treat those who were rude and mean with sweetness and smile a lot, makes you feel good and them quilty. Probably not in this case though.

When his meal came out and Tammy put it down in front of him to refill his soda, she asked, "Is there anything else for you today?"

He snorted at her and said, "Naw this is good," and then waved her away.

Tammy then went over to the end of the counter to talk to the other waitress on duty who hadn't left yet from the morning shift because it was a busy late lunch.

She said softly, "I wonder, Ellen, if that could be the guy Amy called to warn us about, but I don't see a white car out there. I think I saw him get out of that old Ford pickup there, didn't you?"

Ellen answered, "Yeah I did, but he sure is a stranger around these parts, and mean too, I heard the way he talked to you.

"Yeah, he sure is rude, but I smiled more," Tammy said. "What I say if he starts asking about Amy?" she asked Ellen.

"Let's both act like we don't know anyone by that name and never did," Ellen told her. "I don't care he doesn't look right in the head to me; so no matter what, no Amy has ever worked or lived here."

"Okay, that's the plan. Don't leave until he's gone okay, I don't want to be alone with him in here," Tammy said.

"Can I get some more root beer over here or are ya gonna stand over there and jaw all day," he hollered.

"Sure, coming right —sorry," she said when she brought him another full glass of soda. "Are you done here with your plate? Would you like any dessert?" she asked him.

"Naw, just the check. Hey, you guys know if Amy still works here, or is she coming in later tonight maybe?" he asked them as he was paying his ticket.

Tammy looked over at Ellen and said, "No, we don't know anyone by that name that ever worked here or lives here."

"Now I know you bitches are lying to me, I saw her here in this town last year. You'll be sorry for trying to cover that for her when I find her anyway," he said throwing some cash down on the counter with no tip obviously.

He slammed out the door muttering, "Damn sons-a-bitches, I'll find her on my own." I need to find the local tavern and ask around there. Everyone in town knows who the best mechanic is, and who better to ask than a bartender.

He no sooner left, than Tammy was on the phone to the Sheriff to tell him what he said, and what he was driving. She was sure this was the guy Amy had told her about, and that Sheriff Bud should know he's in town. Then she'd call and tell Joe too, so that he would be warned someone in town was looking for Amy.

After she called the Sheriff to tell him what happened and he told her he'd drive around and look for that truck, to keep an eye out for the guy. Tammy then called Amy's house number she still had to see if Joe was there, because he didn't answer his phone at the shop. If nothing else she'd leave a message on her machine

Meanwhile, before the Sheriff went out looking for the guy Tammy had described, he'd call to Twin Falls and talk to Sheriff Marvin Cole,

"This is Sheriff Cole, how can I help you?" he answered his phone.

"Yeah, this is Sheriff Bud Dobbs in Soda Springs, Idaho," he said. "I'm calling to give you a heads up on some information for Amy Winters and Matt Gannett."

"Yeah, Bud what do you have for me? What's going on there?" Marv asked. "Amy and Matt are on there way there now, should only be another hour is all."

"Well, we had a guy show up at the diner here looking for Amy, a real piece of work, he was rude and mean looking. He was driving an old Ford pickup though not a white car that I was told to look out for from Matt, who called this morning," Sheriff Dobbs told him.

"Great that helps a lot Bud. Thanks I'll relay this by radio to my detectives that are behind Amy and Matt helping to keep a look out. I'll have them catch to them now and they can all be ready when they get there. Please not approach this man on your own. He is extremely dangerous and about to be cornered, which makes him more volatile," Marv said.

"Okay you got it, and we'll provide location of suspects vehicle and keep you informed," Bud told him.

He then went out to get in his car to take a drive around town after he stopped at the diner to make sure Tammy was alright and talk to her at length about the guy in question. He figured he needed to know all there was to know about him as he could.

CHAPTER 39

The killer sat in the bar down the street nursing a draft beer and watching the local news on the TV behind the bar. He asked the bartender, "Where's your restroom, I gotta piss; and can't you find anything else on that thing—like baseball maybe?" He didn't want his face flashed all over the news in case that kid in Boise can describe him.

"Sure thing," Mike, the bartender said.

He figured he had maybe a few more hours to nose around town and find that mechanic maybe follow him home and wait with him for Amy to show up. She's gotta come home sometime right. When he got back to the bar stool and sat down he asked Mike,

"Hey, so where can a guy find a good mechanic in this town, my old pickup was starting to act up before I got here. That's why I stopped in to ask around."

Mike says unknowingly, "We got a guy has his own shop down the road by the cemetery, his name's Skylar, something I think. I haven't needed one for a while, but I hear a few of my regulars like him and used him for their farm equipment also."

"Um, yeah good to know, does he have a tow truck also in case I need one?" he asked.

"I'm not sure if he does or not, it's his own business he started it a few months back," Mike said.

Well that might not be the same guy then, he thought. "Has

he lived here a while though before he started the business, maybe worked for someone else first?" the guy asked.

Mike said, "Oh yeah, he's been around here for like 3-4 years I think. He worked for the Highway Department as a mechanic, but then he got laid off is why he started his own shop."

That must be him, he figured he'd better get going over that way. Take the back roads and check it out. Probably park a block or two away and walk around the place before dark, so he'll be ready to get to know the layout by then. That's a plan, he thought and paid with Mike saying, "Thanks a lot, man.'

He went out to get in the truck and pulled further down the alley to take a back street around the block where he thought he saw a sign for the cemetery across the main road. When he looked down the main street to cross, he saw the Sheriff's car at the diner.

Yeah, those two bitches called on him, but he fooled them all and already found out where the mechanic's shop was and now he'll know where they live too when he follows him home. He backed down away from main street and went further down by the overpass to take that road around. He'll figure it out before dark, no problem.

The Sheriff meanwhile, was talking to Tammy to get a better description of the guy and the vehicle. He assured them that guy wasn't going to get to come back there and any harm to them. This all stops here tonight. We'll get him one way or another. He left and thought for a minute about what the guy had told them about them not having any real beer, so he went down the street to talk to Mike. "Hey Mike, how's it going in here today, any problems?" He asked when he went inside to check it out. He didn't see any old Ford parked outside or in the ally either, but you never knew.

"It's all good Bud, only been me and Bob over there all afternoon until a little while ago, some guy left." Mike told him.

"A guy you never saw before? Was he driving an old Ford pickup truck and have on a black sports cap, with a long brown jacket like a rain coat, shaggy brown hair?" Bud asked.

"Yeah, that's the guy all right, only he didn't have on a jacket. He asked for a mechanic saying his truck was acting upon him on his way here today, so I told him where to find Sylar's shop. Why Bud, is there a problem?" Mike asked.

"Oh man, you know the number over at Skylar's, give him a call will you? Yeah, there's a big problem. Let Skylar know the guy's description real good, okay. Thanks Mike, I'm gonna head over that way now too and try to spot him or his truck at least." Bud said.

"You got it Bud, I hope I didn't cause more problems for ya'll," he said concerned.

"No, but one more thing if you see that Wyoming HP car come down the main street, stop him and tell him where I am, okay? He should be here pretty soon. Thanks again." Bud told him as he went out the door.

He stopped real quick to tell Tammy what Mike told him and that he was headed over that way along this side road. If Amy and Matt happen to stop there first, let them know what's going on.

Then Bud went along the side alleyway to the cemetery road, slowly so as to try and spot the pickup truck that might be parked or driving around still.

CHAPTER 40

M att and Amy stopped at the Flying J on US 30 not only to refuel and use the restroom, but also because they spotted a local Sheriff deputy car there and two Idaho state cars. Being as he was curious and a fellow officer of the law, Matt asked one of the state guys what was going on when he pulled next to them in his WHP car.

"Hey, I'm in pursuit of a suspect headed this way, any chance this has to with a white Honda Accord?" I asked the officer showing him my badge.

"Are you Matt Gannett?" he asked me, checking my ID.

"Yes, I am, now answer my question please, I'm in a hurry," I told him politely as I could.

"I got a radio call from two detectives from Twin Falls with a message for you. And yes, this here stolen vehicle has to with a white Honda Accord that was left in the parking lot around back and a 1982 Ford pickup truck, tan with white, Idaho plates 3-JG07K, was stolen and left here approximately two hours ago," the officer informed me.

"Good to know, thanks. What's the other message from the detectives?" I asked.

"I think I can answer that for you Matt," Detective Young said as he came to his car. "Sheriff Cole got a call about fifteen minutes ago from a Sheriff Bud Dobbs in Soda Springs to tell you the suspect has showed up at the diner asking about Amy, he's checking into where he's at now."

"You've been following us, uh? When were you going to let me know?" I asked as I filled my car to go again, this time with lights on all the way.

"I just found out myself and yes, we were going to stop you anyway before getting to the town itself to let you know this is our case, you are our backup," Det. Young told him. "Marv also says to tell you, he informed Sheriff Dobbs to stay clear of suspect and to only follow and observe from a distance. That we were on the way."

"That's fine and dandy and what if he takes someone hostage or kills someone before we get there—then what does he say to do?" I asked him more pissed off now. "You know what, nevermind. Let's go, time is running out. I don't know about you guys, but I'm running all out with lights on, he's already hunting now. So let's get going." I told him and got in my car and left down US 30 headed south going about 95mph with my lights on, as promised.

As we headed down the highway like a bat out of hell, I filled Amy in on what was going on and that Sheriff Bud was hopefully observing the suspect until we could get there.

"I don't care what these detectives have to say about all this, but this guy is ours for the taking. After we get there and take him down, then they can have him in their jail to interrogate all they want. First, he's talking to me and telling me where Hope's buried—if I have to beat it out of him," I said in a rather rampage fashion.

"Let's hope he doesn't find out where Joe is before then and hold him hostage for me or something worse," Amy said looking out the window sadly. She was hugging her purse in her lap more tightly now.

We were making good time of course, as we could go almost 95-100mph on the straight away, but passing other motorists or on a curve I had to slow down a little. Still should be there in about twenty more minutes. Since he's had a head start, but has taken all this time to steal a vehicle, stop at the diner and eat and talk, and whatever else he's doing, gives us time to catch up to him.

I was thinking all this while trying to keep the car under control as this high rate of speed. Keep concentrating, we're almost there.

CHAPTER 47

The killer found a place to park between two old buildings that looked vacant. He got out to walk and put his jacket back on to blend into the darkness of the shadows in the night. He crept around the block to check out all the other buildings close by. It was getting close to dusk now and he had to find the place soon to make his move on the mechanic. He thought about following him home, but he didn't want to walk into any surprises waiting for him there. No, it's best to have the upper hand and in control. This way he can hide out in the shop and wait for this Sylar dude to show if he's not there. He'll be the one with the surprise, he thought to himself with a wicked grin. A few more places to check out, then he would have his prize worth waiting for.

He was sure this side of the road was the one going to the cemetery, but he had to check them all in this area to be sure, since he didn't have the exact address.

Around another corner he quickly ducked back, as he saw the Sheriff's car go by that way. He backtracked around the other way so he'd be behind him and still looking inside the windows as he went along carefully staying in the shadows. The next one over was indeed an auto shop and so he went in the side door, because it was unlocked.

Sheriff Bud drove up and down the side streets leading to the cemetery and Joe's shop, looking in all the alleyways. Nothing yet, no sign of suspect or his truck. He decided then after around a few of blocks to drive down the alley closest to him and that's when he spotted the truck parked between the old abandoned buildings.

He radioed to his deputy who was at the edge of town watching for Matt to let him know his position and that he had the suspects truck in sight, and he was going to verify if it was occupied or not.

Bud got out then with his gun drawn in case, and he crept to the rear of the truck and then along the other side to look in the passenger side window first.

He didn't want any surprises in his face on the drivers' side. He looked in the cab and it was empty. Then Bud returned to his car, radioed his deputy again to tell him,

"The suspects vehicle is indeed unoccupied—repeat no one is inside and that he'd wait there for Matt and other two detectives. Got that Billy, give them my exact position in the alley off 2nd Ave East and Donner Street, suspect must be on foot."

"Got it Sheriff. I think I see someone coming now with flashing lights traveling very fast. Hold on, I'll get Matt for you now, yes it's him," Billy reported back.

Up ahead I saw a Sheriff county car pulled at the edge of the road and someone was waving me down. I quickly braked to come to a fast stop to pull next to the man on the road. He took quite a chance I'd see him in time to stop—must be important.

I got out to ask him, "What's going on? I'm Matt Gannett."

"Yeah, I figured. I got Sheriff Bud on the radio for you, he's found the suspects truck, and no ones inside. He wants to talk to you," the kid told me.

I got on the radio through his open window, "Hey Bud, it's me Matt," I said.

"Thank goodness, Matt. I'm looking at the suspects truck right now, and have verified no one is inside. He must be on foot close by here. Deputy will give you directions to get here, take the back way along Donner street, okay. Amy will know also," Bud said.

"Okay, stay there, we're on the way. Two other detectives are right behind me," I told him.

"Got it," Bud replied.

Then Det. Young and Det. Olson's car pulled up beside me as I was about to get directions from the deputy and Jim rolled down his window said,

"We'll take it from here Matt," hearing the exact location the deputy gave, being as he was driving an unmarked car and I wasn't, of course.

"That's fine with me," I said.

Getting in the car I asked Amy if there was a shorter or better way to get to Joe's shop other than what Bud said to do. "As I see it, Bud gave directions to where he is now with the abandoned truck, I need to go directly to the shop," I told her.

"Yeah, that's where he'll be too, trying to get Joe to tell him where I am, I'm sure of it. So take this next left here coming up slowly until those guys go farther to turn on Donner. We want this one here and it's up this street to the curve in the road we can park by those trees and walk over to the shop from there, it's across the street," Amy explained.

"They're going to be a block over half way down that way east of us and it sounded like in the alleyway. So if he got out to walk this way, he might be close by or be inside by now," she said.

"We'll park here like you said behind these trees and get out to walk around to the back or the side so he can't see us coming through the front windows." I told her as I parked my car, got my Glock 9mm out, checked the load and got out quietly.

"Stay right behind me. No sudden moves or risks on your own. Got it," I told Amy looking right at her, "Promise me."

"Okay, I promise," she answered, hanging onto that purse again. I wonder what she's got in there.

Then we swiftly moved across the street diagonally so as to be close by the side door.

When the Joe had first entered the shop earlier, he had noticed that the lights on his answering machine were on and he was about to turn it on to check them and heard a voice,

"I wouldn't that if I were you," the killer told Joe while pointing his gun at him.

Joe didn't flinch or move a muscle. "What you want? I don't keep any cash here."

The guy laughed, "I don't care about your money, but I think you know what I want, don't you Skylar or is it Joe?"

Joe tensed at the use of his other name that only a few people here know him by. He said, "No, I don't know, why don't you tell me?"

"Get over here away from that desk and those tools. Stand here in the middle, now get on your knees," he told Joe.

He had him tape his own feet and hands together, with the gun pressed to his head, he did as he was told. "Now what, you going to execute me, if you don't get what you want?" Joe asked him.

"Well first, you're going to tell me what I want to know—then I'll execute you, how's that sound?" he said laughing at Joe. "You know I want that sweet little Miss Amy and you're going to tell me where she is or call her to get over here, one way or the other. What's it going to be?"

"I can't tell you something that I don't know, and I can't call her because she's not home either," Joe said.

The guy cocked the hammer back on the his revolver,

"What if I were to tell you we're going to play a little game of Russian Roulette and I'm going to pull this trigger every time I don't get the right answer. How about that? You want to play—hey Joe?" he taunted him.

"Of course you don't, but I do," he told Joe as he pulled the trigger and cocked it again. "That's one wrong answer. Do you want to go for another?"

Joe was shaking now, "Listen, I only know that she went to Boise to visit her parents, but I don't know when she'll be back for sure. Could be today, could be tomorrow."

"Oh, so you like this game ya?" He said pulling the trigger back again with the barrel still pointed at Joe's head. "That's two wrong answers. Do I really need to keep asking and you keep lying to me? Soon it will be over for you, and I'll wait for her here anyway. Is that what you want?"

Joe was visibly shaking and crying now. Crying for Amy as he knew he couldn't stop this crazy maniac from killing him or her either. Crying for himself as he'll never see her again.

CHAPTER 42

Suddenly, the door burst open and Matt said, "Freeze, don't move one single muscle, put that gun down slowly and move away." "Well look who's here Joe, we have more players to our game. Hello Miss Amy, we've been waiting for you—so good of you to come. Who's your other friend? Oh it doesn't matter—more the merrier," he said with a mirthful look.

We were only a few feet away from him, but I couldn't take the chance that the next time he pulled that trigger there would be a bullet in the chamber or not.

"I'm not going to repeat myself again, you're going to put that gun down and move away slowly, or I will put a bullet in your head," I told him ever to firmly and calmly.

"You do that, then you'll never know where I buried your sweet little sister, Hope, now do you? After all that is what you came for, right? Ha, now you have to think about that don't you, well let me help you. I've got some grounds rules of my own," he said with a smirk. "I came for her, so we'll trade—right now, you can have him alive, and I get her."

"You won't get one foot out that door. The place is surrounded with the Sheriff and his deputies and detectives from all over Idaho. You've left quite the trail behind you," I emphasized to him.

He laughs, like he doesn't care at all about any of that, "Who says I'm leaving. I'll do what I want to her right here with you both watching. Like I said, you won't kill me—not yet anyway."

HOPE

I knew the Sheriff and his deputies and the two detectives were right outside listening to the stand-off, as I had seen them running down the alley when I busted through the door earlier. Now I may have blown it for all of us. He knows who I am and why I need him alive, probably seen me talking to people back in Wyoming when I questioned Amy the first time. So if I blow him away before he kills Joe or Amy, then he's right I'll never know about Hope. Or if he's wounded and I get the gun away to keep him alive, is it really worth it in the end, the cost of two more lives.

While I was contemplating my next move, Amy stepped out from behind me with a gun in her hand too, a Walther PK7, small but deadly. It was raised and pointed directly at the guy and she moved ever so slowly, closer saying, "You want me do you, well here I am—now what are you going to do. You see I don't care if you live or die. I prefer you to die. Rid you of this earth forever."

"Ha, little Miss Amy, you haven't the guts to what I do, it's not in you to kill anyone," he taunted her.

But she could tell he war nervous regardless of his bravado. And a nervous trigger finger means a possible dead Joe, she couldn't let that happen. When she stepped forward again to fire her gun between his eyes, it happened all at once.

Joe figured he only had one chance to save himself and Amy too, because it sounded like she was about to do something stupid. He really wasn't too concerned if there was another bullet in the chamber to kill him. What were the odds if had already fired twice with nothing and had four more to go in the chamber, so more than half—it's a one in four chance. He had all this going through his head when the guy and Matt were talking.

Finally he couldn't take it when Amy stepped closer, he threw all his weight back into him to throw the guy off balance. However, that caused him to slip his finger on the trigger and his gun went off, at that very instant Amy's gun also fired into the neck of the killer.

I saw all this happen like it was in slow motion, though I knew it all took less than five seconds to be over. During which time, he also yelled for Amy to stop, "Don't shoot. I got him Amy, I can tackle him."

That was too late, of course. When Joe fell also, Amy rushed to his side to check his wounds. To her surprise and horror she saw that he was bleeding out from the side of his head profusely. She grabbed some shop towels from the shelve and pressed hard to hold against his head to help stop the bleeding.

About this time, the door burst open and Sheriff Bud Dobbs and Det.'s Young and Olsen came rushing in to check on all the shooting they had heard.

"I'll have to take your gun Matt and Amy's too," Sheriff Dobbs said.

He turned to his deputy who was already on the radio to get the ambulance and EMT's here as quickly as possible.

Detective Young came over to where the suspect was, he listened and watched for any response from the guy. The only thing he noticed was a nasty grin, as he had whispered something to me, then nothing. Detective Olson went to assist Amy with Joe, noticing he was in bad shape. Amy was telling him to hang on that help was on the way.

"Please Joe stay with me—you hear me. Don't try to talk, help is on the way. You're going to be okay," she told him.

I walked over and knelt down also as I noticed his eyes were tracking me like he wanted to say something to me, so I bent over with my ear close to his mouth as he whispered, "Please Matt, take good care of Amy. She's stubborn, like I tried to tell you, but she's very lovable," he told me and then he was gone.

I looked at Amy and into her eyes, shook my head no. She cried, "No, it can't be, he's not gone. Please, Joe wake up, I'm sorry. Please, no," with tears rolling down her face. She looked at me with grief and a wishful look as if to say—something—what can I do to make this not happen.

We heard the sirens coming closer now, but couldn't help either one. Both were gone. The suspect finally met his doom, but not without a last taunt to me. He had managed to whisper to me, 'Now, you'll never get your answers.' Then he died with a very satisfied grin on his face.

I am not discouraged however, I will go through every pocket, every piece of paper he has on him to gather more information on where his truck is. That was his lair—that is where he took the girls and I know in my gut, he kept trophies and pictures. He was a photographer after all, where were all the pictures—exactly, had to be somewhere.

When the EMT's arrived and examined both bodies to determine nothing further could be done, the detectives went to the car and retrieved their cameras to take pictures of the whole scene before they could be moved.

Then the Sheriff could take our statements, but before he could get started, I asked if we could go with him to the station to conduct the questioning there, as Amy was too upset and needed to get out of there.

"Sure Matt, Amy let's go to my office and get this report down officially, you ready?" Bud asked her.

I helped Amy over to my car where she sat down with her head in her hands—crying.

"I'll meet you there, Bud. It's okay that I drive, or does she have to ride with you?" I asked.

"No, that's okay Matt," he said, "I'll see you there in a few."

I got in my car and started to drive back to Main Street and Amy raised her head and asked me, "Why Matt? Why did that have to happen that way? I had him, I stepped in to shoot him right between the eyes. Why did Joe have to make a move at the very moment?"

"I don't know Amy, we'll never really know the answers to all the why's. I'm sure in my heart that he was trying to save you though—not caring about himself to do what he thought was right. That's pretty selfless in my book," I told her sadly.

When we got to the Sheriff's Office, I opened Amy's door and escorted her inside. We were met by two very upset looking guys in suits—most likely FBI. One was middle aged, probably, with a short butch hair cut—marine style and very muscular. Why they always look like ex-marines, I wondered.

The other was much younger, must be the rookie who was learning the ropes of field work from the veteran. He looked like a young Tom Cruise, too cute for this type of work. Even Amy looked twice at him in her griefed state of mind. She looked at me and shrugged as if to say—I can look still, I'm not blind.

They introduced themselves as Special Agent in Charge, Dan Booker; and Special Agent, Bruce Carter. I thought 'in training', but didn't say anything. They were going to conduct their interviews of the events leading up to the shooting and including our arrival in Twin Falls and Boise, Idaho.

Bud let us have the only private room he had, his office. As he left, he patted my back saying, "Good Luck."

"First off, I want to say I heard what happened today and that I understand certain events could not have been avoided. However, as you know, we would have preferred the suspect lived to be able to interrogate him," SAC Booker said.

To that Amy said, "And I would have preferred my boyfriend had lived also, we don't always get what we want we."

"My condolences, yes I know. Now, if we can get to the matter of how this all came about. How did the two to you know to come to Boise and why did you follow the suspect here?" he asked looking at me.

"We went to Boise because we were following the evidence, the only tie between the Twin Falls victim and the girl in Boise, the red ribbon tied in a perfect bow around their necks. After we learned other information from Amanda Green at BSU, the person who has possession of Amy's previous vehicle, we were then able to determine the suspect was in search of Amy and concluded he would come here to find her," I explained.

"How did you know he would come here? Had you seen him here before?" he asked Amy.

"Not exactly," she said, "but I knew he had seen me here. I had felt him watching me again."

"Okay, and how did you find this Amanda person in Boise, I understand from her statement you were there only a matter of minutes after the suspect had tried to grab her and assaulted her?" he asked her skeptically.

"That's a little more difficult to explain, but suffice it to say I had a premonition dream, and woke with a urgent feeling to get to BSU. Fortunately, my parent's home is close by and I knew a shortcut," Amy said looking rather proud of herself.

The younger guy, Bruce was taking notes like crazy trying to keep up. When SAC Booker looked at him to make sure he got that, he nodded. Then SAC Booker continued. "When you arrived back here in Soda Springs, were you not told by the two detectives from Twin Falls that they were in charge and that this was their case and the two of you were only supposed to follow their lead—not the other way around. Why did you disobey that order Officer Gannett?" he asked me.

"I was acting on instinct that the suspect was already inside the shop and that I needed to get there asap, not wait for orders to be a back-up. With all due respect, Special Agent Booker, Amy Winters here is my witness and I did all the legwork on this case for three years, gathered the information on the suspects vehicle, physical descriptions, his probable whereabouts. I wasn't about to let someone who didn't know the hostage take over the situation, sir," I told him confidently.

"How did you know that there was a hostage in that building before you got there—another dream Miss Winters?" he asked.

I looked at Amy, who spoke on my behalf. "I just knew, sir, you could call it a vision if you will; and I told Matt to hurry, we had to save Joe."

He seemed to take that reasonably well as well as all her other answers.

"Okay, well let's get to what happened inside the shop then. After your arrival, what happened next?" SAC Booker asked.

"We both approached the building cautiously and listened outside the side door. Then I kicked it in at the time the suspect was about to pull the trigger again with his revolver, as I heard him say he was playing Russian Roulette and I knew Joe's life was in imminent danger," I answered firmly.

"I got that much, but what I don't get is why you let an armed civilian accompany you inside that situation?" he asked looking at Amy.

Before I could answer to take full responsibility of that, she spoke to defend herself.

"Yes, I was armed, however, Matt didn't have any idea of that prior to entering. I borrowed that from my father before leaving Boise, and I fully intended to use it for protection in case something happened to Matt or myself, or as it turned out to try and save Joe. I also insisted on going in when Matt told me to stay in the car, so that I could talk to the suspect. I was the one he wanted after all, and he needed to see me there to think he could still have me," Amy said defiantly.

"Will you walk us through what happened with the firearms being discharged?" he asked me, seeming to be done with Amy for now.

"What I observed when I entered the side door, was the suspect had his gun against the back of Joe's head. Joe was on his knees. I had my Glock 9mm aimed right at the suspect the entire time and advised him to drop his weapon and slowly step away. He then proceeded to taunt and threatened us. After several warnings to no avail, I was about to attempt to wound him when Joe, the other victim, reacted by pushing all his weight back against the suspect. I am sure Joe thought this would cause him to be off balance so that I could subdue him. This must have caused him to slip his finger on the trigger of his revolver, which then went off into Joe's head. At this very same instant, Amy had also fired her weapon which was aimed between the eyes of the suspect. However, since he moved, the entry wound was in his neck also causing his death. My firearm did not discharge because all this happened in less than ten seconds and after that I was trying to ascertain the damage," I explained all in detail as I knew the facts to be.

"Well, on further examination of the suspects weapon, it held another three bullets, so it would not have mattered what you did, he was going to kill his hostage one way or the other." He told us the Sheriff had informed him of this when they first arrived.

"I asked Sheriff Dobbs if he knew of any pertinent information that I needed to know before this interview, and he told me that fact along with his knowledge of the facts you stated by overhearing the conversation outside the door," he also informed me.

"So we're good, we can go now?" I asked him. "I need to examine the inside of that truck he stole and also the inside of the car he rented in Boise to determine the whereabouts of his truck and camper," I said.

He replied, "The detective from Twin Falls may have further questions for you, but as far as we're concerned you can go. We are satisfied that this will be a closed case very soon."

"Not soon enough, until I examine his photos he took of all his victims that must be in that camper," I told him.

"Yes we are trying to determine that also, we've canvassed almost all storage facilities close to where the car was rented in the Boise area. There are quite a few with the right size that would hold a truck and camper. Trying to match the description of the suspects vehicle so we can get a warrant at this time," Booker explained.

"He used several disguises," Amy said, "maybe I can help."

SAC Booker looked at her with curiosity and concern.

"Thank you for your offer Miss Winters, but we have it covered from here," he said, and proceeded to walk out of the door and leave it like that.

Sheriff Bud Dobbs came back in then and asked if we needed anything from him, I said, "No, thanks for all your help Bud, we'll be going now, if you're okay with that?"

"Sure thing Matt, take care of yourself, and Miss Amy stop down at the diner if you can. Tammy is real worried about you all, okay?" he said.

"Thanks Bud, I will," she said sadly realizing she'd have to tell her friends about Joe and then call her parents also.

We got outside as Det.'s Young and Olson pulled up.

"We gave out statements to the Fed's who left. They said we could go," I told them.

Detective Young held out his hand and said, "Thanks for your help on this case. Things sure developed faster after you and Miss Winters showed up. However, next time, if there is one, when I say it's my case; it. is. my. case—no exceptions."

Detective Olson hugged Amy saying, "I'm really sorry about Joe, I wish it could have been a better ending for you." Then she shook my hand too, "Good-bye Matt."

Amy said, "Thanks, me too," as she looked at me over her shoulder.

It was getting pretty late now as we got in the car, I asked, "You want to go to the diner, or give her a call from the house?"

"That's a good idea, I'll give her a call from the house and then stop in tomorrow. I have to call my Mom and Dad still too. You staying at the B&B when you drop me off?" she asked.

"Yeah, it's too late to drive back to Boise now. You coming back with me to stay at your parents place a while—I mean to figure things out?" I asked.

"Yeah, maybe I should. I don't know. I have a lot of thinking to tonight and I need to be alone," she said shyly.

"I understand," I told her. "Here you go, delivered safely at home." Regretting immediately what I had said, because that's exactly the promise I made Joe—to bring her home safely. That was before the new promise to take take of her. They both had a lot of to think about tonight.

I think she realized this too, but only said, "Thank you Matt," as she got out with her overnight bag from the backseat.

CHAPTER 43

Amy opened the door to the little cottage, walked in and stood there— looking at everything and listening to the quiet.

Now what do I do, she thought. Go back to Boise and then what there—feel sorry for myself, hide away at my parents house, or go back to school. That would make them real happy to go to BSU with them. What would make me happy though, she didn't have a clue at this point.

Oh, hell, better make those phone calls. It isn't going to get any better by putting it off. She looked at her phone with the answering machine blinking lights. She didn't want to hear any of it right now or maybe ever. She dialed the diner and talked to Tammy first and told her what happened and that she's at home now, but she'll stop by tomorrow. Next came the call she dreaded to her mom,

"Hi, Mom, it's me Amy," she said, "yeah, I'm okay I guess, maybe not, Joe's dead Mom. He was killed in the shootout by that maniac."

"Are you going to be okay there tonight, dear? Where's Matt, is he with you? Are you coming home soon? You know we love you, we miss you." Her Mom kept asking, and she thought all the questions were coming now. Amy knew she meant well—still.

"Yes, Mom I'll be fine. No, Matt's not here tonight, he got a room at the B&B. I needed to be alone for awhile to think things through. Yes, I'll be there tomorrow sometime to stay for a little while anyways—not sure how long," she told her.

"Okay, that's good, dear. We'll see you then. Are you coming with Matt again or alone? We'll have the rooms ready, don't worry about anything else—get some rest. We love you," her Mom said.

"Love you guys too. Good-night." Amy hung up and went to run a hot bath that she needed to relax in and unwind to think about all that's happened.

Amy fell asleep after a long hot bath thinking of what her life may be like now without Joe, and wishing she could really fall in love truly and forever. She dreamt peaceful dreams for once—no premonitions. Not about her future.

The next morning when she awoke, she knew her next step in her life was going to be an adventure if she didn't dream it, she felt it to be true.

I checked into the B&B again down the street from the diner, Joann's Place. I was able to catch a little leftovers from dinner only because of Joann's generosity when she asked if I'd eaten yet, and I had said, "No."

I asked her if it was okay to bring in a six pack to my room. When she said it was alright with her, I went to get some in order to have one or two to help me relax and get some sleep. I figured I was going to have a difficult time with that. Mostly to get the crime scene out of my head, with Joe dying and his dying request to take care of Amy. That was weird, maybe be sensed that there was something happening between us. A chemistry is there, but who knows if anything will come of it.

How am I supposed to make Amy happy now and take care of her, when she's so sad over losing Joe to that killer, she may feel guilty over it for a long time. The thing was, he thought for sure he was having feelings for her before all this happened, and the flirting was both ways he knew that. He'll have to hang onto the thought that he and Amy can make a go of it. No matter the pain she has now. It will be going away little by little.

I've got to finish this first with Hope and find her and bring her home in order to bring her and my family some peace at last. Then after that, I can fully concentrate on building a relationship with Amy, which I was very much looking forward to.

I fell asleep thinking of ways I was going to make her smile again and be happy with me. Mostly though to bring back that sparkle in her eye when she laughs.

CHAPTER 44

I got up the early the next morning to get going, called Amy to make sure she was awake and would be ready in half an hour. Didn't grab one to Joann's famous breakfast spreads, only coffee in a to go cup and headed out.

Had to get to Boise today and still go over every inch of the vehicles that were towed there yesterday. Apparently, the FBI Offices' there and labs were conducting the forensic evidence reviews to get the answers we all wanted. I got an early call from SAC Booker, he was kind enough to inform me they found the guys pickup and camper in a storage facility there and were going over all of it today if I wanted to be included on that list to observe, I'd better get going.

I picked up Amy, she still needed to stop at the diner and talk to Tammy in person. I was in a hurry, but relented that a quick toast and coffee would get me down the road in better shape.

"How'd you sleep?" I asked her, when she got in the car with her overnight bag.

"Okay, I guess, considering," she said, looking over at me with a hollow sadness in her eyes.

If it's the last thing I do, I will bring back the brightness and sparkle to those eyes, and watch them change color with passion and heat also.

"Yeah, I know, me too. We'll grab a quick bite, refill our coffee and head out then. Get to Boise, because I need to be in on all that evidence discovery. Even without someone to prosecute, I still need to get answers before closing this case. Thankfully, SAC Booker agrees," I explained, pulling up to the diner and we got out.

"Yeah, I can see that," she said. Tammy saw us come in and rushed over to hug Amy fiercely.

"So glad you're okay, and I'm so very sorry about Joe," Tammy said.

Amy sighed, "Thanks Tammy, yeah I'll be alright. It gets better, right?" she said. "We're in a hurry, we're going to grab some toast or muffins and refill our coffees to go."

"Sure, let me get that coffee, how about a nice warm cinnamon roll—fresh out of the oven?" Tammy said.

Amy looked at me, I said, "Sounds good to me." Sitting down and drinking my coffee and proceeded to devour the cinnamon roll, which was very good. Gooey, warm, and baked with chopped walnuts, my favorite.

Amy decided to try a bite of mine was all, "I'm not very hungry, I wanted a little taste. It is yummy," she told Tammy as she refilled our to go cups.

A short time later, we were on the road to Boise again. This stretch of US 30 isn't very fast going, at least not like last time on the way down going over 100 mph. So I drove on with a quiet passenger. That's alright, I thought. I didn't much feel like talking either.

A few of hours later, I stopped to use the restroom and get water—too much coffee I was feeling dehydrated. Then the next stop was Boise, another two hours away.

"You need anything, I'm getting water?" I asked Amy after we both used the restroom and I topped off my gas tank, so we didn't have to stop again.

"Yeah, that's good for me too," she replied.

This time I tried to engage Amy into a conversation, at least to hear her voice if nothing else. Something other than the case or whatever she was thinking about staring out the window.

"You've probably driven this highway a lot over the last, what six or s years since you've moved to Wyoming from Boise, right?" I mentioned casually.

"Yep, I sure have. At first, my parents were okay with me moving away to another state. Then after the first year, my Mom would call me all the time with so many questions that I decided I'd better come back at least a few times a year, so she wouldn't worry so much. She could see me then it was good—Mom's will always worry no matter how old we are, I guess," she smiled.

"Yeah, that's so true. For me, it's been my Dad who wants me to call and check in when I'm back home. I guess because I'm the only one not living on the ranch close to them, they need to hear my voice. I have a place in town, so that I can be closer to the highways to get to work," I told her.

"Do you like this work? This driving the highways all the time— to keep us safe?" she asked.

"Yeah, I do. It's rewarding to me—I know it sounds like a cliche', but I like being able to be outdoors all the time. This is my office," I grinned, waving my arm at the inside of my car.

"Yes, I can see the benefits, all this and the great outdoors, carry a gun, what more could a Wyomingite want?" she laughed.

"There we go, that's what I missed," smiling back at her, "that beautiful, real smile, and laugh."

She looked down at her lap then, "I'm trying Matt, but it's hard, you know."

"Yeah, love. I know exactly how it is—that's why I'm here now," I told her then reached over to squeeze her hand. "I'm here for you."

"Oh God, I'm sorry Matt, all this reminds you of Hope too, doesn't it?" Does the pain get any less with time, as they say?" she asked.

"Yes, with time the pain does ease little each year, at least we have our memories right—remember the good times, that's what I do," I said.

The rest of the trip was small talk, then as I pulled into town, I asked if she knew where the FBI Offices were. She looks at me like, should I—you think, "Not sure, downtown, I assume," she replied.

"Well, you want to go to your parents house first and settle in there? We could call SAC Booker to get directions and let him know I'm in town, and make sure you're allowed to view the evidence as well," I suggested.

"Okay by me, sounds like a plan. You remember to take Broadway Exit?" she said as it was coming up.

After dropping off our bags, I got directions and permission to go directly to the 4th floor of the FBI building downtown. Since I called first and talked to SAC Booker, he said, "Sure, bring Miss Winters with you, I assumed you would. We have a lot to show you."

When we got in the elevator, Amy took my hand, "I'm nervous and a little scared of what we'll find out. I'm not sure I want to see any photos," she said.

"I know what you mean, I want it all to be over," I told her squeezing her hand and winked at her, "I'm here."

Getting off the elevator, we walked through the double glass doors and asked the person at the desk for SAC Booker, who directed to a conference room down another long hallway. After she made a call first to check to make sure we were expected, of course.

When we entered the room, not only was SAC Booker there to greet us, also Det. Young, Det. Olson, and Sheriff Marv Cole, along with the rookie Agent Bruce Carter were in the room.

"We all know each other, let me show you both what we have so far." Booker said as he took us over to three tables full of cameras, notebooks, photos, maps, spool of red ribbon, and various other items they found in the suspects' camper.

"Our evidence forensic room wasn't large enough to spread all this out and examine it closely," he explained.

"Do you have a name yet on who he was?" I asked. Not sure why I needed to know that first, but I did.

"Yes, we do. It was Ted Johnson, ordinary name, but no ordinary man," he replied.

"So a photographer right? Is there stuff here other than pictures of young girls that we can track to where he has been by scenery photos?" I wondered, as I looked at all of it.

"Don't need to, Matt. This pile here of notebooks are meticulous records of names, dates, places, all of it. We've been cross-referencing to lists of missing persons on the dates listed here and that takes time," he showed me.

"Have you looked through it all yet today as we were driving here?" I asked looking over at Amy, who looked a little pale.

"Are you okay, what's wrong?" I asked her.

She shook her head and looked at me, "There's a lot of pain here, I don't think I can do this," she answered, turning away. "Excuse me, where might I find a restroom?" she asked Agent Bruce Carter.

He pointed down another hallway, "that way ma'am, second door on the left," he told her.

I wanted to follow her, but she waved me off, "I'll be fine," she said.

I turned back to the table then wondering why she looked physically ill.

"Does one of these notebooks have the name Hope in it, of about three years ago in Wyoming?" I asked looking at Booker or Marv for any help at all.

It was Marv who answered me, "Yes Matt, there is an entry by that name, but we also need you to identify some photos if you can."

"May I read the notes first, please?" I asked.

"Of course Matt, this is the one you'll want. You can use this other room next door here for privacy," SAC Booker said.

"Thank you, when Amy comes back, have her come in too, okay." I said, going in the other room and closing the door.

The detectives were both at a table viewing more photos and reading journals still after hours of being there. There must have been dozens of victims to identify and find their bodies, he thought. I'm sorry for them too, but right now all I need is this one. I took a deep breath to open the notebook and begin searching the pages for the name and location of Hope's remains. Then the door opened and Amy came in, still pale but not as bad as a few minutes ago.

I got up to hug her, "Are you alright?" I asked.

"No, but it will pass, I'm here for you now too," she said looking into my eyes.

We both sat down and I leafed through the pages slowly. I didn't want to read every entry—only needed one name. Finally, after figuring out the system he used, dates first, then names and locations, I went through all of 1993, month by month.

And there it was, July '93, MS WY, Hope with her horse; and my heart fell to the floor as tears rolled down my face. Unexpectedly, I read the account of my 14 year old sister's final day. Hope suffered beyond my worst nightmare and I sobbed unabashedly for her now with Amy holding me tight as she could and crying also.

After a while, I straightened and told Amy, "Thanks for being here. I wasn't sure I could this alone."

She said softly, "I'm here for you too, big guy."

I took another deep breath, looked through the notebook pages again to find the exact spot of where he buried Hope. It was very precise descriptions, I'm sure I can find it. That's my only desire right now, get back to Wyoming with my team to dig part of a prairie, which is not too far from where they were—close to the Idaho border. I had a milemarker to go by with a dirt road over a small hill. That's where he would find Hope and finally take her home to have a proper burial.

I looked at Amy then, she smiled, "It's going to be alright, let's go."

We went back to the other room where they all pretended not to notice my pain—our pain. Amy wasn't looking much better than I.

"I'm going to need copies of a few pages in here. Is that okay with you, or I need some official request from Wyoming State's Attorney?" I asked Booker.

"There are several adjoining states involved here, for now I can give you what you need. The remaining of Wyoming victims will be verified and sent on to appropriate agencies to notify the families. I'm sorry for your losses, both of you," he said.

I shook my head, "Thanks, what else do you need from me, look at the photos you said? You need me to eliminate Hope from that pile of other young girls, do you?"

"Yes, I do, if you're up to it. We can all break for lunch now if you want and come back to this," Booker said with sympathy.

I looked at Amy for support again, and she smiled. I said, "Let's get it over with."

Then I looked through the stack of photos in no particular order. I insisted Amy not look at any, because she'd already been through a lot of trauma and wasn't looking too good still with whatever it was that happened earlier.

I tried not to really look at any of them, only searched for a familiar face. I didn't really want to find that last look with the red ribbon around her neck. When I did though, I stopped and Amy was shaking beside me, but I stood there and stared at it. Not wanting it to be true.

I felt a hand on my shoulder and Marv said, "I'll take them now, you guys get going and I'll call you later. You'll be at your parent's place, right Miss Winters?" he asked her.

She nodded, a yes. I looked at Marv with a shocked expression I'm sure, when he said, "I know Matt, let's go. I'll drive you."

I felt like I was walking through a fog, we probably looked like a couple of zombies leaving the building, at this moment I didn't care. Amy held onto me tightly, as I did her in the backseat of Marv's car.

Somehow, she was able to give him the address and he dropped us off, "Give me your keys Matt, I'll have someone drive your car over for you later, okay," he said in a reasonable tone.

I forgot I had drove there, "Thanks Marv, "I said numbly.

We got inside and I looked around and at Amy then I said, "It doesn't feel real, does it?"

She answered, "I know, it doesn't. Let's go lay down for a nap.

Neither of us got much sleep last night and I'm exhausted, how about you?"

That sounded wonderful right about now. As we got to the top of the stairs and I let go of her hand to head to the room on the left that I had last time, she took my hand back and pulled me into her room.

"We need to hold onto each other, come on. I won't seduce you, I promise. Let's snuggle and sleep a little while," she said smiling.

"Yes, ma'am," I said. Suddenly too tired to argue or think straight. Besides, how could I resist the offer.

We had taken our shoes off at the front door already, so Amy laid down on one side of her bed a patted beside her. I climbed in and we spooned all snuggled together, then I whispered,

"This isn't exactly what I had in mind when I wanted to get you in bed with me for the first time, but for now it will do fine," as I kissed her temple and she smiled at me.

I did sleep until Amy woke me with a blood curdling scream.

"What the hell, Amy wake up, " I yelled at her shaking her awake.

She was visibly shaking and crying. "I'm sorry, it was so real. My vision, or dream. I was with all these young girls together. They still had on the red ribbons around their necks and they circled me like I was the one who got away, but they wanted to bring me somewhere. One took my hand to go with them, but I don't want to go with them. I don't want to go, Matt, I don't want to," she cried into my chest.

"Sshh, it's alright, you're not going anywhere, you're right here with me, I got you." I told her, trying to reassure her and rubbed her back holding her closer.

She settled down after a bit saying, "But what's it mean, where do they want to take me and why? This has never happened before, I thought maybe it was because I was looking over some of the photos. It's over, isn't it?"

"I don't know love, I can't answer that for you. Have you ever tried hypnosis to get all the dreams to come to you? Maybe there's something we missed," I asked her.

"No, I haven't, sometimes it's too much. I feel too much and it's painful," she said.

"Is that what happened earlier today at the FBI office, you felt them all by being there with all that evidence and the photos, didn't you?" I asked her in awe of her strength.

"Yeah, I guess so. The room was so full of pain that I felt physically ill to my stomach, I thought I was either going to pass out or throw up. That's why I had to get out of there and splash a little cold water on my face," she explained.

I hugged her tighter to me and slowly caressed her back. We stayed that way a while longer, not moving or talking. I had to start thinking of something else instead of her lying here next to me so close, or else I was going to do something we both might regret. I wanted us to be whole and happy again to start new and fresh for ourselves.

"I'm going to have to call home and tell them what was found soon, are you going to be okay?" I asked her but not wanting to move yet either.

"Yeah, lots better, thank you. This feels so good though. Can I have another few minutes please, like this?" she asked.

"Sure thing," I said.

We hugged a little longer and pretty soon we separated a little and she looked at me, I put my hand on her cheek and side of her neck and caressed with my thumb, She closed her eyes for a second and sighed as I kissed her forehead lightly then the tip of her nose.

I said softly, "There will plenty of time for this. I'm not going anywhere away from you for very long."

She smiled and said, "I know."

We heard the front door open and close then and voices downstairs.

"Time to get up," I said, patting her rear to get her moving.

"Yeah, yeah," she smiled.

When we went downstairs and saw her Mom and Dad, her Mom said, "Oh, I didn't know you were home yet honey, we didn't see Matt's car in the driveway," as she came up to hug Amy.

"Uhm, yeah, someone is bringing it back over here for me. I should go call Marv for that I guess," I said, looking at Amy, "and my family too."

"Yeah, sure go ahead in the library, we'll be in the kitchen. I'll make some tea," she said.

As I walked into the next room, I heard her Mom say, "We're so sorry dear, how are you holding up? Can I get you anything else? Here let me make the tea, you have a seat," fussing over her.

I decided to call Marv first to let him know I wasn't such a basket case any longer and that it was safe to bring my car back over here. Then I took a deep breath and called home, Zach answered.

"Hey there bro, I've got some news. Yeah, I'm back in Boise, but I'll be home soon, Can I talk to Dad, is he there?" I asked him.

"Sure thing, but is it more bad news, or relatively better news. We saw the television news reports, there were findings in an ongoing investigation yesterday. Mom was so relieved when you called last night. I don't think she'd survive another death in the family, especially yours, her 'golden boy'. You need to come home," he said as a warning before talking to Dad.

"Thanks for the heads up Zach, and I am headed home after one more stop," I told him, then he put Dad on the phone.

"Hey Dad, I have some news to tell you, we found evidence of where Hope is. Dad, I'm going to get her tomorrow and bring her home to bury properly, okay. Can you get Zach and Drew to help you make the arrangements? Tell Mom I love her too, I'll see you late tomorrow or next day. Call you when I leave Kemmerer. Okay-bye," I told him as calmly and plain as I could.

I'll see them tomorrow or the next day most likely, with Hope finally. I closed my eyes and put my head in my hands and said a small prayer of thanks.

Then I went to the kitchen and found everyone around the table talking about funeral arrangements for Joe. That had to be done also. Amy looked over at me—help rescue me in her eyes. I went over and stood beside her with my hand on her shoulder saying,

"Does this have to be finalized right now. When we go back that way tomorrow, and you can talk to Sheriff Bud Dobbs to release Joe to a funeral home then. I'll go with you to take him to whoever that would be, sound good?" I said to Amy.

"Sounds real good, but you have your own plans to make with finding Hope to take home," she said.

"There will time for that also. I'll take care of that and you too," I assured her, "Don't you worry."

The doorbell rang then and I went out to the entryway as Prof. Winters opened the door and a Boise State Police Officer handed me my keys to my patrol car.

"Thank you sir, I appreciate it," I said.

He said, "No problem, drive safe," adding, "Oh, here are your documents from SAC Booker," handing me a manila envelope.

I went back to the kitchen asked Amy, "Do you feel to heading back tonight? We could get to Pocatello no problem, since it's early still and we did have a two hour nap."

Her Mom looked horrified at the suggestion. "I thought you'd stay the night, get plenty of rest. You both need it. Amy dear, you still have those dreams? You don't look too well. Are you sure you're okay?"

"Yes, Mom. I'm fine really, don't worry. And Matt, yes I can be ready to go, but if it's all the same to you I'd like to sleep in my own bed tonight. Are you up for going all the way to Soda Springs today?" she asked.

"Great, yes I can that, no worries. Let's grab a sandwich to take with us, more water and I'll get gas at the station on the corner. We'll be good to go," I said excitedly. The sooner the better.

Prof. Winter relented to her stubborn daughter and went about making sandwiches for our late lunch to take with us. Amy went to take a quick shower and change into shorts and a tank top, as it was so much warmer here. I went to make another phone call to Sheriff Dobbs to ask if Joe's body could be released to a funeral home so Amy could go directly there to make arrangements.

"I'll see to it myself Matt, thanks for calling," he said. Then I called Marv to let him know our plans and where I'd be if they needed anything else. Within that half hour we were out the door, headed back to Soda Springs. I could probably drive it with my eyes half closed by now, but of course, Amy wouldn't let me try that.

On the way, I told Amy that I had already talked to Bud and he was going to see to it that Joe's body was released to the funeral home.

"Thanks Matt, you have too much to to be worrying about me, but I appreciate it," she said smiling.

"I like to worry about you and taking care of you," I told her, as I reached for her hand to hold.

She looked down shyly reaching for the lunch box her Mom packed for us.

"Are you hungry now, let's see we got a couple of ham sandwiches each, baby carrots, grapes and almonds. She packed enough for a week—mother's always overdoing it. Here's a water, you want anything else?" she asked, munching on an almond herself.

"Thanks, sure the sandwich looks good and some grapes, you can have the almonds," I told her.

"I love these things, better covered in chocolate though. I guess I'll have a sandwich now too," she said.

"Yeah, eat something—you didn't have a breakfast. You need to keep up your strength you know, or you'll be sick. I should have told your Mom on you, she would have made sure you ate before we left the house." I teasingly smiled at her.

"Blah, blah, blah—you sound like her. Thanks for getting me out of there by the way. She's a real worry wart," she said.

"She loves you is all, people show their love in different ways you know," I said with a wink.

She rolled her eyes at me and then we ate our sandwiches in silence. I stopped in Pocatello to use the restroom and top off the tank.

CHAPTER 45

A n hour later we were pulling into town, and I asked Amy if she knew where the funeral home was. She directed me to a side street by a church.

"This is the only one in town that I know of, so it must be here," she said.

We went in to inquire about viewing times for Sklyar Joe Turner. Amy identified herself and wanted to see Joe, the funeral director apologized saying,

"There will be no viewing, we have already taken care of Mr. Tucker as per his wishes," he handed her an urn and an envelope. "I'm sorry for your loss Miss Winters."

Amy held the urn, looked at me saying, "What do I do now?" with a confused look. "I didn't know he wanted this, he never said anything to me about it."

I replied, "Let's sit over here and you can read the note in the envelope first."

We sat down, she put the urn on the side table and opened the envelope to pull out a signed piece of paper and read:

'Amy my love, if you are reading this, then I have left this world before you. I'm sorry I should have mentioned my wishes to you. I had always thought there would be enough time for that later, I guess. Take the urn and let it blow in the Wyoming windswept prairie somewhere out where we used to go rock hunting. Oh, I also have a life insurance policy for you, so check your phone messages at the house too. I know you won't want to listen to any of them right now, that's okay then—soon you'll have to. Please be happy, and go out there to conquer your fears and the world. I love you, Joe.'

Tears rolled down her cheeks as she read and then she put it back in the envelope, held it tightly to her chest, closed her eyes and must have whispered a prayer. I let her have that private moment to herself.

Then she said, "We can go to the house now, I suppose." She got up to thank the funeral director, asking him about paying for this and he told her, "It's all taken care of miss."

When we got to her little house, she put the urn on the table and turned around looking at the blinking light on the answering machine like it was going to reach out and bite her.

"Can I help? What can I do?" I asked her getting more worried, because now she looked pale again.

She sat down in the chair next to the phone, pushed play on the machine. She listened to a few, skipped a few more, then stopped and repeated one to hear again.

"Apparently, Joe had a life insurance policy also that I didn't know about either. And this message here is someone trying to contact me regarding that," she explained. "Well, I'm not ready to handle that right now. We can head to Wyoming now when you're ready. That is also where I need to go to spread Joe's ashes in the wind over the open prairie."

I sat down on the sofa beside her chair and took her hand in mine saying, "We don't have to any of that right now, let's talk about all this and make plans for first thing tomorrow morning. It's been a long enough day as it is. That sound good to you?"

She nodded, "Yeah, it does."

"Come here, sit by me let me hold you for a little while," I told her, as I took her in my arms. "It's going to be okay, we'll figure it out, you can come home with me if you want to."

She sighed saying, "Can't we stay here like this and let the world keep on going outside without us?"

"Sure thing, for tonight anyway," I said holding her closer to me.

236

We stayed like that for a while longer, then I looked at my watch. "Before it gets too much later, I need to call and make excavation arrangements for a forensic team to meet me in the morning at the site described by those notes."

"Yeah, that's a good idea, I'll go see what there is for dinner," she said, as we separated, and she moved to the other room.

When I finished with my personal phone calls, I went into the kitchen to offer Amy my assistance.

"All I have to make is spaghetti and meatballs, if that's alright with you. Help yourself to a beer in the fridge, I'm sure Joe won't mind," then she stopped herself, shrugged her shoulders saying, "He still wouldn't mind."

I gave her a big hug, "Whatever you got to fix is fine with me, but don't go to a lot of trouble on my account. And thanks, I will have a beer." I raised it toward the urn on the table, "Thanks, Joe," I said, and that made Amy smile.

"Will you pour me a glass of wine please, I'll have some with dinner," she said. "It's almost ready, since I used the frozen meatballs and jar sauce."

After dinner and helping with the dishes, we sat down to discuss the plan for the next day.

"It's only an hour to the mile marker and I need to meet the team from Evanston at eight, so we don't need to leave real early," I told her while we sipped our after dinner glass of wine.

"I thought the spot was closer to Kemmerer," she said.

"It is, only 30 miles outside of town, but they don't have the forensic people I need, so I had to call Evanston. Almost had to call Rock Springs too, but Sheriff Colter in Evanston said I could use the local morgue van to take the remains to Rock Springs at least and make arrangements to get her home from there," I explained.

"Tomorrow is going to be another long day," she sighed. "Are you staying here tonight? You can you know—in fact I wish you would."

"I was going to ask you if I could, if you wanted me to be close by in case you had another dream," I said taking her hand in mine.

She smiled, "That's one reason sure, but I need you to hold me till we fall asleep again, like earlier during our nap."

"Be glad to ma'am, I'm at your service," I said watching her smile again.

"Be careful that could be dangerous, offering your services like that," she said with that twinkle in her eyes.

I'm the one who better be careful for what I wish for, she thought. She wasn't about to let tonight to get out of hand, neither one of us are ready for any of that yet.

"Well, I don't offer them lightly," I said thinking that I'm in big trouble. Sleeping in the same bed all night isn't quite the same as a little nap with clothes on. But I'll have to keep some clothes on at least and stop with the wine. I'm relaxed enough now, don't need to be any more horny or I will definitely lose control tonight. Nope, I'm going to be a complete gentleman. If she initiates something, then who am I to refuse.

"So any plans yet to what you're going to when this is all over. You spread Joe's ashes and I take Hope home to have a memorial service, then what should we do?" I asked in a teasing way.

"You probably have to get back to work—real work. Enough time off for you. I need to get back here and sell the shop I guess and then figure out where to go with my life," she said seriously.

"I could come back in a week or so with my horse trailer and pack you up," I offered.

"Your horse trailer, why? Pack me to go where?" she asked confused again.

"We use them to move stuff. I'll wash it out—don't worry about that. To move you to my place—like I told you. You could stay with me for as long as you need, or at the ranch. They have plenty of room there, I'm sure my Mom would be more than glad to have a woman around the house," I told her.

"Wow, I don't know. I sure don't want to be an inconvenience to anyone," she said.

"You could hardly be that if you tried, especially to me," I said, "I really want you close by so we can both determine where this is going with us. You know you feel it too—this electricity when I touch you here and here, and this." As I kissed her softly on the lips, ever so soft lips. And caressed her cheeks and neck, nuzzling her neckline, kissing her earlobe. She shuddered slightly and sighed.

"Matt, we can't get too carried away. I admit there is something here between us. Maybe it's lust or need, but I feel for you enough not to rush into anything. Okay, please," she said smiling at me.

"Damn it to hell," I cursed myself. "I'm sorry, I did get carried away. I really want you to move home to be with me though, will you at least think about it?" I asked, as we walked into the bedroom together.

"I'll think about it, I promise, now let's get some sleep," she said, firmly emphasizing the word sleep.

She opened the window a little to get the night breezes. Then we got on top of the covers with some light clothes on and turned over to get snuggled and I stayed that way holding her to sleep all night. Fortunately, we were both exhausted and Amy didn't wake up with any more dreams.

CHAPTER 46

A my did think about what Matt had offered, in fact she could think of nothing else half the night before finally drifting off to sleep. The next day as they drove to Wyoming, she had concluded that yes, she would move there; but not to live at his place. She didn't want to be a live-in again, she wanted the real thing—the whole nine yards. The ring, the proposal, the happily ever after.

She was ready and she knew she was falling in love with Matt, she didn't think he was with her yet. And she decided that she would live at his parents ranch, until he had it figured out and would come to her.

When she goes home after this and settles all of Joe's affairs, she thought sadly, I'll pack my stuff and call him with my decision but not until then. It wouldn't be fair to Joe's memory or to Matt and his family.

She was quiet all the way there, and of course, so was I. I was thinking about what I would find in the ground up ahead, she must have been thinking about spreading Joe's ashes somewhere.

When I came over a hill close to the mile marker, I saw two cars and a van already there waiting for me. I parked my car off the side of the road and got out, introduced myself and told the Sheriff the spot we need to look for.

"It's been three years, and it's not going to be easy to find, you know," he said.

"I've read the documents that have a pretty clear description of this mile marker. We take this dirt road right here over that little hill, then it's 40 yards from the top that levels off we should see a small outcropping of rocks and it's right there," I told him while walking up the road.

The others followed with the equipment. One carried a small portable machine that detects underground shapes, GPR or ground penetrating radar. The other one carried a camera and a shovel.

Amy and I, with the Sheriff were at the top of this dirt road and stopped and looked down a ways to a leveled off area. Amy pointed to the small set of rocks on the right.

"That's has to be it, we can start there,"

I pointed to the rocks to the analyst with the portable GPR to where to start. He set the machine, turned it on to push it around the rocks in a back and forth pattern. "It works a little like a metal detector, only you have to go real slow because it's sending signals to this little screen here— like sonar—only not in the water," he explained as I watched.

After about five or six times along the side of the rocks he stopped, "Got something here, pretty sure. Yeah, dig here Don," he told the other guy with the shovel.

Fortunately, it's not winter time or fall, and the ground isn't frozen. After about a foot down, it was looser soil, and we started to see something. Then, Don put the shovel down and we all got down on our hands and knees to uncover the bones, so as not to damage anything.

Amy stood to the side and watched the unbelievable gravesite start to open and reveal the bones of Hope Gannett. By this time I was frantic to get all the way to the bottom and get her out. When I saw her skull with some hair still attached, her beautiful light brown hair all stringy, dry and matted, and then the red ribbon still tied in a bow laying there on her neck. I wanted to kill that guy, Ted Johnson all over again.

Amy came over to hold my hand, "Let's get out of the way while they take the pictures and get her out. I saw the Sheriff with a tarp, they're going to lay her out on that to carry her down that way," she said softly.

I said, "Okay, yeah, okay. Best to let them do it, I suppose."

The other guy had already went down to get the van when he put his equipment away. Soon they had her inside and was ready to go at least to Rock Springs. From there, my Captain had arranged to get her the rest of the way home today.

I hugged Amy as we left the gravesite and I told her, "Thanks for being here with me."

"I wouldn't have been anywhere else," she said. "Do you think it's appropriate to remove one loved one from the earth here, to let another loved one go to be returned to the earth?" she asked.

I realized she meant Joe, so I said, "Well it's Wyoming and it's windy, so maybe they will find each other."

She went over to the car and got the urn, while I thanked Sheriff Colter and told him we would meet him in Rock Springs, because we had one more thing to first.

We both walked back up the hill and Amy stood over by the rocks where we had removed Hope, and whispered something as she opened the urn to release Joe's ashes. I held her hand and we said good-bye.

To myself, I thanked Joe for Amy and for him seeing that I cared for her.

Amy said her good-byes to herself also, for her being sorry of not being able to commit and that she promised to be happy and that she had found her true love.

We walked back to the car, I took a deep breath hanging my head and was relieved that part was over. It took over two hours to get all what we needed to get done.

On the way to Rock Springs it was quiet again, each of us in our own thoughts. As I passed Little America, I again thought of

Amy and her being at this place showing off her horse, she was happy then.

"Thanks for being a friend to Hope, she looked to you. I know from what my Mom had told me," I said squeezing her hand.

"We crossed paths briefly, but yes, I will remember her as she was that last day—so happy with her horse and new boots," Amy said smiling.

We got to Rock Springs after the van pulled into the Sweetwater County Coroner's building to transfer the remains of my sister to another van to take her home. I thanked the forensic guys and Sheriff Colter who was in charge of the chain the evidence. Passed along information to send along with that damn red ribbon. No way was I going to let anyone see that. The photos send to SAC Booker in Boise in case he needed them documented with the other victims.

Then I met with another HP Trooper from Rawlins, who caught a ride here in order to drive the van for me.

"I sure owe Col. J.P. Ogden for all this, I'm going to have to work the next 30 years as a volunteer plus overtime," I said to him jokingly.

He laughed, "Do you want to leave right away then or what?"

"Yeah, I got a call to make first then I'll be ready, thanks Travis," I told him.

He replied, "No problem, I'll wait in the van for ya'll."

"I'm going to use the restroom while you call home, okay?" Amy said.

"Okay, I'll only be a few minutes anyway," I said to her going inside to use the phone.

Dad answered on the first ring, "Hi Dad, I'll be home later today, about to leave Rock Springs. Another few of hours okay, tell Mom I have Hope." I said, "I love you too, Dad."

By then Amy was outside, we got in the car and the van followed us out to the highway. We were taking I-80 to Laramie it was faster, since that was where the funeral home was.

Even though we didn't have much of a breakfast, neither of us were hungry or could think of eating anything after witnessing what we did this morning.

Since it was another two hours to where we were going, the officer driving the van wanted to stop and eat lunch when we gassed up. We all decided to take a little longer break than fast food and have something to eat at the Flying J truck stop off I-80 in Rawlins as we needed to head east next anyway.

I planned on stopping at the local funeral home when we got into town, so my parents could set the memorial service for Hope by tomorrow or the next day. Being as the closest place was in Laramie we went there first, which was only another 45 minutes from home anyway.

When I talked to Dad, he said they were expecting us. Fortunately, it wasn't too late, ended up being late afternoon, but someone was there waiting for us as promised.

I thanked Trooper Travis and told him, "You're more than welcome to come back with us to the ranch at Dad's place for dinner."

He said, "Thanks, but I better get on home to the wife." They lived in Rawlins anyway, so he didn't have far to go back that way.

Then we went to the ranch and my family was waiting for us also to sit down together for a late meal. My Mom hugged me so hard I thought she was going to crush herself. Also hugging Amy she said, "I'm so sorry about Joe, there has been too much sorrow and death, it's time we all started living again."

It was like a light had came back on inside of her again, I was so thankful for that at least. Maybe it was the peacefulness in her face that knowing she was finally able to put her baby to rest. I only wished I could have brought her home years ago.

Drew and Zach also welcomed Amy into the family, as we sat at the dinner table to pray. We had small talk for a while to get caught up. I felt like I'd been gone for months, although it was only a few of weeks this time. I couldn't remember exactly when I'd left, too much had happened.

HOPE

"Mom, I told Amy she could stay here before going home to settle some things, and that if she wanted to move here, you'd like that too." I said out loud embarrassing Amy, but not intending to— it came out as wishful thinking.

My Mom said, "Sure thing, honey. You're always welcome here Amy." Looking at me though trying to get a point across. "No hurry, you take all the time you need dear."

"Thank you, Donna. I have some thinking to and things to take care of. Selling an auto shop for one," Amy said.

"Okay then, us girls are going to take our glass of wine into the living room and chat, you guys clear off the table and load the dishwasher. And Matt, go get Amy's things out of the car to put in the guest room," Mom told us in no uncertain terms.

We all looked at her, then at once all got to work with a grin— good to have Mom back with us. Even Dad helped out saying, "What, I'm a guy too, I'd better get to work helping out."

Amy sat down on the sofa with Donna who said, "Now, I know what Matt's thinking. I saw him look at you and if you don't want this move to happen, you tell him right off dear. It's less painful that way for both of you."

Amy smiled and said, "Yes, ma'am, but I think I want to move here— not moving *in* with Matt right away like he suggested. I don't want to be his live-in girlfriend. You understand that don't you? But, yes, I have a lot to consider also. Where will I work, where I store all my belongings? Things like that. He sprung this on me last night out of the blue. Telling me he's going to get his horse trailer to move me right on in with him or here at the ranch."

"Do you have feelings for Matt also? This has been rather fast for you and you just lost someone you loved," Donna asked concerned.

"Yes, I did, I know. But Joe and I were not really committed. He wanted to, but I felt like I was never ready. Well, because he wasn't my true lifelong love. I did love him, not enough I guess. And yes, I have these feelings for Matt—that kind when you know, you know is what my Mom always used to tell me whenever I'd ask her about true love." Amy told her.

This made Donna smile brighter, "Amy, my dear, you can stay here as long as you like or until that knucklehead of a son of mine asks you to marry him. Am I correct on that assumption?" she asked.

"You are absolutely correct and thank you Donna, I appreciate this girl talk," Amy said with a conspiratory wink.

"You bet honey, now you go and take a nice, long, hot bath and take your glass of wine with you," Donna said hugging her good night. "Matt will you show Amy to her room. She's had a long day and needs to get some sleep, as you. Are you staying here tonight or going home?"

"I, uhm, I'm going home I guess. I have to report in to be available to work early tomorrow and make arrangements to get Amy back to Soda Springs," Matt told her.

"Okay, good night then, get some sleep too, love you son," Donna said hugging him.

I turned to Amy, who was waiting for me, "Alright, right this way. Second door on the left here, the bathroom is the next door down," I told her, "you'll like it here, it's very comfortable."

"Thanks Matt, I'm sure I will. Talk to you tomorrow then, when you get off for the service." She said hugging me, "Good-night."

I hugged her back real close and kissed her lightly on the lips. "Sweet dreams—of me," and winked at her.

Then, I left wondering what her and my Mom had talked about. About me, of course, but what was said—I didn't have a clue. They did seem to be pretty chummy.

After a long, hot bath in the deep tub, finishing her wine, feeling fully relaxed; she crawled into the big ol' comfy bed with a ton of quilts on it that she had to remove and open the window for some air. Amy did have sweet dreams of the two of them, she dreamt of sweet pea flowers, fields of wild daisies and of being in love, happy, dancing, playing outside with children she assumed were going to be her own. This happiness was going to last a lifetime with Matt she was sure.

CHAPTER 47

The next day was the memorial service for Hope. Donna had wanted it in the afternoon, so they could all go after chores were done, and all of her friends could attend. It was announced on the radio the day before, and it seem as the whole town were in attendance.

It was a hard day for all of us, but it was also a beautiful service. Then Hope was laid to rest in a proper casket in a proper place to rest in peace. I held onto Amy's hand the entire time. Probably squeezing it until it hurt, but she didn't let go.

Zach and Drew, Mom and Dad sat together. I looked over at them, and they also held hands for comfort. Then for some reason, I noticed Zach looking at this strikingly gorgeous woman across the row from us. Of course, what's not to like—to look at, but he had this big puppy-dog like look to him. When he caught me looking at him staring at this woman, he looked away real fast and put his head down as if to pray. Uh, I thought, I'm gonna have to ask him about that later.

Afterwards, we didn't want a lot of people at the house, so we said our thank-yous and goodbyes' and the cemetery. And then it was over. like Mom said last night—back to the business of living.

On the way to the ranch, I told Amy that I had arranged for her to ride with another Trooper headed that way the day after tomorrow, "If that's okay with you?" I asked her.

"Sure, that's perfect in fact, gives me more time with your family to get to know them better. Who was that very beautiful woman your brother was staring at?" She asked.

"You saw that too uh? I don't know, but I intend to ask him real soon," I told her.

We all had dinner together again that night and I went back to my place alone again. I feel like I might have to start back at square one with Amy, she doesn't hardly give me the time of day with my Mom around to talk to. That's what I wanted right, for them to be fast friends, and for Amy to help my Mom come out of her shell. But that wasn't necessary after that first night back, I saw that right away. Still they're as thick as thieves. I'm going to have to ask one of them what's going on—or ask my Dad—yeah right, like he'd know.

The next day when I came by, I tried to corner Zach about the mystery woman, but he was always busy, so I asked Drew right out, if he knew who she was.

"What you want to know for, I thought you have yours sights set on Miss Amy?" he asked.

"Yeah, I do, I am Drew, but I want to know why Zach looks at her the way he was and who she is to him," I said getting more irritated with little brothers.

"She's nothing to him now, I don't think she knows he exists. She's our neighbors daughter came home from a fancy college in Paris or somewhere. She's been riding that big black stallion around, the one Zach had his eye to buy from her father this whole last year, so he can start his horse breeding business," Drew explained.

"Oh, I see. That's a clearer picture of things now," I said.

"So when are you going to get Amy back here for good and make an honest woman out her?" he asked.

"Soon, brother, real soon," I told him with a big smile.

"Whoa, you better before I jump on the idea," he said teasingly.

"You do, and I'll knock you clear to Texas and back boy," I said while putting him in a choke hold.

I came over early the next morning with my friend, Trooper Rylee Duncan to introduce him to Amy as her escort home. Since

I had taken two weeks off, I didn't have any more allowed personal time to it myself. Rylee happened to be headed to Kemmerer, so I called Sheriff Bud to meet them at the Idaho border to get her the rest of the way home. Since it was at least a four hour drive, they had to get an early start.

"I'll call you everyday, okay with you?" I asked.

"Sure, you better, and I'll call you when I get home," she said.

"You better, I'm going to miss you—not going to see you every day is going to drive me crazy." I said holding on tight and not wanting to let go. Then I laid a really hard, deep kiss on her, that shook us both to our toes.

"Wow, that's sure something to think about," she said.

"That's the idea," I told her, "see you soon I hope."

CHAPTER 48

Amy made it home fine. She didn't think she'd have much to talk about with Matt's friend, so she borrowed a book to read. As it turned out, however, Rylee was a wealth of information on Matt. They have been friends since grade school, and did he have some stories to tell.

Oh yeah, she got to know a lot more about Matt than he was willing to show on the surface. All his old girlfriends, what type of girl he likes, what his aspirations are a WHP Officer. Could that mean more relocating if he was to become a Sgt. or Capt. or Lt. of another division in a different part of the state, she wondered. She'd have to be patient and find out, to stand by her man.

She called Matt first to say she made it home safely.

"Okay, good-night. I'll call you tomorrow, miss you too," she said thinking it was too soon for 'I love you'. Besides, he's going to have to be the one to say it the first time—not me. I already know, especially after spending time with his family and talking to his school buddy all the way home. Oh yeah, he's going to have to realize it now and say it.

She was pretty tired and headed to bed soon after calling her Mom and Dad to bring them up-to-date on what was going on. "I miss you guys too, I'll call again tomorrow after I talk to this insurance guy, okay. Good-night."

That night she had another frightful dream about the deal girls, she couldn't figure it out. They only wanted to show her something or someplace. She almost called Matt to talk to him about it, but she didn't want to worry him either. Eventually, she got a little more sleep before dawn.

The day started like any other, coffee, laundry to catch up on, mail, bills to pay. Finally, she returned the call to the insurance agent and made an appointment to go see him. He was in a local State Farm office close by, she went in on time and introduced herself.

"Hi, Amy, I'm Brad, have a seat. Thanks for coming in, sorry about Joe, he was a great guy," he said. "I have these papers for you to sign, as you are the sole beneficiary of Joe's life insurance," he started to explain. "He didn't have a lawyer, but I have a copy of his living will, if you'd like to look at that too?"

"Yes, thank you. I didn't know about any of this. Can you tell me when he got this?" she asked.

"Uhm, yes right here, he's been paying into this for ten years it looks like. He only changed the beneficiary to you about five years ago though. After both his parents were deceased," he told her.

"Okay, well what you want me to sign for?" she asked.

"That you acknowledge receipt of the total worth of said policy and the payout of $100,00.00. Sign right here and here," he said.

She looked at him with total disbelief.

"What did you say again?" she asked confused.

"I said, it's worth $100,000.00 in your name. Here is the cashier check for you also, to sign for here," he told her.

You're kidding right, this is a practical joke that Joe set with you?" she's said still in shock.

"No, Miss Winters, he was very adamant about all this, and also I may have a buyer for the shop," he informed her. "I know that was not my responsibility, but you know a small town talk and all. I told this gentlemen I'd give you his name anyway and that he's very interested." he said as he shook her hand, "Good luck."

She thanked him, and still in shock, she went over to talk to Sheriff Bud about the gentleman who is interested in buying the shop and gave him the piece of paper with his name and phone number on it, to make sure he's on the up and up.

"You want me to check this guy out for you that wants to buy the shop?" he asked to make sure, because evidently I wasn't making much sense.

Then I guess I better deposit this check, she thought. She stood there on the sidewalk staring at it and she started crying uncontrollably.

Sheriff Bud had seen her from his window and came out to see what's wrong. "What happened Miss Winters? May I help you?" he asked her trying to coax her inside to sit down.

She sniffled and stuttered, "Uhm (sniff),,,,thanks...Bud ..I...have this (sniff)...ch...eck here...for.. $100,000.00 (sniff)....from Joe's... life....in..surance...policy" looking at Bud. "What ...do...I...do...now? Oh ya,...and ....Brad..(sniff) said for me,,,,,to deposit....this.., is... that ...okay?" She finally got it all out, and showed him the cashier check.

"It sure looks legit to me, Miss Winters," he said.

She only nodded, "Pl...ea...se.," still sniffling. He handed her a box of tissues.

"Here you go. Okay, I'm also going to call your back and let them know you'll be in to deposit this check of a large amount," he said.

She nodded again. "Your banker is waiting for you over at State Bank, you want me to call Tammy to come here and go with you or take you—that be okay?" Bud asked her. Not sure what to with a crying woman in his office, so he called the diner looking for Tammy.

"And I'm going to call around on this guy while you go take care of that. Stop back by later today—no I'll call you at home—no need to come back here," he assured her.

A few minutes later Tammy came in. "Oh dear, Amy sweetie, let's go. Where is it you need me to take you—to your bank?" she asked. Amy only nodded again.

"Thanks for calling me Sheriff," Tammy said on the way out. On the way to the bank, Amy got it under control.

"Thanks Tammy, I'm fine now. I got it from here, I'll be right back." She told her, not wanting her to know the amount of the check, though the whole town will know by the end of the say probably. After that, Tammy took her back to her truck that was still parked by the State Farm Office across from the Sheriff's.

"Call me if you need anything at all sweetie, okay?" she told her.

"Okay, thanks again Tammy," Amy said and she got in her truck to drive home. She was sitting there staring into space like a zombie until the phone. It was Sheriff Bud.

"Hey there, Amy you okay now, good. I checked that guy out, he's really interested. He's got all cash money for you and can take it over whenever you want. I would strongly suggest you take the offer, Miss Winters. I gave him your number and he's going to call you, is that okay?" he asked.

"Are you sure Bud, he's legit? He's a good guy, not a con is it?" She asked sounding paranoid to herself.

"No, Amy I know you hear that a lot. I called his banker, he's for real," Bud said.

"Thanks Bud, sorry about earlier. I lost it uh, it won't happen again," she said.

Then she had to wait for the buyer to call her and sell the shop, since all of that went into her name on Joe's death. She couldn't believe the day she's had, she so wished Matt was here to talk to. I'll call him later, she thought. So she checked the rest of her messages on the answering machine while she waited. One was from Sheriff Marv Cole and it sounded important—that had came in yesterday morning.

As she was about to return the call, another call came in, it was the buyer.

"Hello, my name is Mr. Davenport. Is this Miss Amy Winters?" he asked, "I'm looking to buy that auto shop on 3rd Ave E, and I was told it now belongs to you; is that correct?"

"Yes, yes, I'm Amy Winters and I now own or have inherited that auto shop," she said.

"Good, then we have some business to discuss. Will you be home tomorrow around two in the afternoon? I'm driving from Salt Lake City, and should be there by then," he asked.

"Yes, I'll be here. Do I need to have a notary here?" she asked.

"We can sign any agreements at the bank, they have one there I'm sure," he said.

After hanging up from Mr. Davenport, she took a deep breath and called Marv back to see what that message was all about.

"Marv, hi, it's Amy Winters, you left me a message to call you," she said.

"Hi, yeah, thanks for calling me back Miss Winters." he said. "I need to talk to you about your...uhm...dreams, your premonition dreams. Have you had any more recently? Any since we found locations of most of these girls, that is?" Marv asked.

"As a matter of fact I have. Last night and that afternoon we were there in Boise, after I saw the photos," she told him.

"Can you come back here to tell us about them?" he asked.

"Why you ask, what's going on Marv?"

"Well, we're having trouble finding all of the burial sites. We have names and dates, but not all have exact locations. Guess you could say Matt got lucky with his sister, because it's not that way with all of them," he explained.

"How many have you identified from the photos and names matching from missing persons?" she asked.

"We have a total of 17 over a ten year period and that's including Hope. Out of all of them, we have accounted for ten so far. Anyway you could help us out?" Marv asked.

"I'm not sure how or what you want from me, but I'll try to do anything I can," Amy said.

"Great, when can you get here? The sooner the better, of course." he asked.

"I can't until day after tomorrow at the soonest. I have an

appointment I made for tomorrow to sell the shop that was Joe's."
she said.

"Okay, call me before you leave the on Thursday...and thanks
Amy, we'll talk more when you get here. I'll show you our problem."
he told her.

Amy hung up from that more confused than ever. What the
heck am I going to now. Matt wants me to move there, Mom wants
me to move home, Sheriff Marv needs me to come to Twin Falls or
was it Boise, I forgot to ask. Oh man, I need to talk to Matt, if only
he were here, what do I do? she asked herself.

When she sat down again to contemplate what she could do for
Marv, her phone rang. It was Matt, "Hey beautiful, how's your day
going?" he asked her.

"Oh Matt, if only you knew how much I needed you here today."
she answered.

"I miss you too love. I'll be seeing you soon though. I got this
weekend off—amazing uh—I could drive there, load you and be
back here the next day," he told her.

"You don't understand, I went to the insurance office first thing,
right. Joe's policy was for, get this—$100,000.00. Then this guy
calls to buy the shop, since I inherited that too. He's coming here
tomorrow afternoon at two, then I get a message from Sheriff Marv
Cole to call him back—remember him. Apparently, he needs my
help finding the locations of these dead girls. He believes they are
the ones in my dreams that want to show me where they're buried.
Because the notes are not as detailed as the ones you found for
Hope—you were lucky he said." As she explained all this, she was
practically hyperventilating.

"I'm coming there, don't go to Boise by yourself, you understand
me. Wait for me, I'm going with you," he told her.

"But you have to work, and I'm not sure how long this will take.
I can handle it Matt, I'll be fine," she assured him.

"Before you leave, call me I may be able to switch days off with
someone else and call in sick the other days," he told her.

"No Matt, really, I don't want you to jeopardize your job—promise me. This is something I have to anyway in order for the dreams to go away. I had another one last night," she said.

"What and you didn't call me—why not?" he asked sounding upset.

"I didn't want to worry you, like you are now," she said. "I'll go and take care of things and then it will stop. Then I'll come back here to pack and call you when I'm ready, okay?"

"You promise, you swear. You're coming here right?" he asked excitedly.

"Yes, I promise. I'll move in at the ranch house," she said with a smile.

"At the ranch, you been talking to my Mom, haven't you?" Matt asked.

"Yes, we had a few conversations, why what's wrong with that? I thought you wanted me to be friends with her?" She said then, "Look, I'll be gone for a few days is all, maybe to Twin and talk to Marv to get this over with and behind me once and for all, okay."

"Okay, call me tomorrow after the deal with the buyer. I'll see what I can about time off. It could still be official business for me too, if some bodies in Wyoming can't be found, you know. I have to get to work now, I'm on swing shift. Bye-love," he told her.

Amy thought about that too, because Marv didn't really say where they were needing more information about. I'll worry about that on Thursday, right now, I have to get some idea on what the shop is worth for an asking price, she figured.

She went through all Joe's bank statements and personal stuff and found his information on the loan he took out to buy the shop the year before. She called the bank to make an appointment with the loan officer listed on the paperwork, for that afternoon. Meanwhile, she called Brad at the State Farm office to ask about the policy on the business and for how much it a was covered for replacement value. The more information she could get together, the more prepared she'd be for tomorrow.

Her mind was a little more at ease after gathering that information and what the loan officer told her to expect. She then finished her laundry, made a store list to go shopping for dinner and some wine.

She thought a glass of wine would relax her enough to sleep good and to embrace her dreams if they came again to go along with it. Not to be afraid, but try to help them. That's exactly what happened later that night, or rather early morning.

Her dreams started pleasant enough, soft light and foggy. Then instead of all 15 girls around her, there were only seven, the ones that need to be found.

Okay, show me where, take me there. I'll go with you this time. The girls all held hands around her closer together to run in a circle surrounding her, over and over, several times. Amy tried to talk—where are we going, I'm dizzy now, stop running in a circle, STOP—PLEASE—STOP.

Then she woke up, sweating and breathing fast. Her window was open to get fresh air breezes, but it wasn't helping much. It was so hot in here, she thought. What the heck was that all about; if I can't connect with them, then I'm not going to be of much help, she knew that.

She saw that daylight was starting to come in, so there wasn't any use getting more sleep. She got out of bed to make coffee and reflect on what the dream could have meant. She figured she may as well get packing now too in order to be ready to go as soon as she got back from Twin Falls or Boise. Put all this behind her for good.

She couldn't figure out her dreams, she really was going in circles herself. Maybe that's one clue—the detectives were all going in circles, but where do they need to look. I need more information, she thought. Maybe they'll hypnotize me to remember more of my dreams. It's like hiding in my head. Sometimes, I only get bits and pieces anyway, what if the whole story is in my subconscious?

After packing all of Joes' clothes and things first to take to the church thrift store, she went in search of more boxes and ran into

Tammy from the diner. She was so embarrassed after what happened yesterday, she needed to apologize.

"I'm so sorry Tammy, for the way I was acting yesterday. I hope I didn't cause you any inconvenience," she told her.

"Don't worry about it, how are you feeling better, uh—that's good. A lot of money tends to that," Tammy said smiling.

"Yeah, thanks again for your help, I got to get going," she said hurrying to her truck with more boxes.

"Moving are ya, going to take off with that hunk that was here with you last time. I'm sure Joe would be happy for you—get the cute guy and all the money too—lucky girl," she said teasing her, only sounding more mean.

"No, I'm taking Joe's stuff to the church," Amy said.

That shut her up. Amy went back home thinking, if that's what people are saying about her now—well then she's better off leaving as soon as possible. As she continued packing and leaving a few dishes out to cook and eat a few more meals with, she found a particularly favorite photo of her and Joe in front of the dino at Little America, Wyoming. Putting that aside to keep, because Joe will always mean the best part of her past to her.

Then she fixed a ham sandwich for lunch and got her notes together for her appointment with this buyer. He was very prompt, at two o'clock there was a knock on her door, she opened to find a very handsome older gentleman in a nice suit.

"Mr. Davenport, come in. I'm Amy," she said.

"Thank you, Miss Winters for meeting with me, I think you'll be pleased," he said.

"Please have a seat, excuse the mess with all the boxes. I'm packing to move soon. Can I get you anything to drink, tea, water, soda?" she asked feeling like her old waitress self.

"No, thank you, I'm sure this won't take long," he said. "I'm prepared to offer you $300,000.00 for the auto shop, as is with all the tools and current inventory included."

"What was that again, did I hear you correctly? What are you going to with it—for that much money? I can't imagine it's worth half that," she tried not to stammer.

"Yes, it's an investment for me to be honest, and I intend to improve the building and an enlargement of the business, what you say? Do we have a deal?" he stood shaking her hand.

"Yes, of course, let's head to my banker to look over and sign your agreements," Amy answered.

"Great, I'll follow you," he said smiling. Half an hour later with the deposit of his cashier check with what she had deposited yesterday, she almost a half a millionaire. This was one crazy week. Wait till she called Matt to tell him, he's probably already tried to call me by now. He's at work now I bet.

When she got home, she called Marv and asked him if she could drive there now; because she was anxious to find out more information on these girls—maybe that would help.

"Sure thing, Miss Winters, to Twin though, we brought all we could back here to work on it closer to where we need to be. In fact, glad you called, I talked to Matt this morning; he said he talked to you and thought if these girls remains were in Wyoming also, he could get time off to help us out. I told him, no, they're not any more in Wyoming than the ones we already found. So that leaves Idaho, Montana, and Utah." Marv explained they were all supposed to be in a close area.

"Great Marv, thanks, I'll only be a few hours. I can pack an overnight bag and leave here real soon. Bye," she said.

She drove to Twin Falls in Joe's Jeep, it was a little more highway dependable than her ol' truck. She'll have to sell one of them anyway when she gets back, maybe both and get something new for herself. She never thought she'd be thinking of buying herself anything brand new. She's going to have to really consider investing some of that money for her future, a future with Matt—maybe a place of their own in Wyoming.

She got to Twin and went straight to Sheriff Cole's office. The deputy on the front desk called back for her to go on in.

"Hey, Miss Winters, thanks for coming, have a seat," Marv said.

"Please call me Amy, we'll be working close on this and it's easier right, Marv?" she said.

"Okay, Amy, let's go in the conference room with Det. Young and Det. Olson. I'll show you what we have," he told her.

He opened that door, "Jim, Faye, Amy's here to help us out, show her what we have and what we need, okay. I'm going to order a take-out for dinner, any preferences?" he asked.

"Whatever you guys have is fine with me," Amy said, looking at a map on the table. "Are these circles here where you still need to search?"

"Yes, we have seven still to recover; this circle here in northeast Utah, close to the border with Idaho is where three might be. This circle here close to us along I-84 is where three more could be, and this one in the corner of Montana by the Idaho border here is one more," Jim explained.

"What you mean might and could be, don't you have any better details to go by. I remember the notebook Matt looked at for Hope was very meticulous. I can't imagine he got sloppy," Amy said.

"Well, towards the end that's exactly what happened. All these were within this last year," Jim said. "And, of course, you know the last one he tried to bury right here wasn't a very good job either. Even though we found her fairly soon, his notes only say—'along Snake River'—that's it," he added.

"And you know how many miles the Snake River flows through Idaho, approximately 1,000 miles," Faye said.

"Yeah, well you need to narrow that down then, from these notes. May I read the descriptions of a few of these that you need to find?" she asked.

"Sure, we were hoping you'd be willing for a hypnotist to come in—for your, uhm, dreams to help us," Faye told her.

"I figured that's what you might have wanted me to try. You see my dreams are not very clear to me either, not always. Last night, these seven came to me and circled all around me running in circles until I was dizzy," Amy explained.

Jim and Faye looked at her and then at each other, "That's about the way it feels, yes," Jim said. "We're going in circles here. If you're willing, I'll set it up for you tomorrow, first thing."

The door opened then with a delivery for dinner.

"Let's eat now, and then we can look at all this again with fresh eyes," Marv said.

After a feast of Chinese take-out, they get to it. Amy read all the notes relating to these seven girls. She soon realized there was nothing real specific, but he had mentioned close by or on the way to certain towns. The detectives already had those areas circled, so she kept looking and rereading between the lines. She closed her eyes and tried to put herself in that environment to come up with some clue as to where he'd have put them in the ground.

Nope, no luck that way. She said, "I'm going to get a hotel close by and be back in the morning then. I had figured reading these notes over would spark something for me, but that didn't work. Maybe I'll have some visitors in my dreams tonight. Either way, yes, I'll try for the hypnotist."

"Okay Amy, thanks for trying with this. We'll see you in the morning then first thing—after coffee that is," Marv said. "Good-night."

Amy got to her room and it was late, so she called Matt hoping he was home from work by now to let him know what's happening. When he answered, she said, "Hey you, I'm in Twin. I came late today to get a head start on reading all those notes over that they have here. It's going slow that way, because it's not descriptions at all. They want to hypnotize me in the morning."

"Do you really want to try that, I remember how scared you were with that first dream you had in Boise, during our nap," he said to her.

"Yeah, I do too, but I decided to embrace the dreams not run from them. That's why I was calmer early this morning when I awoke after the last one. It was of them running all around me in circles really fast. Still can't figure that one out. Anyway, sorry I missed your call today. I was out getting more boxes to pack my stuff. Then I had that appointment with the buyer, quess what—I sold the shop for $300,000.00, can you believe that? And the payoff on the mortgage Joe had was only $60,000.00. He must have made double payments over the last two years. Anyway, I'm rich—what'dya think about that cowboy?" she said.

"Wow, I'm speechless. I'll bet you're flying high too, or has it all set in yet?" he asked.

"Actually, you're right it hasn't set in yet. I have no clue what I'm going to with all that," she said.

"Well, fortunately you don't have to decide that right now. Concentrate on the business of solving that mystery you have going on there and come home...to me," he said.

"That's exactly what I intend to do, but now I'm exhausted. I've been awake since four this morning. I'll call you tomorrow, okay. Good-night, Matt," she said.

"You better call me back tonight if you have another dream that's upset you, no matter what time it is. Good-night, Amy," he told her.

Amy did have more dreams that night, but they were not upsetting at all. It was calm and serene with mountains streams that bubbled along, fields of wildflowers, blue cloudless skies, open prairie as far as the eye could see. She slept rather soundly in fact, and awoke refreshed. That's what she needed to get ready for this morning hypnosis session. She wasn't nervous about it at all, more excited.

CHAPTER 49

S he showered quickly, dressed and grabbed a to go cup of coffee in her room, then headed over to the Sheriff's office for her appointment with the hypnotist.

"Hello Amy, I'm Sara, and we're going to have a little conversation first, is that okay with with you? Don't be nervous," she said.

"I'm not, excited is all, I've never done this before," Amy told her.

"Good, because there's no need to worry. Now, how long you been having these dreams; the one's in relation to the girls—not all of your premonition dreams?" Sara asked.

"Since that first afternoon in Boise, after discovering and reading the evidence. I've probably have had three of them all together," she answered.

"Do you think you might need to look at the photos again to help your subconscious trigger something?" she asked.

"No, I don't think so, I have their faces clear in my head. but not much else," Amy replied.

"Did you dream of them last night also?" Sara asked.

Amy answered, "No, it was of serene mountain streams, open prairie, field of wildflowers—very calming."

"Good then, you're ready to get started?" she asked.

"Sure, what do I have to do first?" Amy asked.

"Lean back here in the recliner, and relax—that's it, I'll do the rest." Sara smiled. "First I'll touch your arm here to help suggest the trance to go deep is that alright?"

"Sure, whatever you have to do," Amy replied.

"Okay, let's get started. Close your eyes, now picture last nights dream, if you will. The serene comfort and peacefulness of your surroundings. When I touch your arm here, you will go deeper and deeper to look for the real answers I'm going to ask you, okay?" she said as she prepared Amy for what's next.

She touched her arm then and asked her what she saw. Stay nice and calm, relaxed and breath deep and go further into the dream. Now describe what you see each time it may change a little as I touch your arm.

Sara took notes on everything Amy told her, but she also recorded it so as not to miss anything. After about two hours, Sara told Amy she was going to wake up on the count of three. "One...two...three, you can wake up now Amy. All is normal, you're safe."

And at that moment Amy opened her eyes and looked around the room. "Was I of any help at all, what did I say? I don't remember anything," she asked Sara.

"Yes, I know. I put the suggestion to you not to remember any details, so as not to be upsetting to you at a later time," she said.

"Yes, okay, but did you get anything useful, anything at all?" Amy asked.

Sara looked at her notes and said, "Yes, Amy I think I got all we're going to need, thank you."

"That's it then, I'm done. Will I dream any more of those girls, will they need to come back?" she asked hoping this was all over now.

"Yes, you're all done, and no, I don't think you'll have any more dreams of them at least; but you will probably always have premonition dreams. Does that trouble you Amy?" Sara asked.

"No, I guess not. I've made peace with that part of my life," Amy answered. Amy thanked her and left the room, realizing then that it was an interrogation room they conformed for her. Because next she saw Marv, Jim, and Faye come out of the adjoining door.

"So what do you think, I take it you all saw and heard what

happened in there and what I said. Was that helpful?" she asked them.

"Yes, Amy that was very useful and thanks for helping us. We appreciate all you've done. I'm sure we have all we need," Marv said thoughtfully.

"Okay then, that's good. Glad to help and I'm glad to know hypnosis works on me, for future reference that is," Amy said looking relieved walking down the hallway.

She left them there staring after her, Faye says what they were all thinking, "I sure hope she doesn't remember any of that."

Sara came out then with the cassette to give them said, "She never will—not this one anyway."

Jim took the tape and went back to the conference room to the table with the map, "Let's hear this again step-by-step and mark down on here where to search."

Amy didn't have any idea of what she said out loud, but she felt free and peaceful inside, as she headed home to make plans for her life with Matt and her future family. She smiled to herself knowing how hapuppy Matt will be when she tells him it's all over, and she's coming 'home'.

As planned, he came to get her with his horse trailer, on a weekend off. We loaded it and drove her home the next day. He drove us home a few days after Amy came home from Twin Falls and I called to tell him I was ready to come home.

CHAPTER 50

I remember every word Marv told me about her hypnosis. That she spoke in a different voice each time she had an exact location for them. Like it was the girls themselves coming through her to relate what happened to them—all of it—and then to where they were waiting to be found. It was very disturbing to hear and to know that's what was in her deep subconscious. I was so thankful she won't remember that ever. Marv told me I had someone very special and to take good care of her. I told him that I had intended to that.

As we pulled into my place instead of the ranch, Amy raised her eyebrows at me,

"Come on in for a minute, I have something to show you," I told her.

So she got out and followed me inside. "This is a cute little house. It's not as big and homey of course, as the ranch, more like a bachelor pad."

"Yeah, well it's a temporary home, come here," I said taking her hand into the bedroom.

"Really Matt, are you serious, now?" she started to say, as I sshed her with my finger to her sweet mouth.

"Yes, I have to do this right now, and yes, I'm serious." I said, as I reached in my pocket for the antique ring of my grandmothers and got down on one knee.

"Miss Amy Winters, will you do me the honor of being my wife for rest of our lives and marry me?" I asked perfectly polite with my best smile.

"Oh yes, Matt I will. I love you so much; it's crazy, but I do," Amy answered.

"I love you too, so very much. Now I intend to show you how much also," as I put the ring on her finger and picked her up to lay on my bed.

"Oh yeah, is this gonna take long—because I'm so tired," she said yawning, teasing me.

"Only the rest of my life," I said as I began to kiss her face all over slowly and caress her body.

Even through the thin layers of clothing, she responded quickly to my touch as I removed them slowly, touching her ever so softly and finding her sensitive spots. I was enjoying this too much, her eyes did turn a golden speckled brown as her passion began to heat up, as I thought they would.

And her body was hot as liquid fire I found out, as we explored each other through the entire night. I tried to be slow and gentle, but soon we were both feeling the urgency to be consumed by the fire and be united as one huge explosion ripped through us both. The electricity on the surface of our bodies remained long after that as I touched her body all over caressing her slowly and teasing her to aching for me again and again.

"Please don't stop, don't ever stop," Amy whispered.

Matt smiled and said, "I'll remember you said that, because I don't intend to ever stop. I enjoy this too much."

Watching the pure pleasure on her face is all I need to live for, always, and forever.

I wish to thank my brother-in-law, Jess Oyler, for his continued support and expert consultation, regarding all matters for WHP and DCI policies and procedures.

I want to thank my family and friends for their support and encouragement. Most noteblely, my daughter, Shawna Mandros, who is a teacher, and also my teacher friends for their advice on revising and editing my first rough drafts. Eventually giving that part of it up to the professionals, my Editor is Nancy D. Wall. Thank you, Nancy.

I also want to thank the members of Wyo Writers, Inc. for their encouragement and giving me the confidence to strive for the best in myself and my writing. Without attending that first conference, I would not have gained the information and knowledge to pursue my dreams.